ROMANCING TH...

**The royal family of Montebello will send its
best and bravest to seek their missing heir.
The prince's trail is still warm—but the search
is fraught with peril...and with passion!**

Meet the major players in this royal mystery:

Tyler Ramsey: The mission of this mercenary's
career has turned into a double-duty royal baby-sitting
job. Which will be more difficult, finding the missing
prince—or hiding his unwanted attraction to the princess
he's sworn to protect?

Princess Anna Sebastiani: Her brother may be
alive! Nothing will stop her from helping to bring Prince
Lucas home—not even her infuriating new bodyguard,
the only man seemingly able to resist her every whim.

King Marcus Sebastiani: When His Highness hears
just how much his beloved daughter dislikes her new
bodyguard, he knows he's chosen the right man for
her—er, for the job.

Desmond Caruso: Prince Lucas's cousin has taken up
the search, as well. But is his motive to bring Lucas back
alive...or dead?

Ursula Chambers: When the handsome and mysterious
Mr. Caruso appears on her ranch doorstep, where Prince
Lucas of Montebello was last seen, Ursula suspects she
may have found an ally in her plan to be sure the prince
is never seen again. But she'll keep the news of the royal
heir her sister carries to herself for now....

Dear Reader,

Valentine's Day is here, a time for sweet indulgences. RITA Award-winning author Merline Lovelace is happy to oblige as she revisits her popular CODE NAME: DANGER miniseries. In *Hot as Ice*, a frozen Cold War-era pilot is thawed out by beautiful scientist Diana Remington, who soon finds herself taking her work home with her.

ROMANCING THE CROWN continues with *The Princess and the Mercenary*, by RITA Award winner Marilyn Pappano. Mercenary Tyler Ramsey reluctantly agrees to guard Princess Anna Sebastiani as she searches for her missing brother, but who will protect Princess Anna's heart from Tyler? In Linda Randall Wisdom's *Small-Town Secrets*, a young widow—and detective—tries to solve a string of murders with the help of a handsome reporter. The long-awaited LONE STAR COUNTRY CLUB series gets its start with Marie Ferrarella's *Once a Father*. A bomb has ripped apart the Club, and only a young boy rescued from the wreckage knows the identity of the bombers. The child's savior, firefighter Adam Collins, and his doctor, Tracy Walker, have taken the child into protective custody—where they will fight danger from outside and attraction from within. RaeAnne Thayne begins her OUTLAW HARTES series with *The Valentine Two-Step*. Watch as two matchmaking little girls turn their schemes on their unsuspecting single parents. And in Nancy Morse's *Panther on the Prowl*, a temporarily blinded woman seeks shelter—and finds much more—in the arms of a mysterious stranger.

Enjoy them all, and come back next month, because the excitement never ends in Silhouette Intimate Moments.

Yours,

Leslie. J. Wainger
Executive Senior Editor

Please address questions and book requests to:
Silhouette Reader Service
U.S.: 3010 Walden Ave., P.O. Box 1325, Buffalo, NY 14269
Canadian: P.O. Box 609, Fort Erie, Ont. L2A 5X3

The Princess and the Mercenary
MARILYN PAPPANO

INTIMATE MOMENTS™

Published by Silhouette Books

America's Publisher of Contemporary Romance

If you purchased this book without a cover you should be aware that this book is stolen property. It was reported as "unsold and destroyed" to the publisher, and neither the author nor the publisher has received any payment for this "stripped book."

Special thanks and acknowledgment are given
to Marilyn Pappano for her contribution
to the ROMANCING THE CROWN series.

For Amy Reid
You may not have been royally born,
but you're a princess in all the ways that count.
Here's to a future of Prince Charmings, fairy-tale endings
and the best happily-ever-after you can imagine.

SILHOUETTE BOOKS

ISBN 0-373-27200-6

THE PRINCESS AND THE MERCENARY

Copyright © 2002 by Harlequin Books S.A.

All rights reserved. Except for use in any review, the reproduction or utilization of this work in whole or in part in any form by any electronic, mechanical or other means, now known or hereafter invented, including xerography, photocopying and recording, or in any information storage or retrieval system, is forbidden without the written permission of the editorial office, Silhouette Books, 300 East 42nd Street, New York, NY 10017 U.S.A.

All characters in this book have no existence outside the imagination of the author and have no relation whatsoever to anyone bearing the same name or names. They are not even distantly inspired by any individual known or unknown to the author, and all incidents are pure invention.

This edition published by arrangement with Harlequin Books S.A.

® and TM are trademarks of Harlequin Books S.A., used under license. Trademarks indicated with ® are registered in the United States Patent and Trademark Office, the Canadian Trade Marks Office and in other countries.

Visit Silhouette at www.eHarlequin.com

Printed in U.S.A.

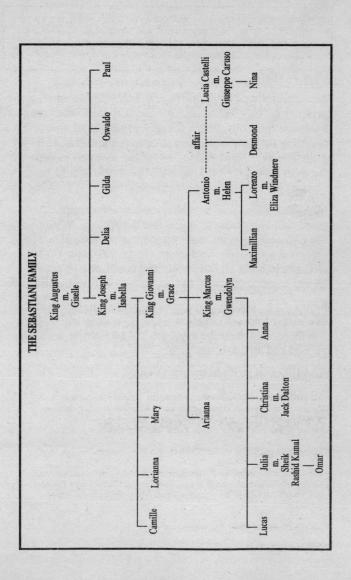

THE SEBASTIANI FAMILY

King Augustus
m.
Giselle

King Joseph
m.
Isabella

Delia Gilda Oswaldo Paul

King Giovanni
m.
Grace

Antonio Lucia Castelli
m. m.
Helen Giuseppe Caruso

------ affair ------

Camille Lorianna Mary Arianna

King Marcus
m.
Gwendolyn

Maximillian Lorenzo Desmond Nina
m.
Eliza Windmere

Lucas Julia Christina Anna
m. m.
Sheik Jack Dalton
Rashid Kamal

Omar

A note from Rita Award-winning author Marilyn Pappano:

Dear Reader,

As a child, I was never the type to buy into the whole princess fantasy. Who had time for fairy tales? Not me. I was too busy climbing trees, playing baseball and rambling through the woods to even think about such girlie things. If some prince had come along to sweep me away to his far-off kingdom, I probably would have blacked his eye and sent him home crying.

I realized, though, as I created the heroine of this book, that I've come to appreciate the fantasy. What forty-something wife/mother/career woman *wouldn't* be intrigued by the idea of such privilege and luxury? Of elegant clothing, crown jewels and handsome princes? Of excitement, glamour and servants at her beck and call?

So if anyone out there wants to offer me a palace home in a sunny tropical kingdom—just for a little while—hey, I'm there. Just send the royal jet. I'll be waiting with bags packed and an ear-to-ear grin.

And I'll even provide my own tiara.

All the best,

Marilyn Pappano

Chapter 1

Anna Sebastiani stood at the window, arms folded across her chest, and stared outside but paid little attention to the lovely view. She'd seen the well-tended gardens and the sparkling Mediterranean beyond practically every day of her life, and though she loved it all dearly, it held no interest for her this morning. The landscape she wanted to see at that very moment was vastly different—miles of barren plains, rugged mountains so rocky that that was the name they bore, forests and glaciers and lakes.

She wanted to be in America, in the state called Montana. That was where her older sister, Dr. Christina Sebastiani Dalton, the esteemed researcher, lived with her husband. It was where Christina had escaped the confines of life in the capital city of San Sebastian and found true happiness.

And it was where their brother, Prince Lucas of Montebello, was reported to have gone.

Since Lucas's disappearance following a plane crash one year past, life for the royal Sebastiani family of Montebello had been chaotic. First Lucas had been believed dead, though the family had continued to hope that he'd survived. Now evidence had surfaced that he *was* alive, though possibly not well. Rumors had placed him in Colorado, and the last people to have contact with him there had steered the search to Montana.

She wanted to be part of that search.

Lucas was the eldest of her siblings and her only brother, and she loved him dearly. Of his three sisters, he'd favored her, and not simply because she was the youngest. They'd shared a genuine closeness that his relationship with the others had lacked, and staying home in Montebello while her father's men conducted the search for him was making her crazy. Those men were paid employees, most of them strangers to her brother, and they would receive the monies due them whether Lucas was found or not. *She* didn't care about money, only about locating her brother. What she lacked in training or expertise, she made up for with love. She was utterly convinced she could help in the search.

And her father would be equally convinced she couldn't.

That was why she'd asked permission to visit Christina in America. Her father would think it perfectly natural for Anna to miss her elder sister and to crave the comfort a sister could give in a time of trouble. He would probably be delighted to send her off into Christina's competent care, leaving him with one less worry at home.

Of course, it was too much to hope that she could escape without a bodyguard, but she'd had no little experience in her twenty-five years in sneaking away for a few hours of freedom. All she need do this time—in the event her father granted permission, which he surely would, for how could he tell the apple of his eye "no"?—was sneak away for a few weeks. Just long enough to visit the sites where Lucas had allegedly gone looking for employment.

Quiet footsteps approached on the marble floor, causing Anna to turn. It was her father's secretary, Albert, a small, bespectacled man who'd held the position for more years than Anna had lived. "Your father will see you now, Princess."

"Thank you." Fortifying herself with a deep breath, Anna crossed the solarium, heading down the long elegant hallway, past the entry foyer to the tall, elaborately carved doors that led into her father's office. On the inside, she might be worrying about Lucas and her plan, but on the outside, she knew no hint of it showed. Her mouth curved of its own accord into an af-

fectionate smile the instant she saw her father, sitting behind a
desk strewn with papers, maps and other necessities for the daily
running of Montebello. To the rest of the world, he was King
Marcus, much-loved monarch of Montebello, but to her, he was
simply... "Papa."

He returned her smile and opened his arms. She embraced
him, then leaned against the desk, her fingers loosely trapped by
his.

"And to what do I owe the honor of this visit?" he asked.

"You know what, Papa. You promised me an answer today."

"An answer? To what?"

She attempted to fix a stern gaze on him, but it was difficult
when the corners of her mouth kept twitching. "To my request
to visit Christina in America."

"Ah, yes, that I did. Such impatience, Anna. The day isn't
even half gone yet."

She didn't hesitate to let her features slide fluidly into a pout.
"Do you know how long it's been since I've seen Christina?"

"Yes, *bambina,* little girl. It was the same time I last saw her.
But will it make so much difference if you see her tomorrow as
opposed to next week?"

Next week? Anna's heart sank. By next week Lucas could be
on his way to any of the other forty-eight states he hadn't yet
been spotted in. He could be getting himself more and more lost.
Naturally she didn't point that out. Instead, she sweetly asked,
"You tell me, Papa. You'll be the one on the receiving end of
my pouting if you make me wait until next week."

He laughed. "You are spoiled rotten, *mia figlia.*"

She gave him an appropriate spoiled-daughter smile. "As you
should know, since you're the one who spoiled me."

"Very well. I'll send you off to visit your sister and get that
scary face out of my sight for a few weeks." He gently pinched
her cheek, bringing a smile from her. "Naturally you'll travel
with an escort."

"Naturally. I thought Roberto would enjoy visiting the Wild
West." Roberto had served the family for years, and his pen-
chant for all things cowboy was well known. John Wayne
movies, Louis L'Amour books, videocassettes of *Bonanza, Mav-*

erick, Rawhide and *Paladin.* Have gun, will travel. He had a
gun, he liked to tease—what bodyguard didn't?—and serving
the royal family certainly allowed him to travel.

"I'm sure he would enjoy it. However, I've chosen someone
else."

He gestured to someone behind her, and instantly Anna became aware that they weren't alone in the room. Ordinarily, she
was more attuned to others' presence than that. She could attribute her lack of awareness only to the fact that these were far
from ordinary circumstances.

Slowly she turned to see the man, his back to her, standing
near the bookcases that lined one wall. Evidently it had been *his*
meeting with her father that had kept her waiting. He turned as
slowly as she had, and her heart took an unexpected leap in her
chest.

Tyler Ramsey! She had just pouted, sweet-talked and manip-
ulated her father with Tyler Ramsey there to witness every word.
Heat surged into her cheeks as she fought the urge to take cover
behind her father's chair. The man was a frequent visitor at the
palace, due to the work he and his brother did for the king as
well as the friendship between his father and hers, but he'd
hardly noticed she was alive.

But *she* had noticed *him.* He stood six feet tall, more than
half a foot above her, and he was—to put it in simple American
terms—to die for. Though he hadn't followed his father and
brother into the military, his auburn hair was military-short. A
few of her friends thought the style too severe, but she thought
it accentuated the clean lines and sharp angles of his face. With
his green eyes and decidedly muscular body, he belonged on a
recruiting poster.

He'd certainly recruited more than a few Montebellans, one
princess included, to the spectator sport of Ogling Tyler Ramsey.

"I believe the two of you have met," her father said as Tyler
came toward them.

"Yes, of course." Anna straightened. Rather than offer her
hand, she tucked both hands behind her back, and since she
didn't offer, neither did Tyler. His own hands were clasped before him—large hands, long fingers, more comfortable with a

gun, according to gossip, than with a woman. Not that there was any doubt of his interest in women. He simply hadn't yet met one who could compete with his fierce dedication to duty.

And that dedication might prove a problem. Escaping Roberto would be child's play. Escaping one as driven by duty as Tyler might prove impossible.

Calling on every bit of regal bearing she'd learned over the years, she inclined her head slightly. "Mr. Ramsey."

He mimicked the action. "Princess Anna."

In the preceding centuries, Montebello had fallen under the control of many peoples—the British, Greeks, Italians, Arabs, and others—so its population was a potpourri of them all. She loved the diversity of the people, their customs and their languages…ah, but there was something special about English as spoken by Tyler Ramsey.

Or perhaps there was simply something special about him, period.

"Tyler was already scheduled to travel to America on business for me," her father said. "If you'd waited one more day to make your request, he would have already been gone, and I would have been forced to turn you down, no matter how prettily you pouted."

"No, Papa," she disagreed. "You merely would have been forced to send someone else in his stead." Like Roberto, Salim, Nikos—any of the guards in the king's employ, any one of whom she could charm as easily as she did her father.

"Perhaps. But since Tyler *is* going, it makes perfect sense for him to deliver you into your sister's care. You get to visit your sister, and I get to know you're safe. We'll both be happy."

"Yes, Papa," she said dutifully. "We'll leave this afternoon—"

"You'll leave tomorrow."

"But I've made reservations!"

King Marcus laughed. "Were you so sure of me, *bambina?* And did you reserve two seats?"

"One for my escort and one for me."

He gave a patient, indulgent shake of his head. "You'll leave in the morning, and you'll take the Gulfstream jet. No arguments. Run along now, Anna. Tyler and I have things to discuss.''

''Yes, Papa.'' Though her ego chafed at her being dismissed like a small child, Anna embraced her father once more, then gave her newly-appointed bodyguard another cool nod as she walked past. ''Mr. Ramsey.''

He nodded, but didn't say a word.

Too bad. She would have liked to hear him speak her name once more. But it was a long flight to America. She would have plenty of chances to listen to the sound of his voice.

Wednesday dawned cloudy, but by 10:00 a.m., it was turning out to be another perfect day in paradise. Just his luck, Tyler thought, since he was leaving for Montana any moment now. Was there any chance Montana in February wouldn't be damned cold and snowy? Not much.

He was waiting on the tarmac near the king's private jet, impatient to board the plane and get the show on the road, and just as reluctant to do so. He was more than happy to follow up the leads on the missing prince for King Marcus. After all, that was part of what he'd trained to do. He just wasn't too pleased to be baby-sitting Princess Anna along the way, even though that was part of what he'd trained to do, too.

Grimly he checked his watch. The princess was already five minutes late. He certainly hadn't expected her to arrive at the airport early, but since this trip to visit her sister was *sooo* important, he'd thought she might actually make an effort to show up on time. Dumb thought.

As he lowered his wrist to his side, he caught sight of the vehicles approaching the heavily guarded hangar where the jet was secured—two four-wheel-drive vehicles occupied by the usual guards and, between them, the royal limo, occupied by the royal brat. The vehicles stopped a short distance from the plane. A guard hopped out of the limo and opened the rear door, and the princess emerged into the bright sunshine.

A low whistle vibrated the air near Tyler's ear. ''If you're gonna be a bodyguard, that's definitely the body to be guarding,'' Jim Wayne murmured appreciatively. ''Just think—you, alone with the royal daughter in the royal plane for six thousand miles. Aw, the trouble you can get into…''

"Knock it off." Tyler scowled at the mechanic, better known as Duke, before shifting his gaze back to the approaching princess. She did look damn fine, he had to admit, wearing a red dress that flattered every curve, with her dark curls in constant motion around her face. She walked as if she ruled the world— and, to some extent, she did. At least, she had the doting father who did wrapped around her delicate little finger. It seemed the king who ran a nation, who stood fast against his enemies and allowed no quarter, couldn't resist a flutter of lashes, a glance from those big eyes and a sweetly uttered, *Please, Papa.*

But what man could—besides Tyler, of course? He had no time in his life for involvement of any kind, but certainly not with King Marcus's youngest daughter. Princesses weren't his type. Neither were spoiled little girls dressed up in women's clothing. He had too much respect for the king, for his own father, and for the job he'd been hired to do.

But looking couldn't hurt…and Princess Anna was well worth looking at. He watched until she disappeared into the jet.

"Play your cards right," Duke went on, "and when this baby sets down in Montana, your future could be assured. Ruin the princess's reputation, and the king would probably be happy to let you marry her—"

"Or maybe he'd cut off my head, along with other parts of my body I'm rather fond of."

"One of those sheiks in Tamir, maybe. But not King Marcus. You'd be living in the palace, gettin' treated like royalty."

He didn't *want* to live in the palace, and he sure didn't want to be treated like royalty. He didn't want servants doing his bidding, bodyguards watching his every move, or to live a life that consisted of a lot of pomp and circumstance. He was a normal person with a normal life, and he preferred to stay that way.

"Time for you to get onboard," Duke said at a signal from one of the pilots. "Tell me all the princess's dirty secrets when you get back—and if she doesn't have any, make 'em up."

"Like I'd tell you anything," Tyler teased as he headed for

the air stairs. He entered the jet just behind the cockpit, nodded to the flight attendant, Mareta, who was busy in the galley, then walked into the cabin.

Oh, the luxury money could buy... When Tyler had flown to Montebello for his last phase of training, he'd flown coach on a commercial airliner, packed like a sardine into seats designed for someone six inches shorter and forty pounds lighter. He'd dated women he hadn't gotten as intimately close to as he had to his seat mates on that flight.

Space definitely wasn't a problem here. The cabin was divided into three separate seating areas, with oversize, plush leather chairs, a conference table, a workstation, a sofa and, at the rear, a lavatory that included a shower. The woods were exotic, the leather soft as butter, the carpet like walking on thick layers of cotton. He'd heard that the Gulfstream company had flown King Marcus to their manufacturing plant in Savannah, Georgia, to pick out everything himself. He'd also heard the plane had cost a cool $45 mil.

People in his world didn't even dream about having that kind of money. Of course, people in his world didn't live in palaces either, or grow up expecting to have every wish fulfilled and every whim obeyed.

Though his luggage had been stowed with the princess's, he'd brought a few items along—a parka, and in a worn gym bag, a couple of books and a portable CD player with headphones. He dropped the coat and the bag on the first foldaway table he came to and started to settle in one of the club chairs that flanked it.

"You may sit back here, Mr. Ramsey," the princess said from the back.

Clenching his teeth instead of grimacing, he left the coat where it was, picked up the duffel once more and went to the rear seating area. There was a sofa with small end tables on one side, plus two club chairs and another foldaway table on the other. She sat primly at one end of the sofa, legs crossed, spine straight. He chose the chair farthest away and immediately removed a book from his bag.

Since he'd been invited to join the Noble Men, a sort of mercenary group started years ago by friends of his father's, he'd received a tremendous amount of training, some of which had focused on guarding dignitaries, called protection details. None of it had centered on baby-sitting spoiled daughters. The important thing to remember, the king had told him yesterday, was that, though Anna was the princess, *he* was the boss. Not likely, he thought with a silent snort. Her own father the king found it impossible to tell her no. What made anyone think she would listen to *him?* He wasn't the king, he was a stranger, and he was only four years older than her.

Thank God this was as simple an assignment as he could have asked for. The flight to Billings couldn't be more secure. Tyler's only job with the princess would be getting her from the airport in Billings to her sister's house. Shouldn't take more than an hour, tops, and then he would be free to do his real job.

That job entailed following up leads that the prince had made his way to Montana. The information was being held in the strictest confidence, known only to the king and queen, the three princesses and a handful of others—Lorenzo Sebastiani, the king's nephew and head of the Royal Montebellan Intelligence; Tyler's brother, Kyle; and his immediate supervisors within the Noble Men. Though Tyler was well aware that true secrets were rare—people always had ways of finding out info—he had no doubt this was one secret closely guarded.

At an announcement from the captain, they buckled their seat belts, and the jet taxied to the end of the runway. Tyler was absorbed in his book when the princess spoke. "Do you enjoy flying?"

He blinked, then looked up. "It beats taking a boat."

"I love to fly. I would learn to pilot a plane myself if Papa would let me."

"I didn't know he ever told you no," he murmured before realizing exactly what he'd said and to whom. He looked at her again, his gaze sharpening, but she merely smiled.

"Not too often. But he's afraid if I learned to fly, I might fly away from Montebello and never go back."

"Would you?"

"Eventually," she said softly, gazing out the window at the island dropping away beneath them.

Eventually fly away? he wondered. Or eventually go back? He wouldn't have pegged her for the type to want to experience life elsewhere. After all, though she would be a princess no matter where she lived, in Montebello, she was *their* princess. The people adored her. They coddled and spoiled her, named their baby girls after her, encouraged their teenage daughters to be like her.

Once the plane reached its cruising altitude, Princess Anna removed her seat belt, then kicked off her shoes and drew her feet onto the sofa. In spite of the casual pose, she still looked every inch the princess. "Tell me about Montana."

Hiding his impatience, Tyler closed his book, his place marked with one finger. "I don't know much about it. I've never been there."

"But you're American."

"And the U.S. is a big country. I've lived a lot of places and visited plenty more, but Montana's not one of them."

"If I lived in America, I would visit every state, especially Texas and California. And Georgia. But maybe not Arkansas."

"Arkansas's not so bad."

"You've been there?"

"Yeah, I've been there."

Silence settled between them. How long did it have to last, he wondered, before he could return to his book without appearing rude? A couple minutes seemed fair enough, but about the time the second minute ran out, she spoke again.

"What are you reading?"

He held up the book. It was a Stephen King paperback, picked up in the airport on the way to Montebello. He hadn't had time since arriving there to get past the first chapter. He'd planned on reading the whole book today, but not if Chatty Cathy over there didn't give it a rest.

"I don't read horror," she said dismissively.

"I don't look at pictures of pretty dresses." He gestured toward the magazine open on her lap.

She smiled brightly, showing off plenty of pearly whites and making her dark eyes sparkle. It was the kind of smile that could make any doting father forget the word "no" for good...or bring any living, breathing man to his knees. "I love pretty dresses, but I brought books, too. I'm too excited about finally getting to Montana to concentrate on reading."

"You must have really missed her."

"Missed her?" For an instant, her look turned blank; then she hastily covered it. "You mean my sister. Of course I have. I've missed her terribly. I can't wait to see her."

Who else would he mean? After all, visiting Princess Christina was the whole point of her trip, wasn't it?

"Are there still cowboys in Montana?"

"I'm sure there are."

"And cattle and ranches and actors?"

"Actors?" Now it was his turn for a blank look.

"*People* magazine says a number of actors and actresses have homes in the state."

"Huh." He didn't read *People,* and he could hardly imagine the circumstances in which he would care where any particular actor lived. Maybe if he was assigned to baby-sit one, God forbid.

The flight attendant chose that moment to come into the cabin. "May I get you something, Princess?"

"A diet soda would be wonderful, Mareta. What about you, Mr. Ramsey?"

"Coffee, please."

"May I call you Tyler?" the princess asked as Mareta left again. When he nodded, she smiled brilliantly. "And while we're alone, you shall call me Anna."

"I don't believe that would be appropriate, Your Highness."

In an instant, her expression shifted from happy to pouty—and damned if she wasn't even prettier with that full lower lip stuck out. "But Roberto does, and Nikos and Salim."

He didn't point out that each of those three guards was old enough to be her father, or that they'd known her since she'd lived in the royal nursery. He sure as hell didn't point out that first names were just a little too intimate for their situation. Anna was someone a man could talk to, have fun with, tease, get to know and call Annie when he kissed her, and the princess was none of those things. She was the favorite daughter of King

Marcus, and Tyler had been entrusted with her safety. Nothing more, nothing less.

"I can't base my actions on what Roberto, Nikos and Salim do," he said evenly. "I can only do what I feel is right."

Her brown eyes took on a glitter of…anger? Annoyance? Maybe rejection? "Very well, Mr. Ramsey. Suit yourself."

That was exactly what he wanted, wasn't it? So why did he feel…disappointed that she'd referred to him formally rather than used his first name?

Nah, he wasn't disappointed. Just…. Truth was, he didn't know exactly what. Annoyed that his first solo assignment from the king was something so simple. Frustrated because he was eager to get on with his *real* assignment—finding Prince Lucas—and this escort job seemed a waste of his training. Troubled that she was so damn pretty and that it had taken less than fifteen minutes alone with her for the idea of kissing her to pop into his head.

That *wasn't* gonna happen. No way, no how.

Mareta returned to serve their drinks, bringing along a tray of the small, flaky, honey-flavored pastries favored in Montebello. The princess took her diet pop but waved the pastries away, so the flight attendant left them on the table next to Tyler. He sweetened his coffee, selected a pastry, then opened his book again.

The silence in the cabin was uncomfortable, and it distracted him from the story. A surreptitious glance at the princess showed she was radiating stiffness. A frown wrinkled her forehead, making his gut knot. If she were a regular person, he was pretty sure he might owe her some sort of apology…but she wasn't.

Ignore her pouts, the king had advised. He could do that. After all, they were going to be together for only twelve hours, fourteen tops.

He could endure anything that long.

Desmond Caruso stood on the terrace outside his quarters, a drink in hand though it was still morning, and gazed at the scene before him. Flowers bloomed in the garden, water bubbled in the fountains, birds sang in the trees, and in the near distance, the palace loomed over him, massive and solid, blindingly white under the Mediterranean sun, a symbol of all he loved, hated, wanted and couldn't have.

When he'd come to Montebello eighteen years ago, he'd thought he had it made. He'd never imagined such wealth and luxury. Hell, he'd been on his own, living hand to mouth, after his old man—scratch that—after his *step*father had thrown him out of the house a year earlier. That was before he'd known that his *real* father was a duke and brother to a king—before he'd even known that he had a real father. If the bastard hadn't died and left him a little money, he probably never would have known, and he wouldn't have been living on the palace grounds for the past eighteen years.

Nor would he be in a position to become best friend and trusted advisor to the man who would likely be Montebello's next king—provided Prince Lucas didn't come back and ruin everything.

He intended to make certain that Prince Lucas didn't come back.

A short while ago he'd seen the most luxurious of the king's private airplanes pass overhead on its way to America, carrying Princess Anna and one of the Noble Men. He wasn't sure which brought the derisive curl to his lip. He despised Anna, a waste of oxygen if ever there was one. She'd been petted and pampered from the day she was born. She didn't have a clue what life was like in the real world and would never have to learn.

He knew. He'd lived in the real world. Scrounged in it. Sacrificed in it. Struggled to survive in it. And he wasn't going to do it again.

He didn't feel any more kindly toward her bodyguard. Noble Men! How insufferably arrogant. How brazen and self-important to proclaim themselves the Noble Men to the world, as if everyone else were anything but. They were opportunists, just like everyone else, and cloaking themselves behind deceptively honorable names didn't change that.

Truthfully, Desmond would feel no more regret if the Gulfstream crashed into the Mediterranean than he'd felt a year earlier when Lucas's plane had crashed into the Rockies. In fact, he might welcome it, for surely the grief would be more than King Marcus could bear. His uncle had turned to him for solace after Lucas's disappearance, and Desmond felt certain he'd advanced his place in the king's affection through that so-called ordeal. Who knew how close they might become if King Marcus lost another of his beloved children?

When he lifted his glass for a sip and found it empty, he went back inside the guesthouse that had served as his home for the past eighteen years. Like everything else on the royal grounds, it was spacious, lavishly designed and opulently appointed—a place fit for...well, if not a king or a prince, someone of royal blood. Priceless rugs were scattered over the marble floor, and works of the old masters hung on the walls. No expense had been spared in the guesthouse, and while he appreciated that, he also resented the hell out of it. All the other royals had their own quarters within the palace walls—the king and queen, Lucas, Anna, Desmond's half brother Lorenzo. Even Julia and Christina, who were now married, retained their private apartments in the midst of the others.

But not Desmond. No, *he* was given a guesthouse on the grounds, separate from the others. The distance from his quarters to the palace served as a bitter reminder that even though he had Sebastiani blood flowing through his veins the same as the others, he *wasn't* the same. None of them—not the king and queen, not the spoiled bratty princesses and sure as hell not Lucas—was ever going to let him forget it.

Except Lorenzo. There were rumors that his half brother well might be named successor to the throne if Prince Lucas never showed up again—rumors that Desmond would do damn near anything to make reality. Rumors that he'd already taken the first step toward fulfilling. On his desk was an airline ticket, final destination Denver, Colorado. From there he would go to the Chambers ranch outside Shady Rock, the ranch where it was now believed Lucas had been living ever since the plane crash.

The ranch where Lucas very well might die.

Desmond crossed to the elaborately carved desk and picked up the envelope containing the ticket. He'd already come up with a cover story—a much-delayed visit to his mother, Lucia, and his half sister, Nina. He'd rarely seen them since his stepfather celebrated his eighteenth birthday by throwing him out of the house. But no matter what Guiseppe Caruso thought of family ties, they were important to King Marcus—or so he claimed. Truth was, blood ties weren't enough. To be welcomed into the bosom of the Sebastiani family, a person needed legitimacy as well as Sebastiani blood. But in keeping with his claim, Marcus would never question Desmond's professed desire to see his mother and half sister again.

And he would never guess that Desmond was, in fact, going to Colorado.

To find his cousin.

And kill him.

With a great sigh, Anna closed her magazine. She couldn't remember a word she'd read in the past two hours or call to mind one single garment she'd looked at, admired or loathed. She was wasting her time, pretending interest in the publication when all she really wanted to do was have a conversation with her reluctant bodyguard.

A glance his way showed that he was having no such trouble concentrating. He'd made good progress on his book without so much as a peek in her direction—or, apparently, a qualm about refusing her request. Her usual bodyguards refused her nothing. In fairness, though, she asked nothing of them that should be refused.

And in fairness, she'd asked nothing of *him* that should have been refused, either. He simply was being unreasonable. American men were sometimes like that…though that fact hadn't swayed Christina from marrying her American. Jack Dalton had been sent to Montana to protect Christina, and they'd fallen madly in love. It had been so romantic…and now Tyler Ramsey was being sent to Montana to protect *her*.

Anna's dreamy smile faded. Tyler didn't strike her as particularly romantic, and he certainly wasn't going to fall in love with her when he couldn't even bring himself to call her by her given name. Besides, they weren't going to be together long enough to pass the polite-strangers phase. As soon as they arrived in Billings, she would escape him and put her plan into motion.

And she wouldn't think about the repercussions of escaping him.

Staring into the distance, she played her favorite scenario in her head—giving Mr. Ramsey the slip, as Roberto liked to say; being truly on her own for the first time in her life—though, of course, she would have to find a way to let her family, especially Christina, know she was safe—making her way through the state of Montana with nothing but a rental car and a highway map, and—the sweetest ending possible—locating Lucas in one of the mining communities where he was rumored to have gone. She had missed him so desperately this past year and couldn't wait to see him, to hear his voice, to hug him around the neck and never let go.

"Your Highness...Princess..."

Giving herself a mental shake, Anna focused on the attendant, who stood in the doorway. "Yes, Mareta?"

"Lunch is served, Your Highness, as you requested earlier. I've set the conference table, though if you'd prefer to dine here..."

Anna smiled. "No, thank you. The conference table is fine." As the attendant turned away, Anna stood and stepped into her heels. Though she wished she could leave her bodyguard behind and eat in private, it would be rude, and she did make every effort to avoid being rude most of the time. However, if he *chose* to remain where he was.... "Mr. Ramsey, you're welcome to join me if you'd like."

Just her luck, he didn't so choose. Setting his book aside, he stood and followed her into the center section of the cabin. There he waited for her to be seated before he sat opposite her.

The teak table had been covered with a black linen cloth, and the napkins at each setting were a rich gold. The antique china bore the royal Montebellan crest, as did the heavy silverware and the crystal goblets. Fresh flowers from the palace gardens were nestled in a Baccarat bowl in the table's middle, with covered serving dishes on either side.

Because she'd received lessons in being a gracious hostess

right alongside math and geography lessons, as Mareta began removing the covers, Anna politely said, "I asked the chef to prepare a typical American luncheon for us. I hope you don't mind."

There was a dish of golden-brown fried chicken, and another held creamy potato salad. There were also baked beans, redolent of molasses and brown sugar, and thick slices of hothouse tomatoes. For dessert a woven silver basket held chocolate chip cookies, each wrapped in a parchment sleeve.

She looked from the food to Tyler, hoping to gauge the chef's success by his expression. He appeared disconcerted.

"Is this not a typical American luncheon?"

"Oh, sure, it's a traditional picnic lunch. I just don't think I've ever seen it served on hundred-year-old china with linen napkins. It's normally eaten off paper plates with paper napkins and plastic forks."

She wasn't certain why he considered disposable dinnerware better suited to the menu, and she didn't bother to ask, as she suspected either she wouldn't appreciate his response or he wouldn't appreciate hers. Instead, as she served herself, she asked in a purely conversational tone, "Do you miss America?"

"Sure. It's my home. Don't you miss Montebello when you're gone for any length of time?"

"I've never been away for any length of time."

"Didn't you go to school someplace else?"

She shook her head. "The others did, but Papa felt I should stay close to home."

"Don't you go on vacations?"

"Of course…but always with Mama and Papa, or with my sisters, Julia and Christina. So many guards, servants, advisors and aides travel with us that it's as if we've taken Montebello along." She assaulted the chicken on her plate with a knife and fork, then, following Tyler's lead, used her fingers with much better results. It was a most inelegant method, but with no one around to comment or chastise, she found she didn't care.

"Where do you live?" she asked while nibbling on her second piece of chicken.

"Nowhere in particular. My parents live in Arizona—that's

where the family business is located—along with my middle
brother, Jake, and my oldest brother, Kyle, and his wife. Since
I went to work for the team, I've spent all my time in training.''

''When you were a small boy, did you always want to be a
mercenary?''

For an instant she thought he might smile. The corners of his
mouth twitched before settling in a level line again. ''Did you
always want to be a princess?''

''No. Actually, Mr. Ramsey, I wanted to be a fairy. You
know, a wee sprite with pointy ears and gossamer wings? I was
approximately seven when I learned that even a king couldn't
perform such magic and I was stuck being a princess.'' Again,
she thought he might smile, but again he disappointed her. ''I
was given no choice as to what I would be. Was it the same
with you?''

''No,'' he answered slowly. ''Probably the only thing my father *didn't* want us to do was follow in his footsteps. He made
a career of the air force before retiring and starting the airplane
parts business, but he steered us all away from military service...though Kyle joined up anyway.''

''And Jake went into the family business, and you...?''

Looking decidedly uncomfortable, he fiddled with the heavy-
handled knife he hadn't touched through lunch. ''I pretty much
did nothing. College bored me. I barely managed to graduate. I
tried a dozen jobs and didn't like any of them. I never had a
clue what I wanted to do until my father offered me this job.''

And did he like it? she wanted to ask. Was that why he was
driven—because he'd finally found his niche? Or did it fail to
hold his interest, as all those other jobs had—and was *that* why
he tried so hard? So as not to disappoint his father? If he were
Roberto or any of a number of palace employees, she wouldn't
hesitate to ask...but if he were Roberto or any of the other
employees, she wouldn't find the question so intriguing, honesty
forced her to admit.

Instead, she directed the conversation toward an earlier comment. ''What jobs?''

Again he appeared disconcerted, a moment which passed
when he shrugged. ''I worked on a road construction crew one

summer—not a lot of fun when it's 120 degrees in the shade. I tended bar for a while, and drove a delivery truck. I taught school for a semester and quit one step ahead of being fired, and I did get fired from the family business. I was a ski instructor one winter, and I worked on a ranch one year. You name it, I've probably done it for at least a week or two."

"I've never held a real job before," she remarked, hearing the wistfulness in her voice and hoping he didn't. "I'm on the boards of several children's charities, but they want my name and title more than they want me. It helps them raise funds."

Apparently, he had nothing to say to that. He simply folded his hands on the tabletop and studied them as if he found them vastly more interesting than her.

His response—or nonresponse—left her feeling a bit melancholy, but she didn't let it show. Placing her napkin on the table, she stood up. "There's a television and DVD player in that cabinet, along with a selection of movies. The stereo is there, too. Feel free to make use of it or not."

He stood, too. "What are you going to do?"

She smiled coolly. "We're on an airplane, Mr. Ramsey. There aren't many options open to me. I'll be back there resting." Slipping past him, she returned to the rear section of the cabin, where she located a pillow and a blanket in a corner cabinet. After depositing them on the sofa, she went to the lavatory to wash up.

When she came out, she stopped abruptly. Tyler was crouched in front of the entertainment cabinet. The position drew his faded jeans taut over long, muscular legs and—a most unprincessly thought—his particularly nice butt. He'd removed his jacket and rolled the sleeves of his dress shirt halfway up his forearms, where the white fabric contrasted nicely against his tanned skin. The brown leather of his shoulder holster contrasted nicely against the white shirt, also.

She had grown up with overt displays of weaponry. Though a number of the guards stationed around the palace were largely ceremonial, many others were loaded for bear, Roberto liked to say. She'd been a not-so-little girl before she'd realized that meant they were heavily armed, rather than hunting bear. Truthfully, the discovery had been a major disappointment, as it had forced her to give up the hope of running into a real, live bear while out playing.

Of all the countless men she'd known with their wide variety of weapons, she couldn't recall ever looking at one of them and his pistol and feeling a shock of arousal shiver down her spine. But Tyler in blue jeans, white shirt and shoulder holster… Ah, yes, she was shivering.

He inserted a DVD in the player, then stood up as the flight attendant approached.

"Can I get you anything, Mr. Ramsey?"

"Nah…but you can call me Tyler."

"And I'm Mareta." She spoke with more warmth than Anna would have thought the woman capable of. "Give me a moment, and I'll clear these dishes out of your way."

"No rush. Have you seen this movie?"

She glanced at the television. "A time or two. I like it."

"Let me give you a hand with the dishes, Mareta, then you can pull up a chair and watch it with me."

"I'd like that."

Feeling unreasonably rejected, Anna waited until they were both on their way to the galley to move forward and secure the accordion-pleated door between the two compartments. Then she settled on the sofa, the blanket spread over her legs, and opened the oversize shoulder bag she'd brought along. On a trip a few days ago to a travel agency in town, she had picked up every brochure they'd had to offer on Montana, and in the privacy of her apartment in the palace, she'd printed off more information from the Internet, including maps. She'd located the three mining operations Tyler was scheduled to check out and had obtained directions to each of them.

Her original plan had called for escaping Roberto, or whomever her father sent along, in the crowded airport—the primary reason she'd booked a commercial flight. It wasn't the best plan, she acknowledged, for she wouldn't have been able to contact anyone until she was certain her escape had been successful, and in the meantime, Christina would have been frantic at her failure to appear. Now that she wouldn't be allowed to set foot in a crowded airport, she needed a new plan.

Montebello was nine hours ahead of Montana, so though it would be approximately 11:00 p.m. Montebello time when they arrived, in Billings it would be midafternoon. She could insist they stop for her first Montana fast-food hamburger, then excuse herself to go to the ladies' room, where she would change into the outfit in her bag. By the time he realized she was taking too long, she would be well on her way back to the airport by taxi-cab to rent a car. And while he looked for a woman in a red Armani dress and black coat, she would disappear into the crowd in her faded Levis, University of Montana sweatshirt, parka and Reeboks.

And frankly, she admitted as she heard laughter—both male and female—from the next compartment, she couldn't care less what the repercussions were for him.

Chapter 2

By the time they landed in Billings, Tyler had one hell of a headache and thought the muscles in his neck were never going to relax again. After resting three or four hours, the princess had given him the royal cold shoulder for the remainder of the trip—which should have suited him just fine but for some obscure reason he chose not to examine pissed him off. He'd discovered too late that, with Mareta, a little friendliness went a long way. She'd wasted no time informing him that the crew was spending the night in town before heading back to Montebello and had made it clear that she wouldn't mind at all spending it with him. On top of that, according to the captain's announcement, it was colder than the North Pole and snowing in Billings.

He'd learned during his winter as a ski instructor that his nature was much better suited to tropical warmth than winter cold and snow.

Thank God the first part of this job was almost over.

The plane landed smoothly and taxied to the general aviation terminal. A black SUV bearing a rental sticker on the rear bumper was parked nearby—the one he'd requested, Tyler hoped. The quicker he could drop off the princess at her sister's, the quicker he could put some mileage between him and her—and him and Mareta—and the happier he would be.

Once the air stairs were locked in place, he pulled his jacket on, then the parka. It was leftover from his days as a ski instructor and immediately brought to mind other ventures, other failures. First thing he'd do after getting rid of the princess, he decided, was dump the coat and the memories, and buy a new one.

The princess came forward, wearing a black coat that completely covered her from chin to foot. She'd traded her red heels for a pair of black boots, better suited to unstable footing, and was draping a black woolen scarf over her hair.

"Wait here while I make certain we're ready to go," he said, slinging the strap of his gym bag over one shoulder, and she nodded once.

The cold air hit him like a punch and made him suck in his breath—not the brightest idea, since it felt as if the air had frozen every particle in his lungs. He spoke to the customs officer, then the rental agent who was, indeed, delivering the black SUV for them. After leaving his bag in the vehicle, he returned to the plane, where the princess waited, gloved hands clasped in front of her. "Are you ready, Your Highness?"

"You may bring my bag," she said, nodding toward the shoulder bag that was bigger than a lot of suitcases he'd seen.

He shook his head. "Sorry, Princess. I'm a bodyguard, not a porter. How can I protect you if my hands are full with your luggage?"

She gave him a look as frosty as the air outside. "And what are you protecting me from in Montana?"

"Did a terrorist organization attempt to kidnap your sister, Julia, a few months ago?"

"It wasn't my sister. Merely a look-alike."

"But the terrorists didn't know that, did they?" He gave her a moment to respond, but she didn't. "If you want to wait here, I'll take your bag to the car, then come back for you."

"Never mind." She picked up the bag and would have pushed past him if he hadn't expected it. He went down the stairs first, then hustled her to the SUV. Onlookers had gathered outside the terminal, curious about who had just arrived among them in a fancy private jet, but the princess was slender enough and he was broad-shouldered enough that he doubted anyone got more than a glimpse of black.

He gave her a hand into the high seat and closed the door, then circled the truck to the driver's side. Fortunately, the rental guy hadn't been waiting long. The temperature inside the truck was about forty comfortable degrees warmer than outside, and the instant he started the engine, hot air blasted from the vents.

"Do you need directions to Christina's house?"

"I have them." And he'd spent the last hour memorizing them. He didn't want to get lost or delay the important part of his trip any longer than necessary—or prolong his time with the princess. Women were a complication he had no time or desire for, and that went double for her.

The roads were clear, and the snow was the tiny, hard kind that was more annoyance than anything else. Still, he was grateful for the four-wheel drive and the heavy weight of the vehicle. Both would come in handy once he got out on the back roads surrounding the mines he was scheduled to check out.

The princess sat stiffly, staring out the side window. Other than loosening her scarf and removing her gloves, he hadn't seen her move at all since they'd pulled away from the terminal. Still ticked off at him, he figured, though damned if he knew for what. He wouldn't waste much time worrying over it, though. He'd never met a woman yet that he truly understood, and the royal pain of the Sebastiani family wasn't likely to be the first.

They were sitting at a stoplight on a street filled with gas stations, fast-food restaurants and strip centers when an abrupt change came over her. Pointing imperiously to a restaurant a block ahead, she turned to him, smiled broadly, and said, "Look! The golden arches! We shall have our first hamburger."

The thought of fast-food anything when his body was still on Montebello almost-middle-of-the-night time made his stomach queasy. "We just ate dinner a few hours ago."

She made a dismissive gesture. "Roasted duckling and wild rice stuffing. We can have that any time. But an honest-to-goodness American hamburger…"

He changed lanes, then slowed to turn into the driveway. "We'll go to the drive-through—"

"I'll go inside." The moment he stopped behind the last car in the drive-through lane, she released her seat belt and was reaching for the door handle.

He grabbed her wrist. "You don't go anywhere alone, Your Highness," he reminded her sharply. With a look in the rearview mirror, he swung out of the lane and into a parking space, shutting off the engine before releasing her.

"May I open the door now, Mr. Ramsey?" she asked in a killingly polite voice.

"No." He got out, zipped his coat, then went around to open her door. They crossed the parking lot together, stomped the snow off their boots inside the door, then headed for the counter. Halfway there, she pulled back.

"Why don't you order while I visit the ladies' room?"

Jeez, she had her own private bathroom on the plane they'd just left, he groused. How could she possibly need to go here? "Why don't I wait at that table right there—" he nodded toward the table nearest the bathrooms "—until you're finished?"

Her smile was cool and disdainful and made his temperature rise a few degrees. "I assure you, Mr. Ramsey, even princesses get to go to the bathroom alone."

He shrugged. "It's your choice. I can wait...or you can."

With her own impatient shrug, she turned and walked up to the counter. She ordered a hamburger and diet pop. He got nothing, but paid the tab and carried the tray to a table. There she undid the wrapper, pinched off a piece of burger and chewed it slowly. "You know, I have traveled with bodyguards my entire life, and you, Mr. Ramsey, are the least pleasant of them all."

He felt a flush of guilt that, damn it, he shouldn't be feeling. He hadn't done anything wrong. He just took his duties seriously—and that was what had her royal nose out of joint. "I'm not trying to be unpleasant, Your Highness—"

"And yet see how well you succeed." She pinched off another piece of bun and meat and delicately chewed it. "I shall tell Papa you're a most unsuitable bodyguard."

Please do, was what Tyler *wanted* to say, because maybe then he'd be spared any future baby-sitting jobs. But King Marcus knew his daughter well and would probably figure that any bodyguard she didn't like was one who did the job exactly the way he was supposed to, and with *his* luck, that would be the only job the king would give him from then on out.

So, though it meant locking his jaws together, he said nothing.

"I shall tell him you were rude and disrespectful, and that you were more concerned with arranging a rendezvous with Mareta than you were with seeing to my safety."

What did she know about Mareta? She was supposed to have been sleeping while he and the flight attendant watched the movie and talked. And what did it matter anyway? As she'd pointed out, they'd been in an airplane. How much more secure could she have been?

"You tell him whatever you want, Your Highness," he said as if he honestly couldn't care less. "But don't force *me* to tell the king that I just missed finding his son because his youngest daughter delayed my departure so she could play with her food and pout."

She shot him a frigid look, then stood up from the table and walked away. By the time he'd gathered the remains of her meal and tossed them in the trash, she'd reached the door and was waiting, her head held high, her expression impassive.

Neither of them spoke again on the drive to her sister's house. The place was located a short distance outside the city in a private community called Eagle's Nest. The Sebastiani-Dalton house was an architectural wonder, all wood, stone and glass, and a security nightmare—though it was a fair bet Jack Dalton had, at the least, made sure all that glass was bulletproof.

Tyler parked in front of the garage, sunk into the hillside beneath the house, and shut off the engine. As anxious as she'd been to see her sister, the princess didn't look too excited to finally be there. Probably still pissed at him, he thought. That was perfectly all right with him. So was the prospect of never being stuck with her again—hell, never even seeing her again.

Though a small voice in his head suggested he was kidding himself on all three counts.

"Let's see if your sister's home, then I'll unload your luggage."

Without even glancing his way, she got out of the truck and

started up the stone path that led to the door. He stayed close behind her, his gaze frequently sweeping over the rocks, the dense trees, the heavy plantings—things that gave the lot much of its appeal and also provided much of the risk. Too many places to take cover, to launch an assault. If he were married to a princess—

His gaze settling on the sway of Princess Anna's hips, unmistakable even under the ankle-length black coat, he cut off that line of thought. He would never marry a princess. Period. Would never date one, sleep with one, even think about kissing one. Never.

Once they reached the top of the path, she was reaching for the doorbell when suddenly the door swung open and, with a squeal of delight, Princess Christina threw her arms around Princess Anna. "I'm so glad you're here! I've been waiting all day!"

He wasn't sure he'd ever seen two women who looked less like sisters. With her fair skin, blond hair and blue eyes, the elder princess took after their mother, Queen Gwendolyn, while the younger had the darker Italian coloring of the king, giving her an exotic air. There was no question, though, they were both beautiful—and no doubt they were genuinely happy to see each other.

The two women hugged and chattered for a moment, then Princess Christina finally noticed him. "I'm sorry to be so rude. My only excuse is I haven't seen my baby sister in too long. Please, come in." She offered one slim hand. "I'm Christina Sebastiani Dalton."

"Tyler Ramsey."

"Of course. I've met your father. Come in. Make yourself at home."

Princess Anna paused at the entrance to the living room. "Your house is beautiful, Christina. Exactly as I imagined it. And the snow..." She gestured toward the tall windows with both arms extended wide. "It's breathtaking."

"We like it," her sister said modestly. "Tyler, can I get you something to drink? A bite to eat?"

"No, thank you, Your Highness."

Her blue eyes gleamed at that. "No one's called me that in

ages. Around here, I'm Dr. S. or just plain Christina. So, please, forget the protocol.''

He didn't know what devil made him do it. One second he was opening his mouth to politely refuse her request, and the next, he heard himself saying, ''If you insist, Christina.''

Princess Anna shot him a look that should have reduced him to a pile of cinders and ash right there on the flagstone floor. Her dark eyes flashed, and her full, kissable lips thinned into a harsh line before she pointedly turned her back on him.

''That's better,'' Christina said, unaware of her sister's temper. ''Take your coat off and get comfortable.''

''Thank you, but I need to get going. If you'll excuse me, I'll bring up the princess's luggage, then be on my way.''

Immediately Christina sobered. ''You must be tired after the long flight and the time change. Why don't you spend the night here, then start your search for Lucas fresh in the morning? You're welcome to the extra guest room.''

Tyler looked from her to Princess Anna, whose back was still to him. The idea of crawling right into bed and sleeping until morning certainly appealed to him...but the idea of sleeping with the prissy princess in the next room sure as hell didn't. ''Thank you, Christina, but I need to make a few stops. I'll check into a hotel in town once I'm finished.''

''Well, if you insist...''

Princess Anna muttered something that sounded like, ''He does,'' before disappearing into the living room.

It took Tyler one heavily laden trip to get the princess's luggage inside. He left the bags at the foot of the stairs, then accepted the hand Christina offered.

''Thank you for delivering my sister safely to me.''

''My pleasure,'' he said. And he really did mean it.

''Anna! Tyler's leaving.''

''Good riddance,'' she replied in a voice meant to carry.

Christina smiled indulgently. ''She appreciates it, too. Be careful...and good luck.''

As he hustled through the snow back down to the truck, he grinned. He was free of the princess, his headache was gone, and the muscles in his neck had loosened significantly. He would even swear the temperature had warmed five or ten degrees since they'd touched down at the airport.

Coincidence? He thought not. More likely the thank-God-that's-over effect.

Now he was ready to get down to some *real* work.

Another perfectly good plan ruined, Anna thought morosely as she waited for Christina to return after seeing Tyler off, and it was all *his* fault. Now she must devise an entirely new plan, one for a situation with a much greater drawback than she'd expected—namely, her sister. Unfortunately, at the moment, her mind was blank.

Hearing footsteps on the wood floor and knowing her sister would have at least a question or two about her uncharacteristically rude behavior, she turned with a brilliant smile. "Where is my handsome brother-in-law?"

The mere mention of her husband brought a sweet serenity to Christina's features as she settled on the leather sofa. "Jack's away on a job. He'll be back in a few days. You know, I lived alone for years, but now, let him go away for more than a day or two and I miss him terribly."

"If he were here, presumably, *he* would be following up the clues regarding Lucas, and there would have been no need to send Tyler Ramsey," Anna remarked. It wasn't until she saw her sister's curious look that she realized how tart her tone had been. With the heat of a blush creeping into her cheeks, she clasped her hands tightly behind her back and offered a question calculated to distract her sister from her all-too-apparent curiosity. "When are you and Jack going to follow Julia's lead and make an aunt of me?"

Now the pink was in Christina's cheeks. "Actually, we're… ah, contemplating—no, that's not the right word. Considering? Entertaining? Laboring toward?"

"Laboring…" Anna stared wide-eyed at her. "You're *pregnant?*"

"Not yet. But I'm confident it's only a matter of time. We're giving it our very best try." Then the esteemed microbial ecologist gave a decidedly unesteemed giggle. "And having a wonderful time at it."

"Oh, Christina, that's fabulous news! Mama and Papa will be ecstatic."

Her sister shook one finger in warning. "Not a breath of it to anyone until the test comes back positive. Promise?"

"I promise. Once that happens, what about Jack's traveling?" She couldn't imagine her sister pregnant and alone while her husband was out saving the world. It had been so difficult for their older sister, Julia, in the months Rashid had been gone, and she had been surrounded by family.

"We've discussed that, and he's already spoken to his superiors about changing the focus of his work for the Noble Men from the field to an advisor/analyst position. That's one of the good things about a former Navy SEAL." Christina's expression turned humorously sly. "He's so versatile."

Partly awed by and partly envious of her sister's obvious love for her husband, Anna completed a slow circuit around the room before letting her hands curve over the back of an antique wooden chair. "Has there been any further news regarding Lucas?"

"You left San Sebastian just this morning, Anna," Christina said gently. "No, nothing else has surfaced in the past fourteen hours."

"Do you think he's in Montana?"

"I don't know."

"Do you think he's all right?"

"I believe so, yes."

"Do you believe we'll ever see him again?" Though Anna attempted to exercise her best princessly control over her emotions, she failed miserably. Her voice quavered and broke at the end, and tears turned her vision blurry.

An instant later she was enveloped in Christina's embrace, with soothing pats and soft words of comfort. After a time, her sister held her at arm's length. "Lucas is a strong, capable man, Anna. He knows how to look out for himself. I believe in my heart he's alive and well and that soon he'll be back with his family where he belongs. I believe," she said fiercely, "and you must, too. Your faith hasn't wavered in the past year. You can't let it start now."

"I haven't. But…it's been so long, and I miss him so much."

"We all do, Anna. And we'll have him back soon." Christina smiled, and her blue eyes silently urged Anna to do the same. "Just think—if Tyler locates Lucas during your visit, you and I will be the first ones in the family to welcome him back. You'll be able to take him home to Mama and Papa."

Oh, she had every hope of doing just that, Anna thought, though preferably without any help from Tyler Ramsey. Perhaps then he would learn to treat her with more respect.

Abruptly she became aware that Christina was watching her with a thoughtful, inquisitive big-sister look, and she realized that the mere thought of her bodyguard had brought a severe frown to her face. She forced her muscles to relax and her teeth to unclench, easing the tension that had seeped through her, and attempted to turn away, but Christina's hold on her tightened.

"Come sit down and tell me about Tyler."

Anna dragged her feet, but she was no match for Christina. Reluctantly she took a seat at one end of the sofa, but she didn't face Christina at the other. Instead, she stared mutinously at the snow outside.

"Come on now. What's the story?"

"No story. Papa felt I needed an escort for the trip here, and he chose Tyler."

"There's more to it than that."

She managed to smile. "What makes you think so?"

"I've never seen you treat an employee so rudely."

Anna shrugged carelessly. "That's because you've been gone from Montebello so long."

"Our mother hasn't been gone, and she would never tolerate your treating anyone in such a manner."

"He's just a bodyguard."

"Just a nobody charged with sacrificing his life if that's what it takes to protect yours, right?" Christina shook her head knowingly. "Come on, Anna. Kick off your shoes, curl up and tell big sister everything. Starting with how long you've had this…thing for Tyler."

Anna opened her mouth to hotly deny having any "thing" for Tyler, except a healthy dislike, when suddenly she realized fate had just handed her the answer to her latest problem. Tyler might have thwarted her plans to escape while they were still in the city, but Christina was going to make everything right. Her sister was unrelentingly sensible, responsible and dependable…and, since falling in love with Jack Dalton, incredibly soft-headed when it came to matters of the heart. Because she was deeply, happily in love, she believed everyone else ought to be also.

And though she detested the idea of lying to Christina, Anna believed in taking advantage of good fortune when it was offered.

She closed her mouth, cleared her throat, then burst into her best spoiled-child pout. "N-not long. It was so easy for you, Christina. You weren't in Montebello, you weren't living in the palace, and you didn't have Papa watching your every move. Tyler and I are fortunate to steal a few moments to ourselves every day or two between his training and my family obligations. And I swear, Papa is deliberately attempting to keep me at home and alone forever! He's much stricter with me than he ever was with you or Julia."

"You're the baby, Anna. What do you expect?"

"I didn't ask to be born last! He alternates between reminding me that there's no reason to marry yet and suggesting that this prince would make an appropriate husband or that duke could prove advantageous, and Mama just smiles and says when it's right, it will happen." She deliberately let her bottom lip stick out. "Not if Papa has his way."

"Have you told him you're interested in Tyler?"

"No."

"Why not? He respects the Ramsey family. He respects Tyler, or he never would have entrusted him with this mission."

"I don't know whether I love him or if he loves me or if it's just…"

"Hormones?" Christina asked with a dry smile.

Finally, something truthful about the conversation! Anna's hormones were certainly stirred up when Tyler was around.

"We—we think we have something special, but we'd like to be certain before we tell anyone, to give it a chance to prove itself. I know Papa does respect Tyler and his family, but that doesn't mean he wouldn't make an effort to sway me if he had the opportunity before I knew for certain how I feel."

"He knows the importance of love as well as anyone," Christina pointed out.

"Yes, but he also knows the value of strong alliances."

"He would never marry you off merely to strengthen an alliance!"

"No, but neither would he have any qualms about giving me a gentle nudge in the direction of a marriageable son and an alliance that needed strengthening." Marveling at how easily the lies came—and more than a little shamed by it—Anna gave a sigh that shivered through her entire body. "If we don't get some time together alone before long, Christina, I fear Tyler will lose all interest in me and find someone who's free to see him at will, and then I don't know what I'll do!"

"If he loses interest that easily, then he doesn't love you."

"Perhaps. Perhaps we're not meant to be…and if that's the case, I can handle it. But if I lose him without ever knowing for sure…"

Christina studied her a moment, then smiled sweetly. "All right. I should have known there was more to your spur-of-the-moment visit than merely a visit. What was your plan?"

Excitement tempered by guilt surged through Anna. She would have to make up to her sister for her deception, she promised herself. She would return for a genuine visit as soon as she was able, and if fortune shined on her, she might just bring Lucas with her. That would surely earn Christina's forgiveness. "Tyler is going to check out the three mining sites to see if Lucas is, or has been, at any of them. It's not a dangerous task. It merely involves a lot of driving, asking questions, showing Lucas's picture, all while being discreet. He thought—*we* thought…well, if I could go with him… We'd have all those days to talk and learn everything there is to know about each other and—"

"And all those nights to not talk and learn everything else there is to know?"

Anna felt her cheeks warm. "Well...we haven't yet...he hasn't...I live in the palace, for heaven's sake!"

"And our father couldn't interfere because he would believe you were spending those days and nights here with your ever-responsible older sister."

"Oh, Christina, I know it's wrong to ask you to lie to Papa, but...I've never felt this way about a man before. When I look at Tyler, I feel..." *Anger. Resentment. Bitterness.* How dare he call her sister by her name after refusing Anna the same request? They were the wrong emotions, but they were passionate, and passion was exactly what she needed to convince Christina.

"I feel as if my life is about to change," she went on, "to become something brighter and clearer and more wonderful than anything I've ever known before. I feel as if I'm on the verge of the newest, riskiest venture I've ever undertaken, and if I lose, I lose everything, but if I win...if I win, I'll be like a real fairy-tale princess who lives happily ever after. Please, Christina...you found your happily-ever-after with Jack. Please give me the chance to find mine with Tyler."

Christina pulled her into her embrace, squeezing her tightly, then said, "All right. I may live to regret this, but...what's the plan?"

What *was* the plan? Since she was making this up as she went along, Anna wasn't entirely certain. What she really wanted was to return to the airport, but Christina would think that was odd, since Tyler had intended to check into a hotel for the night. "I promised him that, if I could get away, I would meet him at the hotel this evening, and then we'd leave in the morning."

"Pleasure before business," Christina murmured. "Are you on the pill?"

"N-no." Anna's face heated again. Though she'd had plenty of boyfriends over the years, she'd never had any need for birth control. Naturally, she could have managed to take a lover at some point if she'd *truly* wanted—she did have *some* privacy from her parents—but she'd never met the man who'd made her truly want. But she certainly wasn't going to admit that to her sister. It made her seem so young, and starting a new adventure wasn't the time to be thinking how inexperienced she really was.

"Make sure he uses condoms," Christina advised. "*Every* time. Come on, now. Grab your bags, and I'll drop you off at Tyler's hotel. Which one is it?"

As Christina pulled her from the couch, Anna closed her eyes, concentrating on the travel brochures in her bag, and blurted out the first hotel name she could think of. "The Radisson."

"Then let's go. Your Prince Charming awaits."

Prince Charmless was more like it, Anna thought to herself. And he certainly wasn't awaiting *her*. When he settled in for the night, it would most likely be with the flirtatious Mareta. The next time she flew on her father's jet with a handsome man, she would insist on a male attendant instead.

The drive back into town to the Radisson was much too long—for Anna found time to have second, third and fourth thoughts about her actions—and much too short, for she and Christina had hardly begun to cover the months since they'd last seen each other. Still, it was with a quiver of excitement that she climbed out of Christina's vehicle at the hotel's main entrance.

Anna turned, ready to say goodbye, but Christina had other plans in mind. She spoke to the valet, as well as the doorman, then hooked her arm through Anna's. "I'll see you to Tyler's room," she said as they strolled into the hotel lobby.

Panic welled inside Anna and caused her to stop abruptly. When her sister stopped, too, and looked at her, she blurted out, "Please don't." Before Christina could respond, she rushed on. "You've been on your own for years, Christina. You came to a new country, attended college, lived by yourself until you met Jack. You're as free as people are supposed to be. But I've never been allowed any independence. I'm twenty-five years old, and I've never gone shopping by myself. I've never eaten in a restaurant without bodyguards nearby. I've never checked into a hotel. I've certainly never met a special man at a hotel. Please don't insist on escorting me to Tyler's room as if I'm incapable of finding my way there myself. Please don't treat me like a child."

"But—"

"Walk me to the elevator. Ride up to his floor with me. But please, please don't make me show up at his door with you at my side. I would feel so incompetent. So foolish."

"But, Anna—"

She gave her sister a beseeching look, and with a sigh, Christina relented. "You're lucky I remember what it was like to have your every move watched like a hawk. Go to the desk and ask the clerk to notify Tyler that you're here. Perhaps he could come down to meet you—" apparently she noticed the distress on Anna's face, for she amended that immediately "—or he could give you his room number and I can escort you to his floor. I won't get off the elevator. All right?"

Anna threw her arms around her in an embrace. "Yes, that is very all right!" Disentangling herself from Christina, she hurried over and joined the line fronting the registration desk. She watched as her sister wandered toward the elevators, then disappeared inside the small gift shop nearby.

In a few moments, it was Anna's turn at the desk. To be safe, she asked if Tyler was registered—it wouldn't do to have him come upon them—then happily thanked the clerk when she replied in the negative and went to meet Christina.

As soon as they stepped into the elevator, Anna pressed a button at random, then smiled broadly. She was so close to success!

As the elevator rose, Christina pressed a small paper bag into Anna's hands. "A gift from your big sister. Just in case."

Anna tore open the bag, and her face turned deep crimson when she saw the box of condoms inside. Quickly she stuffed them, bag and all, inside her shoulder bag. "I—I—"

Christina embraced her. "I don't want you to find he's fresh out and succumb to temptation anyway."

"I— We won't." In fact, with luck, she wouldn't even see the man again.

"And don't let him break your heart."

Anna smiled reassuringly. "My heart's safe."

"Oh, darling, you might think it's thoroughly protected only to discover that it already belongs to him."

Tyler Ramsey wouldn't take her heart even if she begged. Naturally she kept that information to herself.

"Call me."

"I will."

"And be careful."

"I assure you, I will." Anna embraced her once more—one last time—and then the elevator stopped and the doors slid open. She stepped off, then turned to wave at her sister. "Thank you so much."

"You owe me big time."

"I shall repay you big time." Bringing Lucas home was the best repayment of which she could conceive. "Give my love to Jack. I love you. Be careful!"

The doors closed once again and the elevator began its descent. Rather than wait, Anna began her own leisurely descent of the stairs. On the ground level, she peeked through the glass in the door to make certain that the coast was clear, as Roberto would say. It was, and she walked into the lobby proper in time to see her sister drive past outside.

Anna walked out the entrance, where her luggage waited on a cart, then turned in a slow circle. She was free! For the first time in twenty-five years, she was out of the palace, alone and on her own, with no family, no bodyguards, no royal companions! If she wanted to do something, she could do it without seeking permission from anyone. She could walk down a busy street and window shop. Go to a crowded mall and mingle with normal American shoppers. Sit in a cinema and watch the latest blockbuster theatrical releases. Go clubbing.

Ah, freedom! But all she wanted, the *only* thing she wanted, was to locate her brother.

"Ma'am?"

It took Anna a moment to realize the doorman was speaking to her. At home the men she knew called her Princess or Your Highness, and men she didn't know didn't speak to her at all. But this young man with a friendly face didn't think twice about addressing her.

"Can I help you?"

"Yes, please. Could you secure a taxi for me?"

"Of course." He stepped forward to the curb and raised one hand, and immediately a taxicab pulled away from a line of cabs and stopped before her. "Where would you like to go?"

She was about to tell him when she realized the information was best kept to herself. Slipping him a five-dollar bill, she smiled again. "I'll tell the driver myself." What a wonderful feeling to not have to answer to anyone else. To make decisions for herself and carry them through. To be responsible.

She could already guess that she was going to enjoy this adventure to the fullest.

The cab driver took her to the commercial terminal at the airport, where she rented a compact SUV. She disliked that she was required to use her own name, as well as Papa's credit card, as that would assist Papa if he began a search for her, but it couldn't be helped. Rules were rules. Besides, she'd already noticed Americans' partiality for SUVs. Finding hers would be akin to finding a needle in a haystack.

Driving was one of her few freedoms at home, though a bodyguard always occupied the seat beside her. She delighted in causing Roberto to go pale or in wringing a prayer from Nikos's lips as they raced around sharp curves and accelerated down straightaways. In no way was she reckless, though, and she was well aware that snow and ice presented dangers all their own. Why, her speed as she exited the car rental parking lot was cautious, even sedate.

But even that couldn't diminish the exhilaration bubbling inside her. She had made it to America, to Montana, and she was free of all restrictions. While Tyler Ramsey dabbled away the evening with Ms. Come-Fly-Me, she was getting the jump on the search for Lucas. She would locate him—she *must!*—and when she did, she would happily return to Montebello and life in the pretty cage. As long as her elder brother was safe and home where he belonged.

That was all that mattered.

Ursula Chambers hated cattle, mud and dirt and all things rustic, but more than any of that, she hated weepy women. Not that she couldn't cry on command with the best of them—what actress couldn't?—but she admired strength. Backbone. Steel magnolias. She'd played one onstage back when she'd lived in New York, a fitting role since she'd been one all her life. How else had she pulled herself up and out of Shady Rock, Colorado—the most boring small town in America—and made something of a life for herself in the cutthroat world of New York City?

Granted, she hadn't been able to *stay* there, not once that rat of a manager/boyfriend had dumped her for a younger actress with bigger boobs, an emptier head and a wide-eyed eagerness to please. Did the woman have even half of Ursula's talent? Of course not. Did she have a brain in that pretty, fluffy little head? Nope. But she was ten years younger than Ursula's own thirty-five, and she was just so gosh-darn naive that she couldn't see even one of Gardner's faults.

Well, let him have the little twit. Ursula had set her sights on something far more important than the silver screen. She no longer cared about being a movie star, or even a TV star.

She was going to become a bona fide member of the royal family of Montebello.

In the meantime, though, a little acting came into play as she called up the phoniest sincere smile anyone had ever seen for her sister, Jessica. "Is there anything I can get you before I go, honey?"

"No, thank you, Ursula. I'm all right."

All right, maybe, but she looked like hell, Ursula thought unkindly. *She* would never let herself fall apart over some lousy man. Why, she'd been with Gardner for nearly eight years, and the only tears she'd shed at the end of their relationship were for all she was losing—the fabulous apartment, the to-die-for clothes, the A-list parties and premieres. And yet here was Jessica, all weepy and brokenhearted over a man she'd known only a year—a man who'd gotten her pregnant and conveniently disappeared before she could tell him so.

All men were rats.

"I'll be back in a couple days. If you need anything, just see Miz Carlyle next door, or you can call me at the ranch. See you, sweetie.'' She blew a kiss in Jessica's direction, picked up her suitcase and left the apartment.

Her destination was the family ranch outside town. Ursula hated the place with a passion—enough to have left it seventeen years ago swearing she would never return—but she'd promised her sister she would spend a few days there and make certain everything was running smoothly. As if she knew what constituted *running smoothly* on a ranch these days. Erasing all those memories from her mind had been damn near as easy as shaking that dirt from her heels all those years ago. What she remembered about ranching could be summed up in few words—cattle, mud, dirt and all things rustic.

Hated 'em, hated 'em, *hated* 'em.

Who ever would have guessed that horrible little ranch could turn out to be her ticket to paradise? After all, it was the ranch that had brought Prince Lucas Sebastiani, aka cowboy Joe, into Jessica's life. If not for that, they never would have met and Jessica wouldn't be pregnant at this very moment with his royal heir.

It was really too bad that Jessica wouldn't be reasonable about the whole pregnancy thing. What a damn-fool thing to develop a stubborn streak over. It was going to end up costing her dearly…and rewarding Ursula even more dearly.

She had just one stop to make before she headed for the ranch. The house Gretchen Hanson shared with her brother, Gerald, was on the poor side of a poor town. It was tiny, boxy, and hadn't seen a paintbrush in too many years. It would be easy to take care of, though. Just start with a can of gasoline and a lighter.

She and Gretchen had been friends since grade school. Even during her years in New York, she had kept in touch with Gretchen—mostly, she wasn't ashamed to admit, so her friend could be impressed by all the glamour that had filled her life. At the time she'd thought she was being terribly shallow, bragging to someone who had nothing to brag about. But Gretchen hadn't seemed to mind. If she were a spiritual person, she would say fate, kismet or luck had kept them together, knowing that one day Ursula would need Gretchen's help. She wasn't spiritual, though. The only thing Ursula believed in was Ursula. Period.

Wearing a ratty old cardigan pulled tight against the cold, Gretchen answered Ursula's knock and invited her inside. Within minutes, they were curled up on an old sofa that had seen better days, each balancing a mug filled with more Kahlùa than coffee. "What was it you wanted to talk to me about?" Gretchen asked.

Ursula pretended to sip her coffee while studying her friend over the rim of the cup. Gretchen was shorter, thinner, plainer, mousier—just about every negative "er"—than Ursula. She was only one year older, but looked ten. Gretchen's life, she'd confided not long ago, had been nothing but one bitter disappointment after another. She'd never imagined she would be the person she'd become—thirty-six, never been married, a midwife, and caring for her dim-witted younger brother. She'd intended to have a husband, children, a career. How had it all gone so wrong? she'd lamented.

Finally Ursula lowered her cup. "Jessica is staying at the apartment with me for a while."

"Lucky us. You've got your kid sister, and I've got my kid brother. At least your sister can carry on an intelligent conversation."

"She's pregnant. By that missing prince whose plane crashed last winter."

Gretchen stared at her, then her gray eyes slowly took on a sly look. She was reaching the conclusion of what a wonderful thing this could be far more quickly than Jessica the twit had. "Do you know what kind of reward you could get for returning him home?"

"Nowhere near what I could get for delivering his child to the royal family."

After a moment to process that, Gretchen said, "I take it he's no longer in the picture."

"He went missing again. And Jessica says—" Ursula clasped her hands to her heart, let her features sink into distressed lines and in a melodramatic Southern magnolia voice said, "'I shall never, ever use my child to win a place in Joe's life. If he wants to be a father to his son, he must come and claim him.' ''

"Damn. What an idiot. I'd be on the first plane to Montebello and basking in the glow of the king and queen's love for their unborn grandchild before you could say Mother's Day."

"You and me both." Though she didn't show it, Ursula felt a great relief at hearing Gretchen's words. Her friend was going to help. She was sure of it. Still, she took her time. "Have you ever seen pictures of the palace? It's just too incredible. And those people jet around the world, wining and dining with the richest and most famous of the rich and famous. They lavish everything a kid could possibly want on their children. I can't even imagine having the astounding good fortune to be carrying the baby of the heir to the whole damn thing."

"And being stupid enough to say, 'I'd rather stay here on my piss-poor little ranch and struggle to feed my little prince or princess.' '' Gretchen gave a rueful shake of her head. "Have you smacked her upside the head?"

"I've been tempted." Ursula smiled to show that she was merely joking, then went on. "If you can fit her in, Jessica's agreed to have you deliver the baby. This being her first, she's a little anxious, of course. You hear all those terrible stories about how painful childbirth can be, and about women dying giving birth, even in this age of modern medical miracles. Of course, if *she* were to die, God forbid, I'd have no choice but to accept my duty as my nephew's only living relative on his mother's side. And frankly I think I'd have no choice but to take him to his father's family in Montebello. After all, they are *so* much better equipped to raise a child of royal blood than I am. They have nannies, tutors and an unlimited supply of money, as well as all the resources of the royal family at their fingertips. And really—" she faked an innocent expression and tone "—what kind of aunt would I be if I denied the child the upbringing, title and lifestyle that are his birthright?"

"A very bad aunt," Gretchen agreed. She sipped her coffee for a moment, gazing into the distance, then said, "Of course, you would have to relocate to Montebello. Even though he'd have plenty of relatives on his father's side, you would need to be there to keep the memory of his mother alive. A bunch of princes and princesses...they might prefer to forget his mother was a commoner. But you could make sure he never forgot. It would be the least you could do in your sister's memory.''

"The very least.''

After another silence, Gretchen spoke again. "I imagine being aunt to the future king's firstborn son would be pretty damn honorable, too. They'd probably give you a place of your own near the palace so he could visit you regularly. And a staff to maintain it. And they'd probably include you in all their family functions. Introduce you to visiting kings and princes and dukes.''

Ursula nodded solemnly. "And it would probably be a place more than big enough for a dear friend to visit for months at a time, if she wanted. If she didn't want, I'm sure there would be a generous allowance, one that could be shared quite easily.''

This time it was Gretchen's turn to nod—slowly, thoughtfully.

Ursula counted the moments, letting them drag out, before taking a deep noisy breath. "Of course, Jessica's young and healthy. I told her, the chances of anything going so badly wrong are slim. Why, it never happens these days.''

Leaning forward, Gretchen laid her coffee cup on the table, then turned on the sofa to face Ursula. There was a gleam in her gray eyes and a slyness in her expression as she very quietly corrected her.

"Well...hardly ever.''

Chapter 3

Jet lag was hell on a man's system, Tyler decided when he crawled out of bed the next morning. After leaving the princesses the previous afternoon, he'd stopped at a mall and bought a new jacket, then checked into the first motel he'd come to and fallen into bed. He'd slept straight through the night without moving, so now he was not only dim-witted but stiff, too.

But he'd better get used to it if he was going to work for the Noble Men. He very well might be tasked to fly anywhere in the world on a moment's notice and to be ready to work when he arrived. They wouldn't be cutting him any slack for jet lag or too little—or too much—sleep.

He showered, dressed, and walked to the office to check out, then grabbed breakfast to go at the fast-food place next door—a fried egg and cheese on a biscuit and a preformed hash brown, along with a large black coffee. Within a half hour of awakening, he was in the SUV and on his way.

The leads he was following had come from a woman in Colorado by the name of Ursula Chambers. What he knew about her was minimal. She'd been a two-bit actress in New York before returning home to Shady Rock, where she lived in town despite being part owner of a ranch outside town. She'd hired a hand, a drifter by the name of Joe, who stood a good chance, the king's men believed, of being the missing prince. Unfortunately, "Joe" had taken off from the Chambers place, leaving behind only one clue—an inordinate interest in an article on mining operations in Montana. He'd told Ursula he might head that way, to try his hand at something different.

There were a hell of a lot of mines in Montana, but she'd been able to narrow the field for them to three possibilities. According to Ursula, who had been contacted once again by the royal family regarding "Joe"'s whereabouts, Joe had circled the names of three in particular in the article—gold- and silver-producing mines located outside Garden City, Golden and Clarkston. And if those were a bust, he could check out the precious metals operation in Stillwater County, the coal mines in the south-central part of the state, the copper operations at Butte, the sapphire mines scattered through the mountains or the phosphate rock mines in the western and southwestern counties. Hell, he could spend the next six months doing nothing else…and still come up empty-handed.

Or he could luck out and find Prince Lucas, Joe, or whatever the man was calling himself, at the first mine.

He'd decided to check out the Clarkston operation first and took U.S. 87 north out of town. It was about 130 miles away according to the information he'd been given, all of it on local highways. The temperature was only about twelve degrees, but the sun was shining and there was no snow in the immediate forecast. No warmth, either, he acknowledged as he nudged the heater a little higher then adjusted his dark glasses over the bridge of his nose.

Any of that could change in a minute, of course. The sun could disappear behind a bank of leaden clouds, it could suddenly warm into the forties, or a blizzard could blow in from the mountains. Back in his ski instructor days, he'd once spent an entire week snowed in with a pretty blonde he'd fallen for head over heels. With a more than adequate supply of firewood, plenty of candles and oil lamps, enough food to last twice as long and a good supply of condoms, they'd hardly noticed the inconvenience. They'd said goodbye when the snow cleared with every intention of continuing the relationship, but distance had proven to be too big an obstacle. For a long time, he'd thought she'd broken his heart, but he'd recovered…eventually.

If he got snowed in on this trip, there would be no pretty blonde to keep him company…and no pouty princess to drive him nuts. Who said life wasn't fair? he wondered with a grin.

It was noon when he reached Clarkston. A stop at a gas station on the outskirts of town netted him directions to Murchison Mining, which he found with no problem. He followed a red SUV into the parking lot, then turned left when it turned right. Pulling into a space directly in front of the mine's office, he got out and glanced around as he climbed the steps.

He'd never seen a mine before, other than a passing glance at a couple of coal strip mines. This place was big, spread out and busy—and a damn sight less depressing than the strip mines. If anyone had asked him, he would have said the gold rush ended over a hundred years earlier and he wouldn't have bet money that there'd even been a silver rush. But the metals had to come from somewhere, and a fair amount of them, apparently, came from here.

Inside the office, he flashed his most charming grin at the receptionist, who directed him to the human resource office. From there he got bounced upstairs to a paper shuffler, who hemmed and hawed before taking him to the boss.

Cliff Murchison was a big man, silver-haired, in his sixties, but he looked as if he could hold his own in any fight. He sat at a cluttered desk in front of a large window that looked out on his whole operation. With an incoming fax printing on the machine behind him and four lines flashing on his phone, he was apparently a busy man, but there was no hint of impatience in his expression or his voice. "How can I help you, Mr. Ramsey?"

"I'm looking for a man," Tyler said, withdrawing a photograph of the prince from the inside breast pocket of his corduroy jacket. "He's been using the name Joe, though that might have changed. Rumor has it he was heading up this way from Colorado to look for a job."

Murchison accepted the photo and studied it blankly. "This man wanted for something?"

"No, sir. He's been missing a while. His family would like to make sure he's okay."

After a moment, the man shook his head. "There was a time when I knew every single man who worked for me but not anymore. You'll have to talk to my human resource manager." He chuckled. "Used to be, he was called the personnel director. Same job, fancier title, bigger salary. Let me call my secretary and have her take you down to Lyle and see if he can help you out." He pressed an intercom button, then handed the photo back. "Good luck finding him."

"Thank you, sir."

The secretary who came to escort him downstairs was about twenty-five, blond, not pretty but striking, and she looked as if she could teach him a thing or two. He would have been flattered by her interest if she hadn't displayed the same interest in the photograph of the prince, and if he didn't suspect she showed the same interest in every male of legal age she came across.

"Are you going to be in town long, Mr. Ramsey?" she asked as they descended the stairs to the first floor.

"Not too long."

"You might want to visit the Silver Nugget tonight. Real original name, huh? A lot of the miners hang out there—the single guys, and the ones that like to pretend they are. Someone there might have run across your guy." She looked him up and down. "Are you a private detective?"

"Something like that." It had been decided before he'd left Montebello that there was no need to tell anyone he was working for King Marcus. A lot of people probably wouldn't believe him, and there might be more than a few who would try to profit from the royal family's misfortune.

"Where are you from?"

"Arizona."

"You're a long way from home, hon." She pushed open the door marked Human Resource, then gave him a promising smile. "The Silver Nugget's not my regular hangout, but I'll make a point of being there tonight. In case you get lonely." Then she called into the office, "Lyle! Cliff wants you to give this gentleman whatever help he needs."

"Be right there, Cindy," came a reply from the rear of the office.

"See ya, hon."

Tyler watched her walk away with an appreciative smile. "Sultry" wasn't a word to come quickly to mind on a day when the wind chill was down around zero, but Cindy made it happen easily enough. Cliff Murchison might be sitting on a gold and silver mine, but his biggest asset was probably his secretary. The laziest man in Montana would be happy to work if it meant seeing her every day.

Lyle came out of the back office in a short-sleeved dress shirt, a tie that was too bright and too wide for Tyler's tastes, with a half-eaten submarine sandwich in one hand. He looked around, found a napkin to put the sandwich on, then wiped his hands on another napkin. "I'm Lyle. What can I do you for?"

Tyler gave him the same line he'd given Murchison and showed him the photograph, and Lyle gave the same negative response. "Want me to show it to the girls?" he offered, then gestured for Tyler to follow him.

A half-dozen women were having lunch in the employee lounge at the end of the hall. They passed the picture around with little response until the last woman got it. "Hey, this looks kinda like that prince that's missing," she said. "I saw him on TV not long ago. Remember—his plane crashed in Colorado or someplace a while back and they thought he was dead, but then they thought he was alive. He's from Monte Carlo or someplace like that."

"Not Monte Carlo. Monaco," another woman corrected her.

"Isn't Monaco in Monte Carlo? Or is Monte Carlo in Mona— Heck, I don't know. But he kinda looks like that guy." She handed the photo to Tyler. "Is he some kind of royalty? Maybe with a reward for finding him?"

"You'd have the gratitude of his wife and kids," he lied with a smile.

"Heck, if he's married, I don't want him," the woman muttered before picking up her sandwich again.

"Even if he wasn't married, you are, Faye," the second

woman said, "and you've got five kids. When would you find time for him?"

"Honey, I'd leave the kids with my husband and run away with the guy," Faye said with a laugh. "Heck, there're days when I'd leave the kids and run away by myself if I could find the energy."

"Sorry we can't help you, Mr. Ramsey," Lyle said.

"I appreciate your time," Tyler said as they walked to the main entrance. Glancing out, he saw a cluster of men standing in front of the building across the parking lot. "Do you mind if I ask some of your men out there?"

"You can't go in any of the facilities, but...sure. Go ahead."

Tyler claimed his parka from the coat rack inside the door and pulled it on, then drew his gloves from the pockets. The men out front were apparently on their lunch break and had gathered in the frigid weather to smoke. He appreciated a good cigar now and then, but he couldn't imagine developing any habit that he'd want to indulge badly enough to stand outside and freeze off vital parts of his anatomy. The seven or eight burly men didn't seem to even notice the cold, maybe because their attention was riveted on someone else.

One of the men shifted, and Tyler got a glimpse of that some-one, standing in the middle of their circle. Her back was to him, but he'd recognize those dark brown curls and that regal bearing anywhere. Son of a bitch, it couldn't be! He'd left her safe and secure in big sister's care in Billings. There was no way in hell she could be here in Clarkston!

But she was. She turned to laugh at something one of the men had said, and there was no doubt. A hundred and thirty miles from where she was supposed to be and putting him in a world of trouble.

Princess Anna. In the all-too-luscious flesh.

He charged out the door, down the steps and across the park-ing lot, his only thought to grab the princess, drag her royal hide into the truck and get her the hell back to Billings. Before he reached her, though, good sense prevailed. Excluding her, he was the runt in this group. Of course he was armed—he had his Sig Sauer in the shoulder holster, a compact Beretta in an ankle holster and a knife in his jeans pocket—but who was to say these guys weren't armed, too? After all, this was America.

Slowing his steps, he stopped beside the red SUV he'd followed in, its engine making clicking noises as it cooled, and shoved his hands into his pockets. After a moment, one of them looked his way. "Can we help you with something?"

"Nah. I just thought when you were through there, I'd like a word with your friend."

Even though she was bundled against the cold, he could see the stiffness spreading through the princess. She slowly turned, the smile gone from her lips, her demeanor formal and distant. The brat didn't even have the grace to look guilty, he noticed. Instead of at least acknowledging that *she* was the one in the wrong place, she was looking at him as if *he* had no right to be there. "Oh. I'd planned to be gone before you arrived."

"Didn't plan too well, did you?"

The biggest of the men took a step forward. "This guy bothering you, Annie? You know, you don't wanna talk to him, you don't have to."

Annie. Tyler hated the sound of the nickname in another man's voice. *He* couldn't call her that—couldn't even call her *Anna*—and damned if he was going to listen to some good ol' boy do it. Gritting his teeth, he said coldly, "It's time to leave. You have an appointment in Billings, remember?"

She smiled just as coldly. "No one's waiting for me in Billings or anywhere else, for that matter."

"Christina—"

"Thinks I'm with you."

"Why would she—" Understanding arrived about the time the big guy took another step toward him. The princess had pulled off a royal scam! She'd persuaded her father that she desperately needed to see her sister, then convinced the sister that she was going to travel with him, all so she could achieve her original goal—to look for Prince Lucas herself. As if some foolish, empty-headed little princess could accomplish what trained investigators, so far, had failed at. What did she know of conducting a search, an interview or an investigation?

Enough to arrive at this site ahead of him, a small voice pointed out.

"We need to talk," he demanded. *"Now."*

For a moment he thought she would refuse. The desire to do so was obvious in the tilt of her chin, the disdain in her eyes. But after a long, tense moment had ticked past, she turned to the men with a dazzling smile. "Excuse me, gentlemen. This won't take long."

Not trusting himself to touch her, Tyler gestured for her to follow him to the middle of the parking lot. With plenty of angry words trying to break free and not trusting himself to say any of them—*What the hell are you doing here? Are you insane? What kind of fool-minded scheme is this? Does the king have any idea what you're doing? You should be turned over your daddy's knee!*—he just stared at her. And stared.

She shifted uncomfortably, then shuffled her feet. Funny. He hadn't thought she would ever show discomfort to a mere employee. When the wind blew a strand of hair across her cheek, she brushed it back, then pursed her lips primly. "If you have something to say, Mr. Ramsey…"

"I have plenty to say, Your Highness. I intend to say most of it to your father."

Dismay and more disdain darkened her eyes. "Why am I not surprised?" Then… "I'm not going back to Billings."

"No. Obviously, you can't be trusted to stay there."

"You can't send me home. The plane has already begun its return flight."

He smiled. "Don't be so sure, Princess. All it would take is one phone call to departure control at the Billings airport. If they can't get in touch with the Gulfstream, they can contact the air traffic control center that can. The jet can be back on the ground at Billings as quickly as I could get you back there."

She lost a bit of her confidence, because she knew he was telling the truth. "And how do you think you would get me back there?"

"With handcuffs and a gag would be my first choice. Failing that, I thought I'd drive you back in my car."

"I'm not going with you."

"I don't recall offering you a choice, Princess."

She smiled smugly. "If you lay one hand on me, I'll scream bloody murder and my new friends will be more than happy to come to my aid."

She gestured toward the men, all watching them with suspicion, and Tyler noticed once again that the littlest of the eight was about thirty pounds heavier than he was. He didn't have any doubt they were the kind of guys who would act first and ask questions later...and he had plenty of doubts whether she was bluffing. Maybe she was, maybe she wasn't. Maybe she thought they would simply hold him back while she made her getaway, or maybe she knew they'd beat the hell out of him given what they thought was a reason.

"It seems we're at an impasse," she said softly.

He looked at her. With her curls windblown and her cheeks reddened from the cold, she looked sweet, innocent and so damn beautiful...when in fact she was deceitful, manipulative and devious as hell. "I guess we are," he agreed. "And what would be your solution?"

"I'll travel with you."

"No."

"Christina already believes that's what I'm doing. She's covering for me with Papa and Mama."

"No way."

"And I can help you look for Lucas."

"Let me put this simply, Princess—no. Hell, no. No way, no how, not in this lifetime."

She threw his own words back at him. "I don't recall offering you a choice, Mr. Ramsey. I'm not willing to remain in Billings and do nothing while my brother may be out here somewhere. He could be injured, and he hardly knows you. He may not even remember you, and may believe he has no reason to trust you. He may believe you're going to harm him. But I'm his favorite sister. Regardless of what's happened in the year past, he'll trust me."

There was no way in hell he was agreeing to her crazy scheme. After all, he'd done his job. He'd delivered her safely to her sister's. The king couldn't hold him responsible because she refused to stay there.

The hell he couldn't. Maybe Tyler had fulfilled his duty by dropping her off at Christina's, but that didn't mean he was free from responsibility now that he knew she'd left there. Like it or not, he was the only one in the king's security detail—hell, the only one in the king's employ, period—who knew where Princess Anna was. He had an obligation to keep her safe until she was back where she belonged.

Besides, it wouldn't be for long. He would place a call to the king that afternoon, and the king would put an end to this lunacy. The princess might lie to and scam everyone else, but she wasn't about to defy an order from the royal papa, no matter how spoiled she was. Tyler would be rid of her—again—by tomorrow for sure.

He gave her a sour look. "How did you get here?"

"In that vehicle." She gestured toward the smaller SUV. "It's very red, isn't it? Rather like your face."

His gaze hardened, and a muscle in his jaw began to twitch. "Give me the keys and tell your friends goodbye."

She gave him the key ring, then returned to the eight giants. While she chatted with them as if it were the most natural thing in the world, he transferred her luggage from her vehicle to his, then took the keys inside, where he bribed the receptionist with a healthy chunk of cash to return the extra SUV to the rental agency in Billings. When he returned, the big guy was helping the princess into the black SUV. She eagerly waved goodbye to the men as he backed out of the space, then drove out of the parking lot.

As he turned onto the highway, she looked at him. "It's not so bad, Mr. Ramsey. Now you've got a partner."

He scowled at her. A princess for a damned partner. Just what he freakin' needed.

"What exactly have you been up to since I left you at Christina's yesterday?"

Anna didn't need to look at Tyler to know that his fingers were knotted around the steering wheel, or that the muscle in his jaw was jumping, or that his green eyes resembled liquid fire. She certainly didn't need to look to know that he furiously, intensely, didn't want her there, so she gazed out the window instead. "I returned to the airport soon after you left and rented the SUV, and I came to Clarkston. I checked into a motel across the way from the Silver Nugget, and I spent last evening there."

For a moment, she was silent. Then she archly added, "*You,* presumably, were sleeping." With Mareta? She would like to know almost as much as she didn't want to.

"Did you tell those men who you were?"

Though she'd just determined to avoid eye contact, she couldn't resist giving him a scathing look. "I'm not an idiot, Mr. Ramsey."

He murmured something that sounded suspiciously like, "Couldn't prove it by me," and then his mouth thinned in a taut line again. "You never had any intention of visiting your sister, did you?"

"No."

"You lied to your father, your mother, Christina—everyone."

She lowered her gaze to her gloved hands. She wasn't proud of the untruths she'd been forced to tell to get this far...but her cause was just and she would do it again if necessary. She would do *anything* to find Lucas and bring him home!

Deliberately she changed the subject. "I spoke to dozens of people. No one has seen Lucas. We can be in Garden City by six—"

He pulled into the parking lot of the motel where she'd spent the past night and shut off the engine. She glanced around. "Why are we here?"

"We're staying here."

"But I've already spoken to everyone here."

He gave her a cutting look. "Well, Princess, you're not exactly trained to do this, are you?"

"To show a photo? To ask, 'Have you seen this man?'"

"Your father sent me here to follow up on these leads. *Me,* not you. I'm not going to tell him I've done that when I haven't, and I'm certainly not going to tell him I've done it when only you have. If you don't like it, too bad. Get over it…or go back to Montebello. The choice is yours.''

Stubbornly she clamped her jaw shut and stared straight ahead. He waited a minute, then another, then exited the vehicle and went into the hostel's office. He was the most frustrating man she'd ever met. Either it said a great deal for her acting abilities that she'd been able to convince Christina she had feelings for the man, or it was a sad commentary on Christina's judgment that her sister believed she *could* have feelings for the man. Not one of her boyfriends had ever been so stubborn, so infuriating…

Though she must admit, he could certainly be charming when he so chose. Mareta had been quite smitten with him, and the desk clerk visible through the plate-glass window was all but preening under his attention. It was a very good thing he hadn't attempted to charm *her*. His ego surely would be wounded to find she was immune to him.

He came out of the office with two keys and drove to the end of the building. After tersely instructing her to wait, he unlocked each of the last two rooms, took their bags inside, then opened the vehicle's door for her. With a regal sniff, she allowed him to help her to the ground, then in a long-suffering voice, she said, ''I don't understand why we're frittering away precious time here.''

He gestured for her to precede him into the room on the end. The decor was identical to the room where she'd slept the night before, right down to the rather stuffy odor. The door joining her room to his was open, and she could see his suitcase on an identical bed inside.

''Your bag?''

In the palace she was accustomed to servants putting things away for her, and so she didn't hesitate to hand her shoulder bag to him. While she was unbuttoning her coat, he emptied it on the bed, then rummaged through its contents.

''What are you doing?'' she shrieked, frantically reaching for the paper bag containing Christina's condoms. ''You can't—! I demand you stop this instant!''

With one arm, he held her back until he'd pocketed two

items—her passport and her wallet, containing all her money, credit cards and driver's license. Then he politely returned everything else—including the unopened shopping bag—to her purse, secured the clasp and set it on the bed. "Kick off your shoes, Princess. Watch a little TV. I've got to make some phone calls."

She sank down on the bed, infuriated that he'd gone through her belongings, and relieved beyond measure that he hadn't discovered the condoms. Surely he would have commented on her optimism, or would have twisted Christina's precaution into some sort of tawdry character flaw. With her luck, he might even have assumed that they were intended for use with him, and he might have responded in a way that would require she have him removed from this life.

Instead, he intended to remove *her* from *his* life. He would call her father. She knew it as surely as she knew each and every one of the names she'd been christened with. Papa would be furious with her, and he would send the flight crew to pick her up, and he would never let her leave Montebello without him again. Worse, there was nothing she could do about it. She couldn't even attempt another escape. Running away in America required money, and thanks to Tyler she hadn't even the cost of a phone call on her.

Fighting the urge to weep, she walked to the window and stared out. If only she knew how to get hold of Rusty, the largest of her miner friends. He and his associates could persuade Tyler to return her property to her, though she would likely have to stress to them repeatedly that they shouldn't break him. She could probably find them at the Silver Nugget this evening— that was where she'd found them last evening. Perhaps she could persuade them to do something harmless, such as leave Tyler bound and gagged in his room for the maid to find in the morning, while she took her money and his vehicle and continued her search for Lucas. It would be no more than the arrogant man deserved for his highhandedness. After all, he *wasn't* her boss.

Unfortunately, she was quite certain that inciting a group of men to leave another man bound and gagged in a motel room while she skipped town with his rental vehicle would be frowned upon by the local authorities, even if her father had paid for the vehicle. And she had no doubt whatsoever her parents would find such actions thoroughly appalling.

Even if it was no more than the man in question deserved.

Life simply wasn't fair, she thought with a sorrowful sigh.

Life just wasn't fair, Tyler thought as he listened to the hum of the long-distance connection in his ear. Only a few days earlier he'd shared the news of this assignment with his brother Kyle. It was nothing complicated, just a task even someone fairly new to the business could handle, but being selected for it had been a vote of confidence from the king and those in authority in his own organization. It had been important to him, and he'd been certain from the beginning that he would complete it quickly, successfully and thoroughly. He would leave no stone unturned, no question unasked, and would do a job Kyle, their father and everyone else could be proud of, pulling it off without the slightest hitch.

Ha!

That was before Princess Anna had been figured into the equation. Frankly, he couldn't imagine a bigger complication than the delicate, deceptively innocent brat in the room next door.

There was a rustle of sound at the other end of the line, followed by King Marcus's voice. "Tyler. I understand you've encountered a problem. Does it involve my son?"

"No, Your Majesty. It involves your daughter."

After a moment's silence, the king repeated, "My daughter? Which one?"

"Princess Anna."

"She's safe with her sister in Billings, isn't she?"

"No, sir. She's safe in the motel room next to mine here in Clarkston." Grimly, Tyler related the details of finding the princess among her new brawny friends at the mine, her cockeyed proposal that she accompany him to the remaining mines, all but forcing her to leave with him and confiscating her valuables. When he was finished, he waited for the king's response.

It wasn't encouraging.

Laughter rang over the line. "That's my Anna," the king said with no small measure of pride. "She looks most like me, and she thinks most like me. She's very resourceful, isn't she?"

"Yes, Your Majesty, she is, but—"

"Her mother tells me I shouldn't encourage her, and I tell her I don't. She doesn't believe me." King Marcus chuckled again. "So Anna believes she can be of help to you in your investigation."

"Yes, sir. However, I don't *need* any help."

"No, of course not. Still…"

The muscles in Tyler's stomach knotted. He wasn't going to like the way this turned out. He could already tell.

"She is headstrong."

"Yes," Tyler reluctantly agreed.

"And she is her brother's favorite. He would never doubt her love, her loyalty or her trustworthiness."

Of course not. And she was already there, and if she wanted to tag along, how could it hurt? Oh, yeah, Tyler could see exactly where this was going, and he saved himself the discomfort of hearing it one step at a time. "You want me to take her along, don't you, Your Majesty?"

The king chuckled once more. "If you sounded too happy about it, my young friend, I would worry. On the other hand, though, you don't have to sound as if you've just been condemned to a fate worse than death. Anna is quite intelligent, and people like her. They tell her things. I've always found her to be a pleasant companion."

But he didn't want a companion, Tyler thought with a scowl. And of course the king found her pleasant—he was her *father.* Tyler wasn't. He was just a man.

Who'd been thinking about kissing her before they'd even cleared Montebellan airspace.

Who didn't like strange men calling her Annie.

Who wasn't sure he could sleep ten feet away from her.

"Your Majesty, of course I'll follow your orders, but…how can I concentrate on the search for your son if I have to be responsible for your daughter's safety? She has more than one guard any time she leaves the palace grounds, and yet here she is halfway around the world with only me.''

"She'll be fine, Tyler. You'll be fine. It's not exactly a high-risk operation, is it?''

"No, sir,'' he admitted grudgingly.

"And you're able to take care of her if necessary.''

"Yes, sir.''

"And you're willing...if necessary.''

Tyler didn't answer as quickly as he might have if it had been anyone else in the royal family, but he did answer. ''Yes, sir. Of course.''

"Then it's settled. Just do me one favor. Don't tell her you called me. Let her believe you see the logic in her arguments. Extract a few promises from her to be on her best behavior, to obey you at all times, and so forth, then agree to let her accompany you. Let her have her adventure.''

"Yes, Your Majesty.'' *If I have to.*

"Keep in touch.''

"I will.''

Then the king's voice turned stern. "And bring my little girl home safe and none the worse for her adventure.''

Which translated roughly to, You lay a hand on her and I'll throw you in the dungeon. "Yes, sir.'' Tyler hung up, then fell back on the bed.

Life was so damn unfair, it sucked.

Royally.

"Are you ready?''

Anna was lying on the bed, staring at water stains that spread across the textured ceiling, when Tyler spoke from the connecting doorway. "For what?'' she asked morosely. To return to Billings, where the Gulfstream would be waiting to take her home in defeat? She would never be ready for that.

"I can't look for information on your brother if I don't leave the motel and talk to people, and I can't do that if you don't go with me.''

Abruptly she sat up. "You didn't call my father?''

"I called my brother, and I spoke to Lorenzo.''

Kyle Ramsey was one of the Noble Men, and her cousin, Lorenzo, was head of intelligence in Montebello. It was logical that he would report to both of them. "And did you tell them I was here?"

That muscle in his jaw jerked again as he scowled. "No. Call me crazy, but I'd rather not get yanked from this assignment before I have a chance to complete it. It wouldn't do much for my reputation…not that covering up for a runaway princess is going to help, either."

It took a moment for his words to sink in, and another for her to rise from the bed. "Thank you," she said fervently. "You won't regret it, I swear. You won't even notice I'm here, and I promise you, no one will ever know. Thank you so much."

Acting purely on impulse, she raised onto her toes and pressed a kiss to his lips. It was chaste, innocent, and over in a heartbeat, and it left him, for one satisfying moment, looking dazed.

As she turned away to pick up her coat and handbag, she felt neither chaste nor innocent. Her lips were tingling with an unfamiliar buzz, and there was a sweet heat seeping through her. And all from a sisterly kiss! she marveled. Who knew how she might respond if he ever truly kissed her, the way a man kissed a woman.

They left the SUV in the parking lot and set out along the narrow sidewalk. He'd said he wanted to talk to people, and that was exactly what he did for the next few hours. They went inside every shop, every business, and showed Lucas's photograph to every person willing to look at it. By the time they returned to the motel, she was certain she could repeat the standard questions, and everyone's answers, in her sleep.

"What now?" she asked as she preceded him into her room.

"We might as well get some dinner, then call it an early night. How's the food at the Silver Nugget?"

As she began removing her coat, gloves and scarf, she glanced out the window at the establishment across the way. It was built to resemble an old mining shack of some sort, but inside it was pure cowboy bar, according to Rusty and his companions. The air was smoky, the music loud, and the action tended to get a little rowdy. As for the food…. Granted, the palace's staff of chefs had certainly spoiled her palate, but she was quite certain that, even among the town's meager offerings, the Silver Nugget's cuisine didn't shine.

"It's edible," she replied with a shrug. Her dinner the previous night had consisted of a steak on the chewy side, a baked potato on the mushy side, and corn that she was fairly certain had come from a can. And she hadn't cared at all. It had been her first steak in her first American cowboy bar with her first American beer from a long-necked bottle on her first night of freedom, and she'd been thrilled with every bit of it.

"You want to go someplace else?"

"The Silver Nugget's fine." She gave him a sly look. "Maybe we'll see Rusty and his friends there."

Tyler's gaze hardened, and his jaw clenched. "Maybe we will. Do you need to change clothes or anything?"

She looked down at her sweater and slacks, then ran a hand through her curls. *Did* she need to change clothes or anything to make herself presentable? she wanted to ask, but wouldn't give him the satisfaction. "It won't take but a minute."

With a nod, he passed through the connecting door into his own room. The instant the door was closed—or rather, pushed up apparently as far as he intended to close it—she removed an outfit from her bag and went into the bathroom to change. A moment later, she came out again and studied her reflection in the mirror above the sink. Her makeup required only a minor touch-up, then she combed her hair with her fingers and sprayed herself with perfume created exclusively for her by the queen's favorite parfumier in Paris.

After a time, she acknowledged that she was dawdling merely to keep Tyler waiting. She walked to the connecting door and called that she was ready, then slipped into her coat once again, belting it tightly.

"Only a minute, huh?" he remarked dryly when he came into the room.

She didn't deign to answer.

The winter sun was low on the horizon, and the sky was quickly turning the hue of ancient pewter. Without the sun, the air seemed immeasurably colder, though realistically she guessed the temperature hadn't dropped by more than a few degrees. Even so, she was happy to match the rapid pace Tyler set as they crossed the parking lot, then the street.

They were among fewer than a dozen customers in the bar. A waitress who introduced herself as Suz showed them to a table along the wall. She wore a short, tight denim skirt and a red cowboy shirt with fringe following the yoke that dipped across her breasts, and after depositing two stained menus on the table, she sashayed off, her short red cowboy boots clicking on the wood floor. Anna watched her go, wondering where she could get an outfit like that for the next charitable costume ball she was forced to attend, and whether she could possibly remain in Montana long enough to learn how to sashay like that. She wasn't entirely certain her hips would move in that manner. Perhaps it was something bred into a woman.

She chose the chair with its back to the wall so she would have a good view for people-watching when the customers began arriving for their evening's entertainment. To her dismay, after removing his coat, Tyler chose the chair next to her—presumably for the same reason. Not out of any desire for proximity to her.

"What's good on the menu?" he asked as he opened it.

"Rusty says the fried pickles are good, but I didn't give them a try. The buffalo wings with blue cheese dressing are quite tasty, but they're actually chicken rather than buffalo."

"Yeah, I knew that."

She didn't like it when he used that dry tone with her. If he was dryly amused, that was one thing, but when he was dryly making fun of her...though a furtive glance suggested he was amused this time.

Suz returned to deliver utensils wrapped in paper napkins, then drew an order pad from its spot tucked into the waistband of her skirt. With the skirt fitted so tightly, Anna wouldn't have thought there was room to tuck in a breath, but she would never presume to comment on it. "What can I get you folks?"

"Are your hamburgers as greasy as the steak I had last night?" Anna asked.

Beside her, Tyler made a coughing sound, but Suz didn't take offense. "I imagine they probably are," she replied, then drolly added, "I only work here. I *don't* eat here."

"Good. The best American hamburgers should be, you know. I'll have one greasy burger with cheese, and some of those French fries with fried onions and peppers, and one of those American beers I had last night."

"I didn't wait on you last night, honey. I have no idea what kind of beer you had."

"It was very cold, and it came in a brown bottle with a long neck."

"Just bring her whatever you have," Tyler said. "And make it two on everything."

"The staff at the palace always remembers what I eat, what I like and what I don't like," she remarked as the waitress left.

"Well, she doesn't work at the palace, and her universe doesn't revolve around you."

She granted him an aloof stare. "I'm well aware of that, Mr. Ramsey. I was simply making a comment."

"Call me Tyler."

"No, thank you."

"You can't keep calling me 'mister' or people will get suspicious."

"Then I won't call you anything," she announced. Before he could respond, she gestured. "See that man behind the bar? His name is Toy. Isn't that an unusual name for a man of his stature? I'd wager *he* recalls what kind of beer I ordered last night. And see the man seated on the stool? His name is Slow. Of course, that's a nickname. Americans have a fondness for nicknames, don't they? Rusty's name is actually Dudley, and I seriously doubt Suz—" she nodded politely to the approaching waitress "—is her given name."

The waitress smiled as she served two bottles of cold beer. "You're right, hon. It's short for Suzannah. What's your name?"

She had introduced herself the previous night as Anna Peterson, Peterson being her maternal grandparents' surname, but Rusty had been quick to christen her with a nickname of her own. She happily used it now. "Annie. Which is short—er, rather, long for Anna. And he's just Tyler."

"Is that a first name or last?" Suz asked.

"Makes no difference," Anna replied before he could.

"As long as he knows to come when called," Suz said with a laugh. "That's all that matters, isn't it, Annie?"

Chapter 4

Tyler pushed back in his chair so he could see the princess better, then rested one ankle over the other knee. So the name issue was still a sore point with her. Maybe he'd handled it the wrong way. Maybe, when she'd asked him to call her Anna in private, he should have agreed, made her happy and then made a point of not using any name at all when they were alone.

It was too late to do that now. With that mile-wide stubborn streak running through her, the only way she was going to call him by his given name was if he used hers so often it became second nature. Familiar. Friendly.

He didn't want to be friendly, damn it. He only wanted to do his job and do it well, without complications or emotional entanglements.

He was looking around the room for a diversion when the scrape of chair on floor beside him brought his gaze swinging back to her as she stood up, inches closer to him than he'd expected her to be, and loosened the belt that secured her coat. With easy, graceful movements, she shrugged out of the garment, then leaned to drape it over the chair on the opposite side. The movement gave him a moment too long to gaze at faded denim molded over a shapely derriere, then she straightened and gave him a better view of rounded breasts, a narrow waist and womanly hips. The T-shirt and jeans couldn't fit any more snugly if they'd been made for her body, and they could put a man in mind of all sorts of things, starting with taking them off of her...slowly.

He tried to swallow but couldn't, reached for his beer but grasped only air. Forcing his gaze away from her as she settled in the chair again, he found the beer and drank half of it in one swallow, but it did nothing to ease the heat building inside him. He wanted to order her to put the coat back on, to flag down Suz and tell her they would take their food back to the motel...where they had connecting rooms...with beds....

"Do you like my shirt?"

He stared toward the bar. "Yeah, sure."

"You didn't even read it."

How could a red-blooded man who'd been alone a long time be expected to notice what was on the shirt when he'd already noticed what was under it?

He glanced at it, then had to take a longer look to actually read it. There was a photo of a man, head tilted, cowboy hat tipped low to hide most of his face, and the legend, I got lucky at the Silver Nugget. He might have been amused if he wasn't aroused, and if she were Cindy, Suz or any other non-royal female in the world. Instead, he finished off the beer and signaled Suz for another before asking, "Do you know what getting lucky means, Your Highness?"

"My command of the English language is as good as yours, Mr. Ramsey," she said with exaggerated patience. "Perhaps even better. 'Getting lucky' refers to having good fortune."

"Your command of the English language probably *is* better than mine," he agreed. "But your command of English slang isn't. Having good fortune is one meaning. 'Scoring' is another. Getting laid. Having sex." He half expected her olive skin to turn deep crimson, or the smug superiority in her expression to shift to dismay.

Instead she smiled—a sly, subtle I've-got-a-secret sort of smile—and murmured, "So that's what Rusty meant. He gave me the shirt, you know. Last night—or, actually, early this morning. When he left the motel."

Tyler was stunned at the intensity of the jealousy that settled in his gut. The thought of her with the big, brawny redhead who'd called her Annie was enough to knot his muscles and stir a few murderous impulses. Not that it was any of his business. He was protecting her from those who might threaten or endanger her life, not from herself. Even back home in the palace, she had the freedom to carry on affairs, as long as she did so discreetly. The king and queen might not like to acknowledge it, but those apartments were private for a reason.

The hell it wasn't any of his business! Back home in the palace, help was never more than the push of a button—or a scream—away. Security was strict, and it was a damned island, which made it easy to lock down. Here *he* was responsible for her safety. *He* was the one whose career and life would be over if anything happened to her.

He was the one who wanted her for himself and couldn't have her. Damned if he would stand by and let good ol' Rusty take what he was denied.

Suz brought their meal, along with another beer, and they ate in silence. The princess had been right—the greasy burgers were good. Now if he could just find a way to get her back to the motel while he passed around her brother's picture…not that sending her back would necessarily make her safe. Rusty could find her there easily enough. She could call him or any of her other new friends, or could slip out and wander off.

Too bad handcuffs and a gag really were out of the question.

He was morosely considering that fact when a warm hand touched his shoulder. "Hi, darlin'," Cindy murmured, leaning close enough for him to smell her cologne and get an indecent look down her blouse. "I was hoping I'd find you here."

Without waiting for an invitation, she slid into the chair opposite him. "Things won't really pick up in here for another hour or so. There's gonna be a local band playing tonight. What they lack in talent, they make up for in enthusiasm. I hope you're planning to stick around so I can give you a tour of the dance floor."

Instinctively he knew her style of dancing was suggestive and intimate—exactly what he might need if he was by himself. But he wasn't alone, and no way was he going to let himself be dragged off in Cindy's clutches and leave the princess alone for Rusty or any other cowboy to make a move on. *Another* move, apparently, in Rusty's case.

"Sorry," he said. "I don't dance."

"Why, of course you do," the princess said innocently. "And quite well, too. Go ahead. Drop a few coins in the jukebox and show her."

He gave the royal brat a warning look. "I can't leave you alone here," he said, his tone neutral for Cindy's sake but his gaze threatening.

"Don't worry about me. My friend Rusty has just arrived." Smiling, she waved at the red-haired miner, who picked up his beer from the bar and headed their way. "You two go on. Enjoy yourselves."

"I really don't like to—" Tyler broke off as he moved against his will. How had Cindy gotten a death grip on his arm and pulled him to his feet and halfway to the dance floor, with a stop at the jukebox, in a matter of seconds? And what the hell was the princess doing, laughing at something the big guy had said and laying her hand on his arm as if he deserved it?

"Sorry, Cindy, I don't want—" He got about three steps away before she swung him back around.

"Relax, darlin'. All this tension isn't good for you...well, except in certain places." With a devilish smile, she wrapped her arms around his neck, stepped in close and began moving in time to the music.

Because it appeared he had no other choice, he settled his hands at her waist and tried subtly to put some space between them...with emphasis on *tried*. For such a slender little thing, Cindy was stronger than she looked. "How well do you know Rusty?"

"Jealous, darlin'? Don't be. He's just a friend." She slid her fingers into his hair, leaned even closer and brushed a kiss to his jaw.

The action annoyed him. Hell, the whole scene annoyed him—the fact that a stranger could insist he dance with her, that she felt entitled to touch him intimately, to kiss him as if she knew him, to rub against him as if she had the right. And that was *all* that was annoying him. He didn't care that the princess was still laughing with Rusty, or that she looked like she was having a better time with him than she'd ever had with Tyler. He for damn sure didn't care that she was still touching the guy, or that she'd apparently done a hell of a lot more than touch him last night.

Yeah, right.

Cindy slid her hands down from his neck, rubbing his spine with easy, sure touches, when suddenly she stopped. Her arm was pressed against his side—more accurately, against his shoulder holster. She blinked in surprise, then gave him a lush, sexual smile. "Hmm…what other surprises do you have for me, darlin'?" She slid her hands lower, as if she intended to find out. Over at the table good ol' Rusty stood up and took the princess's arm as she got up, and Tyler decided he'd had more than enough.

He untangled himself from Cindy, crossed to the princess in four strides, removed her from Rusty's grip and swept her back to the table with him. There he tossed down enough money to cover their bill, grabbed their coats and pushed her ahead of him to the door and outside.

"Well, that was certainly—"

He raised a hand in warning, and the princess fell silent. Ignoring new customers arriving, he helped her into her coat, shoved his arms into his own jacket, then headed for the motel.

"Rude," she finished once they reached her room. "You were very rude."

He unlocked and opened the door, then made a big gesture for her to enter. He followed right on her heels, locked the door, then turned on the lights in his own room before facing her. "What? Were you planning another late evening with Rusty? Maybe this time he'd pay you with something more than a cheesy T-shirt."

For a long time she simply looked at him. Even in a badly lit, badly furnished cheap motel room, she looked every bit the elegant, well-bred, privileged princess she was, and with nothing more than a look, she made him feel…undeserving. Unworthy. "Rusty gave me this shirt because he thought I would get a—

a kick out of it. He didn't ask for anything in return, and I didn't offer him anything other than my thanks.''

"Call it what you want, Princess. It doesn't matter to me." Turning into his room, he jerked off his parka, then the sports jacket underneath it. He didn't hear any sounds but the ones he was making—the rustle of clothing, his uneven breathing, the anger and jealousy and frustration boiling just below the surface—but suddenly she was in the doorway.

"You think I 'got lucky' with Rusty last night? You think I had sex with him?''

He couldn't look at her because his face was hot, so he kept his back to her and pretended that unpacking the smaller of his bags was vital at that moment. "I don't care what you did with him last night—'' liar "—but whatever it was, it's not happening again.''

"You do," she repeated, her voice soft and underlaid with surprise. "You think I was intimate with Rusty and you're—''

Before she could say "jealous," Tyler swung around to face her. "Do you think I give a damn if you were *intimate* with every man in that bar? I don't care if you've slept with every man you've ever met, but you're not doing it on my watch! Your father entrusted me with your safety, and I'll be damned if I'll screw up my career because you like to bring men home from bars with you! The extracurricular activities are over until you get back to Montebello. Get used to it, Princess.''

She stared at him, regal and cold, no doubt thinking of all the royal punishments she'd like to condemn him to. Then, without a word or even so much as a blink, she turned, went back to her room, and closed and locked the connecting door on her side.

Muttering curses, he went to the door, but he stopped short of banging on it, yelling out his frustration or demanding she unlock the door immediately. Instead, he leaned against the unyielding steel, cool against the flush of shame that warmed him, and closed his eyes.

What the hell was wrong with him? He couldn't talk to the king's daughter that way! No matter what she did, no matter how he felt about it, he owed her the respect and deference her title commanded. He couldn't yell at her, insult her, criticize her—and he damn well couldn't do any of that merely because he was jealous. She was out of his league. He had no right to even want her. He had a career to consider, and she had a father who could destroy him. Hell, *she* could destroy him.

He rubbed his hand over his face. It was just a matter of perspective. He needed to remember that he was a professional with a job to do, that she was a privileged princess whom he never would have gotten near without that job. This was a protection detail, no different than if the protectee were her sixty-some-year-old father or her months-old nephew.

Perspective. Pure and simple.

By the time Tyler knocked at the door the next morning, Anna had been dressed, packed and ready to go for more than an hour. She ignored his subdued greeting and made a production of putting on her coat, scarf and gloves while he delivered their luggage to the vehicle. As she adjusted the black wool scarf over her hair in front of the mirror, she searched her reflection for any outward indications of the restless night she'd spent. No reddened eyes from the tears she'd shed in the shower before bed, no dark shadows from the hours of tossing and turning— at least, none that a deft hand with cosmetics couldn't disguise.

When was the last time a man had made her weep? Of course she'd cried many tears upon hearing the tragic news of Lucas's plane crash. She'd been unable to believe that the elder brother who'd doted on her since birth had been taken from their lives, and at times she'd thought she couldn't live without him. But other than that…when had she last cared enough about a man that he'd had the ability to bring her to tears?

The memory came to her with astonishing clarity. She had been fifteen, and he was seventeen, and she'd nursed a schoolgirl crush on him through the entire year. He'd given her reason to believe that he was going to invite her to their end-of-the-year dance, an event akin to an American school prom, and she had been breathless with excitement…right up to the moment he'd asked her best friend instead.

That had been her first and last broken heart. No way was

she allowing Tyler Ramsey to become the second. Her feelings for him were as foolish and pointless as her crush on that boy had been. And look at her now. Neither the boy's name nor his face would come to mind.

She couldn't fathom ever being unable to recall Tyler's image.

Even as that stubborn thought popped into her mind, his image appeared in the mirror next to hers. "Are you ready?" He sounded cool, polite, deferential—as he should.

She didn't trust herself to speak at all. Instead, she picked up her bag and followed him to the vehicle.

They ate breakfast in awkward silence at a restaurant on the outskirts of town, then took a highway in a southwesterly direction. Their next destination was Garden City, located practically in Wyoming, only miles from Yellowstone. Lucas had spent a week there once and had returned with a fuzzy stuffed bear for her as a souvenir. Someday, he'd said, they would visit the park together and he would show her the mountains, the geyser called Old Faithful and, with luck, one of the black bears after which her stuffed one had been modeled.

If only *someday* could be today!

Their route took them between the Big Snowy and Little Belt Mountains. Perusing the atlas she'd found between the seats, she located the Castle Mountains not far out of their way, near a town called Castle Town and another named Buckingham, and south of that range was the Crazy Mountains.

For a time she allowed the names to distract her—allowed her mind to roam six thousand miles home to Montebello. No doubt it was a sunny, warm day on the island—probably seventy degrees warmer than it was in central Montana. It was late afternoon there, and her mother would be preparing for whatever guests the palace would entertain that evening. Whether Anna's presence would be required would depend on the nature of Papa's business with them. Often he requested that she join them, but just as often she was free to entertain her own guests in her apartment or to go out clubbing with her friends.

To hear Tyler tell it, she went out only to collect new men so the revolving door on her bedroom wouldn't grow rusty from disuse. If he knew the truth, would he be ashamed of his unkind thoughts? She didn't know. She did know, though, that she cared not one bit what he thought. He was less than nothing to her. An employee, and a temporary one at that.

Though she vowed she would stay on Montebello forever before she would accept him as a bodyguard again. There was no place on earth she wanted to go badly enough to go with him.

"Are you warm enough?"

She refused to look directly at him, though she did turn her head enough to catch a glimpse of him from the corner of her eye. "If I weren't, I would increase the temperature," she replied haughtily.

He grew silent again for a mile, perhaps two, before speaking again. "If you get tired, you can recline that seat and take a nap."

"Yes, I am well aware of that."

After another mile, he cleared his throat. "Listen, about last night…"

She gave him a frigid look. "I am also well aware they teach you in your training that, except for an emergency, you're not to speak to the dignitary you're protecting unless he or she speaks to you first. I haven't spoken to you first even once this morning, and yet you persist in your awkward attempts at conversation. If I want to talk with you, Mr. Ramsey, I'll let you know."

His cheeks flushed heatedly and his ears—at least, the one she could see—turned red as his fingers clenched the steering wheel. He clamped his jaw shut, but that didn't stop the muscle there from twitching as it had done repeatedly the two days previous. His dark glasses hid his eyes from her, but she didn't need to see them to know the derision that clouded them.

Foolishly she felt the urge to weep again, and she turned to stare out the side window to hide it from him. As the scenery flew past unnoticed, she wished she were home in Montebello, with Christina in Billings—anywhere other than here, with anyone other than Tyler.

She was lost in regretful thoughts when abruptly he swore aloud, stomped on the brake and steered the vehicle to a shuddering stop on the shoulder of the highway. While she attempted to gather her wits—had he seen something? had they hit something? was there a problem with the vehicle?—he jumped out of the driver's seat, slammed the door hard enough to rock the SUV, then stalked around to her side. Before she could react, he jerked her door open, grabbed a handful of her sweater and hauled her—as if she were no more than a sack of grain!—out of the vehicle and set her on the ground.

"I'm sorry, okay?" he shouted, leaning menacingly close to her. "I'm sorry I refused to call you Anna. I'm sorry I wasn't as friendly as you wanted. I'm sorry I dragged you out of the Silver Nugget last night, I'm sorry I said the things I did, I'm sorry if I hurt you, and I'm *damned* sorry I can't do this—"

And just like that, he kissed her—hungrily, greedily, possessively, as no man had ever kissed her before, as if he'd waited forever to do it, as if he'd wanted forever to do it. He slid his arms around her and pulled her against him, lifted her with one hand so her hips pressed snugly against his, and tangled his other hand in her hair, and he thrust his tongue inside her mouth, probing, stunning, melting her. Her arms automatically wrapped around his neck, and her body rubbed against his as naturally as breathing. Though the air around them was frigid, heat radiated through her, along with need, hunger, pleasure and an immeasurable sense of rightness. His arms about her, his tongue in her mouth, his arousal searing her...nothing she'd ever known had felt so right, so special, so...perfect.

And then, as abruptly as he'd taken her, he released her, put her away and took steps to move himself even farther away. She stared at him, dazed, aching, wanting nothing so much as another of his embraces, another of his kisses, and more, everything more he could give. And he stared back, appalled, angry...and still noticeably aroused.

After a time he dragged his hand through his hair and swore. "I'm sorry. I shouldn't have done that."

The words hurt, but this time she didn't turn away to hide it. She touched her fingers lightly to her lips, still able to feel the tingle from his mouth, to savor the taste of him, then regretfully asked, "Then why did you?"

Anger flared in his green eyes as he all but growled, "It won't happen again."

"To me it felt very right," she said hesitantly, gently. "Was it so different for you?"

"You're a princess, damn it!"

She was well aware of that—though, obviously, not as much as he was. She'd known people who sought her friendship merely because of her rank, as well as people who'd wanted nothing to do with her merely because of her rank. It always hurt, but it was a fact of royal life. She couldn't change that people judged her on her position within the monarchy and not on the woman she was any more than she could change the fact that she *was* a part of the monarchy.

But for this man—this man who could kiss her as no other man she'd ever known—to so judge her.... An ache settled in her chest.

Though she feared he would reject her, she closed the distance between them and clasped his hand in hers. She was right. He shrugged off her touch as if he found it unpleasant. "Does it matter so much to you—my being a princess?"

"Yes, it matters," he replied with a harsh scowl.

"And if I weren't...would you kiss me again?"

"If you weren't," he said harshly, "we wouldn't be having this conversation."

He walked away, heading for the opposite side of the vehicle, but she moved only to watch him. Folding her arms across her chest to combat the sudden chill shivering through her, she called after him, "What does that mean, Mr. Ramsey? You wouldn't have looked twice at me if you weren't being paid to do so?"

He stalked back, coming right up to her, so close she could feel the tension vibrating through him, and he glared down into her face. "It means I would have you stripped naked in the back of that truck and we wouldn't be talking at all. And my name is Tyler, damn it!"

She couldn't help it. Even though he appeared more intimidating and commanding than virtually any man she knew besides her father, she smiled sweetly. "Call me Annie, and I'll call you Tyler."

He glared at her mutely, and she smiled back. After a long moment, he turned his back on her, drew a deep breath, then swung around to face her. "We need to get going. It's cold out here."

"You don't look chilled. Your cheeks, ears and throat are flushed red. Permit me to determine whether you feel chilled." She reached out to lay her hand against his cheek, but he grabbed her fingers an instant before she made contact.

"I'm not chilled," he growled.

"No, I didn't think so. You rather look as if you might give off steam, Mr. Ramsey."

He wrapped his fingers around hers and used the hold to back her toward the SUV. "Tyler."

"I believe we're both well aware of your given name, Mr. Ramsey."

"Say it. *Tyler.*"

"Not until you call me Annie."

Feeling the cold metal of the vehicle at her back, she could retreat no farther, but that didn't stop him from advancing. He pinned her to the side panel with his body and slid both hands into her hair, anchoring them in the curls, tilting her face for his kiss. Her blood turned hot and sluggish and her lids fluttered shut as his mouth brushed her temple, the corner of her eye, her cheek. "Say it, Princess," he demanded in a husky whisper. "Say my name."

He traced her ear with the tip of his tongue, and she whimpered deep in her throat. Her fingers clutched handfuls of his shirt as if he might save her from floating away on a tide of sensation, and she whimpered again when at last he touched his mouth briefly, chastely, to hers. "Say my name, Annie," he groaned, his mouth so near that she tasted his words. "Please…"

"Yes…Tyler…" She couldn't think of any other words to add—pleas, demands, needs—but that was sufficient because the instant she whispered his name, he kissed her again, and she lost the ability to speak at all.

She was filled with aches to which she had no means of giving voice when the sound of a clearing throat penetrated the haze that had enveloped her. It startled her, but not nearly as much as it startled Tyler. He spun around, pushing her behind him at the same time he reached inside his jacket where his weapon was holstered, then stilled when he saw that the intruder was a policeman.

"I thought you folks might be having some trouble," the gentleman said with a broad grin, "but it looks like you got it straightened out on your own."

Peeking around Tyler, she smiled. "Yes, we're fine, but it was very kind of you to stop and check."

"Nah, just part of my job. You're not from around here, are you?"

"No." She sidestepped Tyler's restraining arm and moved to stand beside him. "We're from Arkansas. Have you ever been there?"

"A time or two."

"It's not so bad."

"No, ma'am," he agreed with a chuckle, "I suppose it's not."

"I'm sorry, deputy," Tyler said, attempting to unobtrusively nudge her toward the open door of the SUV. Stubbornly she planted her feet and refused to be nudged. "We're up here on our honeymoon, and we stopped to look at the mountains out there and just sort of…forgot where we were."

The deputy grinned again. "Those are the Crazy Mountains. You can't pick 'em out from here, but there's one at this end called Loco Mountain and one farther south called Crazy Peak. Kind of appropriate for the situation, huh?"

"Very appropriate." Tyler's smile wasn't very convincing…but his blush was, Anna thought. "Why don't you get in the car, Princess, so we can all be on our way."

He boosted her into the vehicle, then closed the door before she could do more than wave goodbye to the policeman. After fastening her seat belt, she held her icy fingers to the hot air blowing from the vents and wondered how a simple matter such as a kiss could so thoroughly change the nature of a word. Tyler calling her princess before the kiss had been unwelcome. Tyler calling her princess after the kiss was unbearably sweet.

When he got into the driver's seat, he gave her a triumphant look. "You called me Tyler."

"Yes, I did." She waited until he'd pulled back onto the highway and resumed speed to add, "But not before you called me Annie."

"Did I?"

"Yes, you did." In a pained groan that had made her legs go weak and her body feverish. After that husky, pleading *Please*…she would have given anything he wanted, would have done anything he asked.

"Hmm. But don't get too smug, Princess. It won't happen again."

"That's what you said about the kiss."

"Yes, but this time I mean it."

She didn't doubt his conviction at all, but neither was she troubled by it. Now she knew how amazing their kisses could be. She would give a great deal for another one, and she suspected he would do the same.

And when the time was right, she would prove it.

A couple of hours on the two-lane state highway led them to Interstate 90. Tyler set the cruise control on eighty to knock a little time off their trip, then glanced at the princess. She'd been quiet since their little exchange at the side of the road, but it wasn't that wounded silence that made him crazy—rather, a thoughtful type. If he were a smart man, that would probably make him crazy, too, since he was coming to realize that with her, *thoughtful* equated planning, plotting and scheming.

But if he were a smart man, he wouldn't have kissed her back there.

If he had even a passing acquaintance with *smart,* he would have taken one look at her in the king's office and turned down this assignment. He should have known she was trouble from the start.

Now it was too late for *would haves* and *should haves.* The best he could hope for was that this trip would end before he did something incredibly stupid like seduce the king's youngest daughter.

Like perpetuate his father's disappointment in his youngest son.

Like end his career before it really got started.

Seducing the king's daughter... A couple of days ago, the thought had never crossed his mind. He'd seen her around Montebello, always with her bodyguards, often accompanied by a girlfriend or two, and he'd thought she was awfully pretty, awfully young, awfully spoiled, awfully not his type. He hadn't known her or wanted to get to know her.

A couple of brief kisses later, and, man, did he want to get to *know* her!

Seeking a distraction in exactly the wrong place, he glanced at her again. For the last few miles, her royal nose had been stuck in a travel guide, though she looked up often to gaze around. Given a choice, she would probably visit every tourist site in the state, stop at every historical marker and tramp through every museum. As it was, she seemed determined to absorb every bit of information she could find on the state.

"Can we talk, Your Highness? I realize I'm only supposed to speak when spoken to, but I'd like to ask you a few questions."

Closing the travel guide, she slid it between the seat and the console, then twisted to face him, her dark eyes shadowed with embarrassment. "My remarks this morning were rude and inappropriate. Officially your protection detail ended when you delivered me into my sister's care. You're no longer my bodyguard, and it was improper of me to treat you as such. You may speak whenever you like and say whatever you like."

It was a prissy little speech, but he didn't focus on that. Instead, he wanted to press for clarification. *Whatever? Then how about finding a place where we won't be disturbed so you can give me a taste of what you gave Rusty night before last? Where you can make me forget you were with Rusty last night?*

Just a taste. That would be enough to satisfy him.

It would be enough to hang him.

He was considering the trade-off—intimacy with the princess

versus his best chance to prove himself worthy of a place in the Ramsey family—when she politely cleared her throat.

"You had something to ask?"

He shook his head to clear away the image of her, eyes closed, lips parted, holding on to him as if she would never let go, and asked the question that had been on his mind earlier. "Did your brother ever express any interest in mining?"

"No, never. I was surprised when my cousin Lorenzo returned from Colorado with the report that Lucas might have come to Montana to work in a mine. Lucas's interests were more...recreational in nature."

And the prince's favorite recreation had been busty, blue-eyed blondes, Tyler dryly agreed, followed closely by busty, brown-eyed brunettes and redheads of every eye color and cup size.

"Of course, who would have thought Lucas might work on a ranch?" she continued. "And yet if this former employee at the Chambers ranch *is* my brother, that's exactly what he's been doing for the past year." She fell silent for a moment, and when she spoke again, her voice was softer, more hesitant. "Do you believe it is Lucas?"

He shrugged. "Lorenzo seems to think the odds are pretty good."

"But if this man is Lucas, why is he calling himself Joe? Why was he employed as a cowboy, and why would he want to work in a mine?"

Those were questions that had been debated long and hard by the king, his intelligence people and every mercenary involved in the mission, and they'd come up with two likely answers. "Maybe he believes his life is in danger—maybe the accident was no accident—or maybe...he doesn't know who he is."

"Amnesia?" She gestured dismissively. "A common plot device of books and movies."

"But if it didn't exist for real, it wouldn't have become a common plot device. It's a legitimate diagnosis—a rare one, but it happens."

"My brother would never forget his family."

"It's not usually a voluntary thing," he patiently pointed out.

"Your brother was in a plane crash. He might have suffered head injuries that caused him to forget."

She was stubbornly shaking her head before he finished speaking. "He would never forget *me*. I'm his favored sister. He adores me. No injury could wipe clean his memories of me."

"No shortage of ego here, is there?" he murmured.

She flashed him a smile. "I'll locate you in six months and see how easily you've managed to forget me."

Tyler's expression turned grim. Easy to forget? Not likely. Not in six months or six years. Probably not in a lifetime.

"Do you believe we'll find any clues to Lucas's whereabouts at these next two mining operations?"

"I'm just here to ask the questions. I honestly can't guess."

"What if we don't? Then what?"

"Then you return to Montebello."

Her features took on an obstinate look, but she didn't argue the point. "And you?"

He drew a breath. "I go wherever they tell me to go." It could be Montebello, or it could be a world away. Truth was, he might never return to the island again. Might never see Princess Anna again.

Two days ago he'd told himself he was looking forward to that prospect.

Even two days ago he'd known it was a lie. He knew it even better now.

"Is that the life you want? Going where someone sends you? Always following orders? Living nowhere in particular, and having no one to miss you when you're gone?"

Though he didn't much feel like it, he grinned. "Sounds like heaven, doesn't it?"

She made a prissy face. "It sounds lonely."

He wasn't lonely, and he wouldn't be. Traveling was better than staying in one place. Everyone took orders—even King Marcus devoted much of his time to keeping the queen and his three little princesses happy—so why shouldn't Tyler take his doing something he enjoyed? Living nowhere in particular meant nothing to tie him down, and as far as someone missing him...women were a complication he had no time or desire for. Zip. Zero. Zilch.

"And you think your life is ideal? Living in the palace? Bodyguards escorting you everywhere you go? Being at risk for no reason other than who your father is? Having your every move scrutinized, criticized or analyzed by your public?"

Distance crept into her gaze as if, instead of snow-covered ground outside the SUV, she saw her paradise island home. "Of course it isn't ideal. Nothing is."

"So change it. Your sister did."

Her smile came quickly, lightening her expression, making her radiant. "Christina is brilliant. She's a microbiologist, and is the best in her field at the university, you know."

"No, I didn't know that. And what are you? The village idiot?"

She laughed, and damn it, he would have been better off not hearing it. It was too cheerful, too pleasing, too easy on a man's ears. *"No,"* she chastised him. "I'm as smart as I want to be, but I'm nowhere near brilliant."

"You're bright enough to avoid the subject. If life were ideal—"

"It isn't."

"But if it were—"

"It's impossible."

He rolled his gaze skyward. "Hypothetically, let's pretend, make believe...if life were ideal, where would you live and how?"

The distance returned, joined with a little wistfulness. "The where and how are unimportant. It's with whom you live that matters." Deliberately, badly, she changed the subject. "This is our exit," she said with a gesture toward the highway sign they were approaching. "According to the guide book, there's a restaurant in the first town we'll pass through that serves buffalo. Can we stop there? I've never dined on buffalo before, and I would like to be able to tell Roberto I'd done so."

He could think of any number of creatures he'd rather eat than buffalo, but he didn't say so. Instead, he slowed to exit the interstate, then turned south. "What's the name of this restaurant?"

She looked it up in the travel guide, but within a quarter mile they discovered it wasn't necessary. The place was the only restaurant in town, and even if it hadn't been, the ten-foot-tall fiberglass buffalo out front was a dead giveaway.

He found a space in a parking lot filled with pickups and eighteen-wheelers, then shrugged into his coat before opening the door. The princess didn't wait for him to help her out, but slid to the ground and belted her own coat around her narrow waist.

"This cold is amazing," she remarked as they made their way across frozen gravel and dirty slush. "If I were a native, in winter I would move to the tropics."

"Montana only has two seasons, you know—winter, and winter-will-be-right-back." Tyler kept a straight face as he went on. "Not everyone can afford to move south for the winter. The ones who do are called snowbirds, and an awful lot of them wind up in my home state."

"Can we visit Arizona?"

"Nope." Not that he wouldn't mind seeing a few familiar places once he was finished with this assignment. "Arizona's a good long drive from here."

"Everything in America is a good long drive. You have cities larger than my entire country."

"Yep." He opened the restaurant door, then followed her inside. It was no fancier than its name—Buffalo Bill's. Everything from the tables to the decor to the staff was worn and years beyond its prime, but the aromas were good enough to make his mouth water, the place looked clean and the customers looked satisfied. What better endorsement could a man ask for?

There were only a handful of empty seats in the dining room, and he checked them out before steering Anna toward a booth against the far wall. He took the bench facing the door, sliding in after removing his coat. She pulled off her coat to reveal faded jeans and a red University of Montana sweatshirt worn over a white turtleneck. Too bad it was sized more for him and didn't even hint at what it covered.

"When did you find time to buy that shirt?" he asked as he opened the menu.

"It was a gift from Christina. She sent it to me several years ago. It was to be part of my disguise."

He looked up from his study of the usual diner fare and scowled at her. "Your disguise?"

"To escape you." She smiled guilelessly. "When we first arrived in Billings and stopped for a hamburger, I intended to go to the ladies' room while you ordered. There I would change into this outfit, which was hidden in my bag, and then I would sneak away. While you searched for a foreigner in a red dress and black coat, I would pass for a Montanan in a sweatshirt, baseball cap and jeans, and I would begin my search for my brother."

His gaze narrowed. How panicked would he have been if he'd lost the princess at a fast-food restaurant only a few miles from the airport? He would have called Princess Christina, the local police, his brother, and his father, and everyone would have realized that he didn't have what it took to succeed in the Noble Men. Caved under pressure, they would have said. Wasn't cool in a crisis. He would have had to move quickly to quit before they fired him.

She slowly grew more serious. "You're not amused."

"No, sorry, I'm not. I would have been the biggest failure my father and his partners have ever seen."

"They wouldn't have blamed you."

Whether they blamed him was inconsequential. He would have blamed himself, rightly so.

Her smile was faint and coaxing. "As I pointed out, even princesses are allowed to go to the bathroom alone."

"Maybe not anymore," he muttered. Maybe he would invest in a pair of handcuffs and attach one end to her wrist and the other to his own. Maybe then he could make absolutely certain that she didn't try anything.

When the waitress arrived to take their order, Anna smiled gratefully as if she'd just received a reprieve. She scanned the menu, then asked, "What do you recommend?"

"That you eat someplace else," the gray-haired granny said

with a cackle. "But if you're too famished to wait, you're probably safe with a few of Bill's dishes...long as you don't have too strong an aversion to gettin' your stomach pumped."

"I want to try your buffalo. How should I order it?"

"In English gets you served quicker, seein' as how I don't speak anything but. Scoot on over, honey, and let me tell you about our buffalo." As soon as the princess slid farther across the bench, the waitress sat down beside her. "Now, ol' Buddy was meaner 'n a rattlesnake and tough as rawhide. Why, it'd be easier to take a bite out of ol' Burke's hide out there—" she waved toward the fiberglass buffalo outside the plate-glass window "—than to chew a steak cut from Buddy. This fine sunny morning we've also got burgers ground from Bob and stew from Betty Lou. Our sirloins come from Bronc and our short ribs from Barney, and we've got a particularly tasty chili from Barbara."

Anna glanced out the window—whether at Burke or the cloudless gray sky, it was hard to tell—then leveled her gaze on the waitress again. "You're teasing me, aren't you?"

The old lady raised her right hand in testimony. "I never ate a buffalo I didn't like. Except for ol' Buddy." Then she laughed again and elbowed Anna. "You're right, honey. I'm pullin' your leg. The only buffalo 'round here with a name is ol' Burke outside—and Bill, who's the chief bottlewasher and cook in this here establishment. He has a head hard as a rock and empty as a broken egg. He also happens to be my husband of fifty-two years, and I'm beginnin' to think maybe this marriage thing just might work out." She paused for a breath. "You two just passin' through?"

"More or less." Before Tyler had guessed her intention, Anna pulled a photo of the prince from her bag. "We're looking for this man. Have you seen him?"

The waitress picked up the picture and studied it a moment, then transferred that alert gaze to Tyler for a moment before turning back to Anna. "You got him, and you're lookin' for a replacement? What's wrong? Don't all his parts work right?"

Anna's cheeks turned a delicate shade of pink. "Presumably...except for also having a head as hard as rock. This man is my brother, and he's gone missing. We're simply trying to locate him, to make certain he's all right.''

"Haven't seen him in here, darlin', and if them doors are open, I'm here.'' The waitress returned the photo and picked up her order pad and pen. "Now...if I haven't scared ya off from eatin', what can I get ya?''

Chapter 5

Garden City was located in the Gallatin National Forest, south of the Absaroka Range, southeast of the Absaroka Beartooth Wilderness and just north of the Wyoming state line and Yellowstone. The town appeared to be more than double the size of Clarkston and supported more of a tourist trade. Fortunately, the season for their activities, primarily camping, hiking, fishing and such, was long over, which meant fewer people to question, as well as fewer strangers in town to go unnoticed.

Anna waited impatiently in the vehicle while Tyler asked for directions to the mine. She wished the cell phone in her bag would ring and her father would be on the line, announcing that Lucas was alive, safe and on his way home. Even though it would mean a reassignment for Tyler. Even though she might never have another opportunity to spend time alone with him.

The thought made the muscles in her stomach tighten and caused her to catch her lower lip between her teeth. Thus, when the cell phone in her bag did ring, it startled her and she bit her lip hard enough to draw blood.

Quickly, she rummaged through the large bag, reaching straight to the bottom where the phone always seemed to migrate. Her fingers closed around it, she pressed the button to receive the call and raised it to her ear, her hand trembling apprehensively.

"You promised you would call me," Christina said reprovingly by way of a greeting.

"Oh, Christina, it's you!"

"Of course it is. Anyone in San Sebastian who wanted to reach you would naturally try my house, since that's where they believe you're staying. Anyone...oh, I don't know...such as Papa?"

"Has he called there?"

"Quite early this morning. He wanted to see how you're enjoying our visit. I told him you were sleeping. Considering the hour, I assumed chances were better than even that I wasn't lying. Do me a favor and call him back at a time when you're certain to awaken *him* in the middle of the night."

"I will," Anna murmured. She could pretend she had forgotten about the time difference, tell the staff not to wake him and simply leave a message. She liked that idea better than outright lying to him.

"So...how's it going?"

There was a teasing note in her sister's voice that Anna hadn't heard in a long time, and it made her realize how much she'd missed Christina's presence in the palace all these years. Growing up, she, Christina and Julia had been so very close—playmates in the nursery, best friends and confidantes. Julia, being the eldest, had naturally been the first to grow away. Though her family remained important to her, they'd been displaced somewhat by her new husband, Rashid, and their baby. Then Christina had not only grown away but gone away as well, coming to Montana to continue her studies. Like Julia, she still loved her family dearly, but Jack and the children they would soon have came first in her life.

Anna gazed at Tyler, visible inside the gas station, studying a wall-mounted map with the attendant. It was true enough that she liked him, and certainly true that no man's kiss had ever affected her as his did. But that was a sad substitute for the depth of emotion shared by Julia and Rashid, and Christina and Jack. Would that depth come? Could he be the one? Or was she naive enough to mistake another schoolgirl crush for the real thing?

"Aaan-naa," Christina called in a singsong voice. "Come down out of the clouds and get your feet on the ground again. I assume from your silence that it's going quite well. Tyler hasn't disappointed you?"

With her free hand, Anna touched her lips and imagined she still felt the tingle from this morning's kiss. "No," she said softly. "Not in the least."

"He seemed a polite young man."

"Oh, he can be so polite, I want to choke him."

Christina laughed. "I know what you mean. But consider it from his point of view. You *are* the youngest and most protected daughter of a powerful king in a region of the world known for rather…er, harsh punishments. There are some countries nearby where, even today, he could be put to death for what he's doing with you."

"But Montebello has never been that rigid. And there are some who think Papa would breathe a sigh of relief to receive an offer for my hand in marriage."

"You mean an offer that you might conceivably accept."

"Is it wrong to want a proposal of marriage to be wildly romantic and based on love rather than a business proposition?"

"No, Anna. It's not wrong at all, and don't ever let anyone convince you otherwise. Marriage is too difficult and much too important to do it for the wrong reasons. Hold out for love—and trust me. It'll come."

She watched Tyler laugh at something the station attendant said, then walk out the door and come toward her, his strides long, his boots splashing in the dirty slush that covered the ground. Was it possible he was the one for whom she should hold out? The one meant to displace her family, to brighten her life, to father her children?

The idea sent a shiver down her spine and heat curling deep inside her. Even if he wasn't *that* one—the love of a lifetime, the happily-ever-after one, the fairy-tale prince for a real-life princess—she was fairly certain he *was* the one for whom she'd been saving the intimacy. Powerfully intense, tingling, hot-and-shivery kisses might not provide much of a basis for love and marriage, but they seemed the perfect reason for the king's most-protected daughter to give up her virginity.

"You're drifting again, Anna. Try not to sound so dreamy and love struck when you speak to Papa, and you'd probably better not speak to Mama at all. She knows the symptoms all too well."

"Tyler's coming back, so I'll talk to you later, Christina. I'll call you. Really, I will. I love you."

Frigid air blasted into the SUV as he opened the door. His cheeks reddened by the wind, Tyler glanced at her, then the phone. "You calling somebody?" he asked, then blew on his ungloved hands to warm them.

"No. Christina called. My sister. In Billings."

"I know who and where Christina is, Princess. What'd she want?"

"My father called to inquire whether I'm enjoying my visit. I should contact him after we check into our lodgings for the evening."

He glanced at his watch. "It's already eleven o'clock there. If you want to catch him before bed, you should go ahead and call him now."

"No, thank you. He awoke Christina in the middle of the night, and she'd like me to return the favor."

"Huh. You're just afraid to talk to him when he's wide awake and coherent, aren't you?" He fastened his seat belt, then pulled out of the gas station and onto the street.

Not afraid to talk to him, Anna silently acknowledged. She simply preferred to not lie to him directly.

Garden City was at a higher elevation than Clarkston had been, and had received some heavy snowfalls recently. The worst of it had been removed by snowplows, though the streets were far from clear. There was a thick pack of dirty snow, rutted and slick, but the SUV handled it beautifully...and Tyler handled the SUV beautifully.

"Where is the mine?"

"Changing the subject?"

She smiled brightly. "You noticed."

His corresponding look was less than amused...though his

green eyes couldn't hide the fact that he found *some* humor in the conversation. "It's about ten miles out of town, but we may not get there today. The guy at the gas station says there's snow moving in. Before we head that way, we're going to find a place to stay for the night."

"Oh, I hope it does snow. It's so beautiful," she said. Then, with a grin and a shrug, she added, "Besides, this is Montana. What's a little snow?"

Within the hour, she learned the answer to that. They'd checked into the guest lodge the gentleman at the gas station had recommended—owned by his brother and sister-in-law, as it turned out. Compared to her accommodations the two nights previous, she had found the cabin luxurious. It was built of logs and set among a forest of pines, and from the outside it looked like every frontier cabin on the old television shows Roberto so favored. Inside, there was one large room—living room, dining room and kitchen—and the bedroom was tucked in a small loft upstairs.

The only down side was that Tyler's matching cabin was a dozen feet away.

Ever since he'd mentioned that small detail, she'd been debating how to persuade him that two cabins were unnecessary. She hadn't found the answer yet.

Minutes after they'd set out for the mine the snow had started falling—heavy, fat flakes that turned everything in their path into cold, white lumps. For the first ten minutes it had charmed her, as she watched the flakes melt the instant they landed on the warm glass of the windshield. Then the wind had picked up, and the flakes had stopped melting so quickly, and before long they weren't melting at all. She imagined the SUV resembled a great lumbering white beast, thoroughly covered except where the windshield wipers labored to keep the glass clean. With all the other windows coated, though it was late afternoon, inside the vehicle it seemed well past dusk.

"Hell." Tyler slowed the vehicle to a crawl, carefully steered onto the shoulder, then swung the steering wheel hard to the left. "Sorry, Princess. I don't want to get stuck out here in this. We've got to go back."

She sighed with relief, then felt her face heat with embarrassment when he glanced at her.

"You nervous about this?"

Sheepishly she shrugged. "I live on an island where the sun shines three hundred days or more a year. Wintry weather is a whole new world to me."

"You should have spoken up."

Once again she shrugged. "I assumed you knew what you were doing. If you thought the trip too dangerous, you would postpone it."

"Glad to hear you have such faith in me," he said dryly.

"Of course I have faith in you. If you weren't well trained and more than qualified to handle this assignment, the Noble Men never would have given it to you, and my father never would have entrusted you with protecting his daughter or locating his son. There's no reason—"

"Princess," he interrupted, releasing the steering wheel long enough to raise one hand, palm toward her, in what might have been a signal to stop...or a gesture of surrender. "I was just kidding...but thanks for the vote of confidence."

"I don't imagine you ever lack confidence." She tried to make her voice sound as dry as his had moments earlier, but wasn't sure she'd succeeded. In spite of his comment at Buffalo Bill's that afternoon—*I would have been the biggest failure my father and his partners have ever seen*—she didn't believe he ever doubted himself.

"Then your imagination's not too lively for someone whose life goal was once to become a fairy."

For some silly reason, she was touched that he remembered her comment. Being the youngest, the most sheltered and the most spoiled of the royal children, she'd learned over the years that many people treated her the least seriously.

And why shouldn't they? She wasn't in line to someday ascend to the throne, as Lucas was. She hadn't produced a new heir for the neighboring nation of Tamir, as Julia had. She wasn't a brilliant researcher making life better for everyone, as Christina did. She was just Anna, the baby, who made public appearances on behalf of the king and sat on the boards of charities which had never bothered to discover whether she was capable of giving them anything more than her name.

Thinking back to his comment about being a failure, she quietly asked, "How important is this job to you?"

For a time he appeared to concentrate intently on the road ahead of them. The snow swirled and blew, severely limiting visibility. In places there was nothing ahead but a swath of white that stretched from the timber line on one side to the corresponding line on the other side. All he could do, she supposed, was drive slowly and hope he managed to remain on the indistinguishable road.

At last, when she'd assumed he wasn't going to answer her question, he spared her a quick glance. "*This* job? Right here, right now? Or the whole thing?"

"The Noble Men. Following in your father's and brother's footsteps. Do you enjoy it? Is it a career you can see yourself pursuing in five or ten or twenty years?"

"I haven't really done enough yet to know."

It was an easy answer, but by no means complete. She wondered if he would ever trust her enough to confide the rest. If he never did…well, that would answer her earlier question about whether he might be the one, wouldn't it?

Even considering the possibility stirred an ache in her stomach…which also might have some bearing on the answer to that question.

After what seemed interminable hours, they reached the town. Just ahead on the right, not yet visible through the blizzard, was their lodge. Tyler, however, turned left, into the parking lot of a busy supermarket.

"Why is everyone shopping in such bad weather?" Anna asked as the SUV slid into a parking space.

"They're stocking up on supplies, in case they get snowed in. That's what we're going to do, too."

Anna had never been in an American supermarket before. This one wasn't as big as some she'd seen in Billings, but it pleased her. Tyler took charge of gathering the real food, while she focused on treats. She'd been indulged since infancy with the best desserts a small army of pastry chefs could produce and so had never truly experienced American junk food. She intended to make up for lost time.

By the time they paid for their purchases and lugged all the bags to the vehicle, the snow was blinding. They hurried to the lodge—if the grand speed of two or three miles an hour could be considered hurrying—and parked in front of her cabin.

She filled both hands with the handles of plastic grocery bags, ducked her head and followed Tyler to the cabin steps. The drifts reached to mid-calf and were building with every gust of wind, and snowflakes stung her face and coated her lashes.

When she missed a step and her feet went out from under her, she found herself lying on her back, snow falling inside her coat, creeping between her socks and jeans, clinging to her hair and neck and hands. Gazing up at the angry winter sky, she sighed softly. "I believe I have seen enough snow now. Please stop."

"Sorry, Princess. I don't believe Old Man Winter is one of your loyal subjects. I doubt this'll stop until he's ready to stop it." Tyler bent to give her a hand up, lifting her easily to her feet. "You okay?"

"Yes, quite," she replied, though she sounded breathless. Because he'd pulled her up so effortlessly...or because he was standing so close? Still holding her hand. Looking at her.

For a moment she clung to him, and he appeared content to let her cling while they stared at each other. Granted, she wasn't particularly experienced with the physical aspect of romance, but she wasn't totally naive. He wasn't looking at her bodyguard to princess, or even Noble Man to employer's pesky daughter. No, he was looking at her the way he had that morning, just before he kissed her. The way a man looked at a woman he felt something for.

A woman he wanted.

Was she looking back at him the same way? she wondered.

Sadly, the moment passed when a great shiver passed through her. He gave a shake of his head. "Come on, Annie," he said abruptly. "Let's get inside before you turn into a Popsicle."

Come on, Annie. Simple words, but they chased away her chill and even warmed the snow that was melting inside her clothing. Who needed shelter and heating systems and dry clothing to stay warm? Tyler could accomplish the job for her with no more than a look, a touch, a quiet husky word, and she would be delighted to return the favor.

As he helped her up the steps, she cleared the hoarseness from her voice and spoke brightly—perhaps a bit too brightly—to hide the direction of her thoughts. "Popsicles...I bought some banana Popsicles. I wonder which bag they're in..."

By the time Tyler got the last of the groceries and the princess's luggage inside the cabin, the snowstorm had become a bona fide blizzard. He dropped his load inside the door, then stomped off the snow that clung to him in layers. If he had any sense, he would take some of the food and get the hell over to his own cabin before it disappeared in the swirling snow. But the truth was, he wasn't totally comfortable with the idea of going over there at all. What if something happened in the night—if Anna needed him? She could get sick. Someone could break in. More likely, the power could go off.

"Oh, good, you brought my bags." She came from the kitchen, padding across the wood floor in bare feet, and hefted one of the suitcases. "My clothes are damp. I'm going to get changed."

"I can take that—"

She waved him off. "You're not a porter, remember?"

She was halfway up the stairs when the phone rang. He glanced at it, on a desk not five feet away, then said, "Go ahead. I'll get it." It had to be someone at the motel office, since no one else in the world knew where they were. After stomping again to dislodge some of the snow starting to melt, he took two strides and picked up the phone.

"Mr. Ramsey, this is Gemma Lee in the office. I wanted to remind you that you've got a big supply of firewood on the back porch, and there are emergency supplies, including plenty of canned food, in the pantry off the kitchen."

"Yes, I remember." She'd explained that to him when he'd paid for the two cabins.

"Of course. Also...well...we have a bit of a problem, Mr.

Ramsey. You see, we're booked up solid on account of the bad weather, and the highway's been closed down, and...well, we have one more family than we have cabins. Now, we can put 'em up here in the office, but they've got three little ones, including a baby, and..."

Tyler's stomach knotted. He wanted to save Miz Gemma Lee from beating around the bush, to say, Sorry, your problem, not mine—to remind her that he'd paid for two cabins and by God he was going to use two cabins.

But nobody had asked for this blizzard—well, except the princess, who thought it was so beautiful. And how could he insist on having two cabins for the two of them while a family of five camped out in the motel office, with no beds, no bathroom, no diversions for the kids—all because he was afraid to spend the night alone in a cabin with Annie?

Not Annie. Anna. Princess Anna. Her Royal Highness.

As if mere words could make him forget the way he'd kissed her that morning, or the way she'd clung to him. He wasn't a man who liked clingy women, but there was something different about *her* clinging. It made him feel like he was doing something right and good. Like he was...worthy.

"Mr. Ramsey? Are you there? Oh, darn, I hope the phones haven't gone out. I swear, this is gonna be—"

"I'm here, Gemma Lee. I take it you'd like to give my cabin to your late guests."

"It would sure be a help to 'em if you don't mind."

"Send them to Number 12. Ms. Peterson and I will stay in Number 11."

"Oh, wonderful! Thank you so much, Mr. Ramsey."

He hung up, pulled on his gloves one more time, and went out into the snow. As big as he was and carrying an extra seventy pounds in luggage, it was a struggle to get back inside. One more trip, he promised himself as headlights weakly penetrated the snow, and then he was staying inside by the fire until all this was over.

A small SUV was parked haphazardly in front of Number 12 when he reached it. He didn't waste time on introductions or anything else—just called over the wind, "Need some help?"

The woman climbing out of the passenger seat gratefully pushed a small child into his arms—a boy, judging by the superheroes on his coat. He took the kid inside, returned for a little girl dressed in pink and purple, then brought in an armload of luggage while the father brought in the mother and the baby. He and the father made one last trip for the rest of the luggage, then the inability to feel his extremities sent him double-time back to Anna's cabin.

She was kneeling in front of the fireplace, coaxing a waxy firestarter to life underneath a towering pile of logs. When he burst into the cabin, she looked startled, then immediately recovered. "I thought you'd gone on to your cabin without even saying good-night."

"I—I—I w-was h-helping th-the neigh-b-b-bors." He peeled off his gloves, yanked off his coat and hung it on the doorknob, then pried off his boots without bothering with the frozen laces. After so much in-and-out, his jeans felt like ice, and his heavy denim shirt had long since lost whatever warmth-giving capabilities it might have possessed.

She watched him remove his outer layer, then politely said, "Take your coat off. Make yourself comfortable."

"D-d-don't be a—a sm-sm-smart—"

"Aleck?" she provided helpfully.

He glowered at her, then tried to decide whether to go for dry clothes and then the fire, or thaw first and worry about dry clothes once he could feel again. Thawing won.

She scooted to the side as he approached. The firestarter was burning now, and bright flames licked over and between the logs, making them crackle and sizzle. He sat down on the hearth, and she wordlessly handed him a towel apparently used to dry her curls, because it smelled of her shampoo. When had he become familiar with that scent? he wondered as he dried his face, then rubbed the towel over his hair. He hadn't really been close enough until this morning when he'd kissed her...and God knows, shampoo hadn't been uppermost in his thoughts at that time.

As the fire burned stronger and hotter, she nonchalantly remarked, "I noticed you brought your luggage in by mistake."

"No mistake. The motel's booked, and they needed my cabin for a family that got stranded. I've got to bunk over here...unless you object."

Her smile was cool and distant. "And what would you do if I did? Bunk in the vehicle?"

"Nope. But I would apologize for the inconvenience and the impropriety, and I would assure you that my behavior would be above reproach."

"And I would inform you that I don't require any such assurances."

Meaning what? he wondered. That she trusted him to behave? Or wouldn't object to a certain amount of misbehaving?

Leaning back on her elbows, she propped her feet on the hearth. Though he tried not to look, he couldn't stop himself from gazing at her, starting with her tight damp curls, moving down to the red sweater that ended an inch or so below her waist, sliding over snug black sweats and finally reaching her feet. Her socks were red and black stripes, with individual little knitted toes that she wiggled as if to absorb the fire's heat more quickly. With the tousled hair, the makeup worn away to a memory and the ridiculous socks, she looked incredibly young and innocent...and beautiful and desirable.

"How old are you?" he asked wryly. "Thirteen?"

Her full lower lip easily slid into the pout her father had warned him about. "I'm not so young."

"Oh, yes, you are, Princess. You're *very* young."

"It's a proven fact that girls mature more quickly than boys, which means that even though you're a few years older, you're less mature. So if I'm very young, then so are you."

"But you're not a girl. You're a princess. And princesses are spoiled and pampered and mollycoddled."

"Or wonderfully composed, grown up, responsible and self-possessed."

"Wrapped in cotton batting and protected from life."

"Baptized as a babe in the concepts of duty, obligation and position."

"Innocent."

She laughed. Stretched her arms high above her head, tugging the ribbed hem of her sweater inches higher, exposing creamy golden skin he had no need to see, and laughed. "Would you like to wager on that?"

It was amazing. One instant he was too cold to feel much of anything, and the next he was hot and sore and damn close to making steam rise where he was damp. He had to try a couple of times to make his voice work, and then had to clear his throat before the words could come out. "Sorry. I'm not a betting man."

"Why does that not surprise me?" she asked dryly.

He wasn't sure if her words actually held a bite, or if he felt one where none was intended. He didn't know why he would even care. He had no desire to surprise her. He wasn't concerned with what she might or might not think of him. All he cared about was keeping her safe, completing his assignment and returning her home safely to her father...how had the king put it? Oh, yeah. *None the worse for her adventure.*

Honor demanded that he return her unharmed. Reality suggested that he might go crazy by then.

When the heat had soaked through his extremities, he eased to his feet, took a clean set of clothes from his suitcase and went into the bathroom angled under the stairs to change. When he came out, the princess was still lying on the floor, curled on her side, head pillowed on her arms, gazing dreamily into the fire...or dozing dreamily in front of the fire, he realized when he got closer. Seconds ticked past unnoticed as he watched her— just watched, with a jumble of emotions he wouldn't identify if he could—until suddenly he realized that the side of him nearest the fire was hotter than the flames. At least, that was the excuse he accepted, and he refused to wonder why the side of him away from the fire was just as hot.

He forced himself to move away, to cross the room to the luggage near the door. Carrying her remaining bags upstairs, he listened to the steps that creaked under his weight. The loft was small, with a rough-hewn railing overlooking the rest of the cabin and narrow windows on three sides. There was room enough for a queen-size bed, the headboard and footboard made of solid rounds of natural-finished pine, a matching dresser, an armoire that bore the marks of a lifetime of hard use and a night table that consisted of a pine top supported by what appeared to be elk antlers. It was very likely the ugliest piece of furniture he'd ever seen. And back in college, he'd lived in a house decorated completely with other people's throwaways, so he'd seen some damned ugly stuff.

After leaving the princess's bags next to the bed, he checked out the bathroom—small, cozy, but with a shower and a tub—then returned to the living room to stretch out on the sofa and read.

Not to watch the princess sleep.

Not to consider how damn pretty she was.

Not to think about how much he wanted her or how wrong it would be to have her.

Just to read.

Right.

Anna awakened slowly and came alert even more so. Why was she sleeping on the floor in front of a fireplace that radiated mind-soothing heat? Why was the room so unnaturally quiet, and why weren't they canvassing the town, asking about Lucas?

Then she sat up and saw Tyler's boots and coat near the door and the snow still falling heavily outside the windows, and she remembered the blizzard. She combed her fingers through her hair, fairly confident it looked frightful since it had still been damp when she'd lain down, then looked around for Tyler. He was sprawled on the sofa, wearing sweat pants that were black like hers, but much older and in a much more disreputable condition, and a white T-shirt that showed a cartoon of a bicycle and its rider huffing up a mountain trail, underscored with the question, Are we having fun yet? His feet, propped on the coffee table, were bare except for a pair of thick white socks.

He looked quite appealing.

Lowering his book, he regarded her solemnly. "It's about time you woke up."

"Have I slept away the day?"

"Nope. Just the afternoon and part of the evening. You hungry?"

She considered it a moment, then smiled. "Yes, I believe I am."

"I don't suppose you cook."

She would love to be able to say, *Of course, I can throw a few things together,* and then prove it by making the best meal he'd ever eaten, but the sad truth was no, she didn't cook. Couldn't. Had never even made toast. Regretfully, she shook her head.

"So it's up to me to keep us from starving to death." He laid his book aside—the same Stephen King novel he'd been reading on the flight from Montebello, practically finished now—and headed for the kitchen.

"Starving?" she echoed as she stood up. There was a half-empty bag of potato chips on the coffee table, alongside an apple core and the wrapper from a chocolate-iced cream-filled cup-cake. She followed him into the kitchen, where she discovered he had finished putting away the groceries while she napped. Now he was gathering an assortment of items on the counter—aluminum foil, a package of chicken breasts, an onion, two sweet peppers, a carton of mushrooms and a box of rice.

"May I help?"

"You ever use a knife?"

She smiled sarcastically as she slipped past him to wash her hands. "I'm well aware it's used for chopping."

"That's not what I asked," he pointed out. "Which is an answer in itself, isn't it? Maybe I should chop the vegetables while you clean the mushrooms. Wouldn't want you to cut off your royal finger."

"Or stick it between your commoner shoulder blades." Tearing the plastic wrap from the mushrooms, she was about to hold the box under running water when he pushed it away.

"Get a paper towel, wet it and wipe the mushrooms clean."

"That's not very efficient."

"But it's the right way."

"According to whom?"

"My mother, who's the best damn cook in all of Arizona." He tore a sheet of toweling from the roll, moistened it, then handed it to her before returning to the peppers lined up on the chopping board.

"Funny. I never thought of you as having a mother," she remarked as she followed his directions meticulously. She wasn't aware he was looking at her until she'd thoroughly cleaned two mushrooms and started on the third, and his scrutiny caused her to shrug. "Of course I knew you had a father—I've met him. And I've met your brother, Kyle, and heard about your brother, Jake, but I don't believe I've ever heard any mention of a mother."

"Did you think our father just built us out of spare parts?"

If that were the case, she knew a great many young women who would happily pay Edward Ramsey premium prices for similar models of their own. The idea made her giggle, which made him scowl, though not seriously. "Of course not. Don't be silly. I presumed you were genetically engineered in some ultra-secret laboratory somewhere."

"Well, sorry to disappoint you, Princess, but we all came about in the old-fashioned way—mother, father, sex. My mother's name is Beatrice. She's always been a stay-at-home wife and mother. When my dad was still in the air force, she considered it her job to make the rest of his life as uncomplicated as possible so it wouldn't interfere with his career. That meant she did all the cooking, all the cleaning, most of the raising-of-the-kids and handled all the problems, while he went to work, came home and relaxed."

"You sound almost resentful."

"I'm really not. If she'd wanted him to be different, he would have changed, and would have thought it was his own idea. She has a lot of power in their relationship. She just wields it subtly."

Anna cleaned the last mushroom, moved them next to Tyler, then circled the island to sit on a stool on the opposite side. "What does she think of you and Kyle following in your father's footsteps?"

"She'd rather have us both living close to home, especially now that Kyle and Joanna are married and there's a grandbaby.

But as long as we're doing what we want and we're not taking any unusual risks, she's satisfied.''

"And if you were taking unusual risks, she would never know, would she?''

He looked up, a grin softening his features. "I'd never tell. Funny thing about mothers, though…they tend to figure things out on their own.''

Anna thought of Tyler putting his life in danger for someone else, for some noble cause, and her stomach turned a somersault. If she were in Beatrice Ramsey's position, she would hate her sons' careers with a passion and would do her best to discourage them from continuing in that field. If *she* had any right to an opinion at all, she would voice it…but two small kisses gave her no such right.

Deliberately she returned to his earlier comment regarding being conceived the old-fashioned way. "I learned where babies come from in school, but when I realized that meant *all* babies, including Lucas, our sisters and me, which meant that *my* mother and my father had done that…I was appalled. I simply couldn't—wouldn't—imagine my parents sharing that kind of intimacy. After all, they were the king and the queen of an entire nation. Heavens, I couldn't imagine *myself* doing such a thing. It was unthinkable.''

"And then you did it and it wasn't so appalling anymore, was it? At least, not if it was done right.''

She watched as he tore off large pieces of the heavy-duty foil, then divided the chicken breasts, vegetables, spices and a sprinkling of bottled Italian salad dressing among them. Should she play along with his assumption and hope that sometime before this journey was over, he would find out firsthand how wrong he'd been? Or should she be honest and forthright with him, and risk destroying that hope for all time? Some men, she was well aware, liked bedding virgins—took it as a challenge and saw the results as proof of their sexual prowess. Others had no desire whatsoever to deal with inexperience, fears and pain. Which was Tyler?

"You're awfully quiet,'' he said as he laid additional pieces of foil over each chicken breast, then folded the edges to make an air-tight packet. "Does that mean you've never experienced it done right?"

Which *was* Tyler? She supposed she would soon find out, though she couldn't bring herself to look at him as she carelessly replied, "Actually, it means I've never experienced it at all."

He stared at her. She felt his green gaze on her, creating a heat that started somewhere around her cheeks and spread in every direction. Suddenly it seemed overly warm in the room, and she wished for a bit of the chill she'd felt when she'd fallen in the snow. But she didn't wish she could take back the words. If they were going to have any sort of relationship—and that was quite an if—it must be based on honesty. His career and her place in the royal family put enough obstacles in their way. Better that an unwelcome surprise—if that was how he viewed this—come sooner rather than later.

"You're—you're a—a—"

Barely able to breathe, she managed to smile and answer lightly. "It's not such a difficult word. Virgin. See?"

"Not such a difficult word," he muttered, "but one hell of a difficult concept." After a long still moment, he gathered the foil packets onto a baking sheet and put them in the hot oven behind him, then came back to the counter, resting his hands flat on the surface. "You're teasing, right?" he asked, then demanded, "Look at me."

Slowly she raised her gaze until it locked with his. He studied her long and hard, then his face paled and his jaw tightened as he answered his own question. "Aw, hell, you're not. Jeez, last night...the things I said...the way I acted...you must have thought..."

She waited a polite moment before finishing for him. "That you were temporarily gone feeble-minded? Yes, I did." In some tiny hopeful place deep inside, she'd also thought he was jealous, and she'd liked thinking it—liked thinking he cared enough to care.

"But...the T-shirt...and you said Rusty stayed with you at the motel..."

"I *said* he gave me the shirt when he left the motel that morning. It was late when we left the Silver Nugget, after midnight, and he escorted me to the motel to ensure I got there safely. He bought the shirt as we were leaving and gave it to me when we reached the room. He thought I would get a kick out of it—which is slang for enjoying something, I believe.''

"Close enough." Tyler dragged his hand through his hair, the gesture taut with frustration, embarrassment and surprise. She truly had shocked him, Anna thought, and wished she knew whether that was good, bad or in between. "Jeez, Your Highness, you're twenty-five," he said as if that was somehow significant.

"I'm well aware of that."

"And you've had opportunities."

"A few," she replied dryly.

"So why…?"

"Why not? Is it wrong to wait until it means something?"

"Of course not. It's just…rare."

"Believe me, I know. My girlfriends all think it's most strange. Even my sister, Christina, believes that I'm—" Blushing, she broke off, but it was too late.

"That you're what?" When she didn't answer right away, his gaze narrowed, and that muscle in his jaw twitched. "Even your sister believes what, Your Highness?"

"That I'm…uh, we…that is, you and I are…" She saw when he fully understood—saw the dismay and something very close to horror that turned his gaze to emerald stone. Once upon a time, the idea of having sex had appalled her. Now the idea of having sex with her clearly appalled him.

Biting her lip and finding it sore from when she'd bitten it earlier that afternoon, she slid from the stool to her feet and retreated to the living room side of the cabin, where she added a log to the fire, then turned on the television. She found nothing but static on the regular channels, so she selected a video from the cabinet and inserted it in the VCR before making herself comfortable on the couch.

In her peripheral vision she could see that he hadn't moved and that he didn't appear any less repulsed by the idea that someone thought he might actually, willingly be her lover. It wasn't so far-fetched! Men had tried to seduce her before, and that very morning Tyler himself had said if she weren't who she was, they would have been in the back of their vehicle having fabulous sex instead of arguing at the side of the road.

Very well, so he hadn't said fabulous. In fact, he hadn't mentioned sex at all. Specifically, he'd said, *I would have you stripped naked in the back of that truck and we wouldn't be talking at all.* Perhaps her English wasn't as good as his, but she knew what that meant.

But she was who she was, and he clearly had no intention of ever forgetting it.

"Listen, Princess..." His voice was quiet, his tone regretful.

Stubbornly she increased the volume on the movie. It didn't deter him one bit.

"Look, I'm sorry for...hell, I don't even know what. I didn't even say anything."

But his look had said plenty, and it had hurt more deeply than she'd dreamed possible. She was only grateful that her eyes were dry. She couldn't bear it if she burst into tears in front of him.

He crossed to the television with long strides and pressed the mute button. She responded by raising the volume once more, and he responded by snatching the remote control unit from her hand and shutting off the television entirely, then placing the unit on top of the cabinet out of her reach. "I'm trying to talk to you, and I'll be damned if I'm going to yell over the TV. When we're done, you can watch your movie, but not until then."

"We are done now." Regally she rose from the couch and started toward the stairs. When he caught her wrist and brought her sliding to a stop, she spun around, her free hand raised in anger.

His features hardened, but he didn't release her. "Don't even think about it, Annie," he warned in an icy low voice. "It seems I've spent about half my time with you apologizing or groveling, and I damn well don't like it. There's no way in hell I'm going to stand here and let you slap me without spanking you like the spoiled brat you are."

"Spoiled brat?" Slowly she lowered her hand and raised her chin, managing to look down her nose at him in spite of the fact that he was half a foot taller. "Then we are a fine pair, for *you* are an ill-mannered boor."

For a moment he didn't react, then a frown wrinkled his forehead. "An ill-mannered boor? Is that the best you can do? Try a damn fool bastard. Or a stupid son of a bitch."

She blinked. "My mother says a lady never swears. Besides, I have no reason to cast doubt on your parentage and no desire to insult your mother."

"Neither of those names has anything to do with my parentage or my mother," he explained with more patience than she expected. "They have to do with me being an idiot."

Once more she blinked, feeling oddly unbalanced. "But you're not an idiot."

"Yes, I am. Trust me."

She did trust him—there was no doubt of that—but she also knew he was quite intelligent and competent...at least, when not dealing with her. She gazed up at him, her eyes wide, and softly said, "I trust you, Tyler. Honestly, I do."

Chapter 6

Her words, quiet, simple but sincere, made a lump form in Tyler's throat. He knew well what a difficult proposition trust was—knew how many people gave it, lost it, betrayed it. He imagined Anna, sheltered though she was, had seen her own trust betrayed more than most, and yet she could so innocently offer it to him.

And he didn't deserve it. He'd spent half their time together wishing she were anywhere in the world but with him, and the other half wanting to make love to her until they both forgot who and what she was. A princess. The treasured daughter of his father's friend. A virgin. And the woman he was lying to. Who didn't know he'd already betrayed her by calling her father yesterday from Clarkston.

Slowly he became aware of her pulse, steady and strong beneath his fingers. He looked down at her wrist, so small and delicate in his grip, and knew he should let go. Should quit touching her so much. Quit looking at her. Quit wanting her.

Yeah, and for his next trick, he would stop the snow, make the sun rise at midnight and turn the dead of winter into hot, hot summer.

"You said you wanted to speak with me," she said politely.

He vaguely remembered telling her that after she'd dropped her bombshell and before he'd called her a spoiled brat. After she'd tried to slap him and before he'd grabbed her. After he'd brought that stricken look to her face that had wiped away her smile and dimmed the light in her eyes, that had made her full lower lip tremble and left him feeling as if he'd just kicked an innocent puppy.

Sliding his hand down until his fingers were twined with hers, he drew her back to the sofa, seated her at one end, then went to stand in front of the stone fireplace. The mantel consisted of a massive piece of wood, rough-hewn with the axe marks still visible, and when he touched it, it was warm with the heat from the fire. Lined up along it were pieces of locally made pottery, offered for sale in the motel office. He drew his finger over the graceful curves of one tall vase, then took a breath and faced Anna.

"You asked me a question on the way back into town this afternoon. I…didn't answer it."

"I asked you several questions. You didn't answer any of them." She smiled faintly, and he realized that even without looking at her, he would have known she was smiling. He had come to recognize it in her voice. "You make a habit of doing that."

"I suppose I do. I'm sorry about that." After a moment, he sat down at the opposite end of the sofa, and she immediately turned to face him. Part of him wished she hadn't. "You asked how important this job is to me—whether I enjoyed it and could see myself still doing it in ten or twenty years. My father decided when he was a little kid that he was going to be an air force pilot when he grew up, and damned if he didn't do it. When he retired, he decided to start a successful business, and he did that, too. He always knew exactly what he wanted, and he always got it.

"Well, except when he tried to convince Kyle not to go into the service and to take over the company instead. The only reason he lost then was because Kyle was just as determined and stubborn. Jake's like that, too. They're all so sure of what they want and how to get it—so confident and single-minded and decisive. And then there's me."

Though he wasn't looking at her, he knew Anna's gaze hadn't wavered. He wished it would—wished she would turn those dark eyes toward the fire or the snow outside. He'd never talked to anyone about this—not the mother who'd raised him while his father was off saving the world or the brothers who'd taught him all the important things that their old man hadn't been around for, like throwing a football, sliding into home and being prepared for a date. Certainly not with Edward himself on those occasions he was home.

"My mother says I never knew what I wanted from one day to the next. I never could decide which toys I wanted for Christmas, which food was my favorite, which girl I liked better, which college I wanted to go to or what I wanted to major in while I was there. After I graduated, I never knew what I wanted to be doing next month, much less next year. All those jobs I told you I'd done...some of them I knew were just temporary, but most of them I really intended to stick with...at least until I got bored. I started and quit or got fired from so many jobs that it got to be a family joke. It made Mom and Dad crazy. Hell, it made *me* crazy. She thought I was wasting my life. He couldn't decide whether I just wasn't living up to my potential, or whether somehow a son of his could possibly not *have* any potential."

"Not everyone is born knowing what they want to do or who they should be."

"Every Ramsey is," he said with a wry grin. He'd always felt as if he didn't quite fit in. He'd been the only one without ambition in a family driven by it. The only one content to drift where life took him rather than forge his own trail over, around or preferably through any obstacles. The only procrastinator in a bunch of hard-chargers. Hell, he didn't even look like the other men in the family. Kyle and Jake had their father's brown hair and gray eyes, while his hair was auburn and his eyes green, like their mother's.

He'd stuck out like a sore thumb. The indecisive one. The unreliable one. The disappointment.

"I don't know what prompted my old man to offer me a job with the Noble Men. Maybe he thought it would force me to grow up, or maybe it was his last attempt to turn me into a credit to the Ramsey name. Hell, maybe he wanted to prove once and for all that I couldn't cut it in his world. Whatever his reason, I like what I do...finally. It's important to me—damned important—and I would very much like to be doing it in ten or twenty years. But...I can't afford any mistakes. This is my last chance to be a son he can be proud of, and if I blow it, that'll be it. I *can't* screw up.''

Finally he looked at her. She was studying him with sympathy and other emotions he didn't want to identify. ''Do you understand what I'm saying, Annie?''

''Yes,'' she murmured even as she shook her head no.

''This job is the most important thing in my life,'' he said quietly, carefully. ''I have to concentrate on what I'm doing. I have to prove myself to my father, to the Noble Men, and to myself. I don't have time for distractions.''

''And I'm a distraction.''

''Yes.'' Hell, yes. Of the worst kind. ''That's why I reacted so...strongly when you said Christina believes we're...'' He couldn't bring himself to say the word and half expected her to finish it for him. *It's not such a difficult word. Lovers. See?* But she didn't speak up, so he left the sentence hanging. ''If she lets it slip to your father or anyone else, I'm screwed. I can kiss my career goodbye. I can't let that happen, Annie, not when it took me so damn long to figure out what I wanted to do. *Now* do you understand what I'm saying?''

For a long time, she sat still, her dark eyes shadowed with hurt. Then she raised her chin an inch or so, straightened her spine a few degrees and, through sheer will, apparently, forced a wintry chill into her gaze that could hold its own against the cold outside. ''You flatter yourself, Tyler,'' she said frostily. ''No one who knows me would believe that I might seriously entertain the notion of a relationship with you. Even Christina believes I'm merely using you for sex. After all, you're already on my father's payroll. Why shouldn't I get his money's worth from you? That's what she did with Jack Dalton.''

Tyler's gaze narrowed, and a pain started deep in his gut. ''She *married* Jack Dalton.''

She laughed at his unspoken suggestion that if it happened to Christina and Jack, it could happen to them. ''My father has princes, nobility and sheiks asking for my hand in marriage on a regular basis. They offer power, riches, influence and alliances that could strengthen Montebello well into the next century. What could the Ramsey family joke offer that could possibly compare?''

Her words hurt more deeply than he'd thought they could. It

was only the tears suddenly brimming in her eyes that stopped him from retaliating. There was no need to retaliate. He'd already hurt her enough.

He stood up, retrieved the remote control from cabinet, turned on the television and started the tape, then laid the unit on the coffee table. Then he went into the kitchen, through the well-stocked pantry and out the back door, where the cold hit him with the force of a freight train.

Snow that had drifted onto the porch soaked through his socks, but he hardly noticed. Except for a narrow passageway to the steps, the entire porch was stacked with firewood. Miz Gemma Lee believed in being prepared for just about anything. Come the spring thaw, she didn't want to find any of her paying guests long past suffering from lack of heat or food. That might give the place a bad name.

For a long time he stood there, staring out at the snow. Periodically a crack would echo through the forest as a tree branch gave way under a load too heavy to bear. If he weren't too cold to feel much besides rotten, he might consider doing the same.

He hadn't meant to hurt Anna. He'd just wanted her to understand why he'd reacted the way he did in the kitchen. He'd wanted her to know that no matter how damn much he wanted her, no matter how much she enjoyed amusing herself with him, there couldn't be anything between them. How the hell had he wound up bringing her to tears?

Shivering, he grabbed a load of logs and stacked them on the pantry floor. Before heading out for more, he strained to hear something besides the TV—but please, no tears, no sobs, no whimpers. Laughter would be good. Angry curses would be better.

He couldn't make out a thing.

He brought in several more loads of firewood, then closed the door with more force—more noise—than necessary and jerked off his wet socks before cautiously entering the kitchen. There he started the instant brown rice cooking, then sneaked a look over his shoulder at the princess. She sat in the same rigid, regal position, her attention riveted on the TV. If she was crying, it was the quietest, most elegant crying he'd ever witnessed.

When the timer rang for the rice, he turned off the heat, then removed the chicken from the oven. Hoping he sounded halfway normal, he called, "Dinner's ready," without looking in her direction, then began transferring the food to plates.

"You may serve my meal over here," she announced coolly.

Tyler's first impulse was to snidely point out that he wasn't her servant, but he clamped his jaw shut before the first word escaped. If acting out the part of spoiled princess helped her to cope, more power to her. She could put him in his rightful place, and he could get pissed off with her condescension and eventually get back to thinking of her as the royal pain in the ass that he had to endure until this job was over.

Maybe.

Like a good servant, he located a serving tray in the pantry, then carried her food, utensils and diet pop to her. He passed behind the couch, so he wouldn't block her view of the television, and offered her the tray without a word. Seconds ticked past—five, ten, then twenty—before she finally deigned to raise one hand in a gesture so careless it was insulting.

"Place it there."

He considered *placing* it upside down over her head and seeing how she liked wearing chicken and rice a la Beatrice. But once again he resisted the impulse, set the tray on the end table, then returned to the kitchen for his own food.

He ate at the dining table, his fork in one hand, his book in the other, but by the time he finished eating, he hadn't read more than ten words or understood even one of them. He'd just stood up to return his dishes to the kitchen when she broke her silence once more.

"Take this away. I'm finished."

Grinding his teeth, he collected the plate and found she hadn't taken more than a few bites of her meal. His patience strained, he dumped the food into the trash, then gripped the edge of the sink with both hands. He could get through this. He was a Ramsey, and Ramseys could endure anything.

In fact, *when* he got through this, he had no doubt he would have suffered so much that he just might be the toughest damn Ramsey of them all.

The worst of the snow dissipated sometime in the night, though Anna could just barely tell that when she awakened Saturday morning. The long, narrow windows that circled the sleeping loft were coated with snow on the outside and a thin layer of ice on the inside. She felt something of a kinship with the glass. Though she had no snow on her outside at the moment, she certainly had the ice inside.

If she were home in Montebello, she would go to her favorite spot on the island, a small beach not far from the palace, made private by rocky outcroppings on either end and kept that way by palace security. As a child, she'd learned to swim there and had built castles in the sand—as if the real-life castle in the distance could have been improved upon. As a teenager, she'd passed many solitary hours there, reading, letting the sound of the waves relax her and sweep her away to someplace in her imagination. Now she needed to lie there under the Mediterranean sun and absorb the heat, the peace, the easiness, of nature into her heart and her soul.

Instead she was snowed in, in a cabin that was much too small for two, that had lost all of its charm in the aftermath of last evening's conversation.

She was ashamed that she'd taken words Tyler had said to her in confidence and thrown them back for no reason other than to wound him. If asked, she would have been confident she was above such petty, mean-spirited behavior. It wasn't a welcome discovery to find that she would have been wrong.

Down below the sofa springs creaked as he shifted positions. When he'd first informed her they would be sharing the cabin, she would have happily offered to share the bed, too, and when he turned that down, she would have offered to sleep on the sofa, though he likely would have turned that down, also. By the time bedtime had arrived, they'd been ignoring each other too carefully to even speak a civil good-night. She had lain in the center of her comfy, queen-size bed—princess-size, in this case, she thought with a faint smile—and hoped he would sleep poorly and awaken stiff and cranky, and know he had only himself to blame.

She should be ashamed of that pettiness, as well…but she wasn't.

The sofa creaked again, followed by a rustle of bedding and a grunt. Rolling onto her side on the edge of the bed, she could just see Tyler, standing beside the sofa, arms over his head in a stretch. His arms were bare, and so was he—at least, what little she could see, though she had no doubt he wore *something*. Sleep naked in the same cabin in which she slept? Ha! No doubt, he would be appalled by the very idea.

She drew her covers tighter, tucking them high around her neck so camouflage would be a simple matter if he should look in her direction, and she watched as he moved to the fireplace. Last night's fire had burned down to a pile of ash-coated embers that showered as he tossed a couple of logs on top, then held his hands out as if to coax them into flame.

She could see now that she'd been right—he'd slept in the same disreputable sweat pants he'd worn the evening past. Of course, that could have been for warmth as well as propriety. Heat rose, and while she'd been toasty comfortable in the loft, no doubt the temperature had been significantly cooler downstairs. The waistband of the garment had slipped below his own waist and gave her plenty to peer at through barely opened eyes—lots of skin a few shades lighter than her own, nicely developed muscles, broad shoulders, strong arms.

Interesting how her own temperature was starting to increase.

Once the logs were burning brightly, he disappeared into the kitchen, then returned a moment later with a cup of microwaved coffee. This time he presented his back to the flames, which presented her with a nice view of his front. He was the epitome of lean, strong and healthy…and he had placed himself off-limits to her.

Slowly, when it seemed he'd run out of anything else to look at, he raised his gaze to the loft. She closed her eyes quickly and regulated her breathing, steady and easy. She needed a plan for dealing with him over the next few days. She couldn't lie in bed and ogle him every time he wasn't looking, and she certainly couldn't pretend to be asleep every time she thought he might glance at her.

She could be civil to him, though it was the last thing on earth she wanted. Her mother had taught her to be most pleasant with those whom she liked least. She'd witnessed the queen playing gracious hostess with people who, had they not held some position of authority somewhere, wouldn't have been deemed fit to venture into polite society. If the queen could do it, so could Anna. After all, in spite of her insult the previous night, Tyler was neither ill-mannered nor a boor. He was an exceedingly polite man with an excessive sense of duty and a compelling motivation to do his job properly. He would make it easy for her to be gracious.

Unable to put off her morning needs much longer, she made a big show of awakening—rolling onto her back, fumbling with the alarm clock, yawning loudly—then sat up and swung her feet to the floor. A sidelong glance down below showed that he'd hastily turned his back to her.

A shower did much to energize her. After she dressed in jeans and a Hard Rock Café T-shirt, she took socks and a pair of boots downstairs with her and left them near the coffee table. "Good morning," she said, reminding herself to emulate her mother. Cool, polite, gracious.

Tyler had pulled on his own shirt and was in the small kitchen, and his tone was guarded when he replied, "Morning. What do you want for breakfast?"

She considered everything they'd bought the previous afternoon—bacon, eggs, ham, cardboard tubes containing preformed biscuits, cereal and milk—and said, "Ice cream with fudge topping."

He blinked once before opening the freezer, then placing a carton of ice cream next to the jar of topping. She knew, though not from experience, that ice cream was not so unusual a Saturday morning breakfast for children in America, but apparently not in the Ramsey household. Beatrice Ramsey, according to Tyler, was a very good cook—no doubt forced to become one by her family of big healthy strong males with healthy strong appetites. Well, *she* was a healthy, pampered female who didn't fly planes, handle weapons, run miles, lift weights or save the world, and she wanted ice cream.

Though she wished she could seat herself on the couch and let him wait on her as she'd done last night—it had certainly kept him too annoyed to even consider any attempt at a cease-fire—she simply couldn't do it. She was spoiled, yes, but she didn't overly take advantage of it, except with her father, and no matter how deeply Tyler's words had hurt, she didn't want to treat him badly because of it. It wasn't his fault he didn't reciprocate her feelings, and it certainly wasn't his fault that he equated her with words like mistake, screwup and distraction. It wasn't even his fault that she'd made it necessary for him to tell her so.

But she still didn't want to get close to him.

In her best imitation of Queen Gwendolyn, she went into the small kitchen, took a bowl from the cabinet and a spoon from the drawer. Tyler was cracking eggs into a larger bowl and frying a slice of ham in a skillet while biscuits baked in the oven, and she felt his wary gaze on her as she dished up a generous portion of chocolate-covered cherry ice cream. She concentrated on ignoring the fact that he was less than four feet away as she returned the carton to the freezer, even though she could smell his cologne and could feel the heat radiating from his body.

Holding the jar of fudge sauce in one hand, she tried to open it with the other, but her best efforts failed. Perplexed, she studied the lid, then gave it another mighty twist, but still it refused to budge. Having no idea what to do next, she was on the verge of mentally revising her menu to plain ice cream when Tyler reached around her, took the jar and opened it with ease, then set it in front of her. Set it there and retained hold of it, which kept him standing immediately behind her, so close that his shirt tickled against her bare arm. So close she was convinced she felt his breath stirring her hair.

When she realized her hands were trembling, quickly she lowered them to her sides, but when the trembling spread through her entire body, there was nothing she could do. She knew instinctively the only thing that would stop it was Tyler, holding her close, and there was no way he intended to do that.

"Thank you," she said, attempting to sound untouched and reaching for the jar from an angle calculated to minimize the risk of physical contact with him.

His fingers tightened around the jar when she pulled. "Annie." His voice was warm, husky and filled with regret.

"Princess," she corrected him quickly, shakily. "I believe it would be best if you refer to me by my title."

He withdrew emotionally before he drew back physically. She was filled with regret, also, but it was his doing. *He* was the one who thought she would destroy everything he was working for. *He* was the one who placed more importance on his father's approval than on the potential between them. "Sure, Your Highness," he said flippantly. "Anything you say."

His sarcasm made her mouth compress in a tight line and provoked her temper no small bit. But she wasn't going to respond. She was merely trying to place this disaster of a relationship on a footing which they could survive until the snow melted enough for her to depart, and she would not give in to his childish urge to see who could wound the other the most until then.

She spooned sauce over the ice cream, then replaced the cap. "Thank you for your assistance," she said politely as she left the kitchen.

He watched until she sat down on the sofa, then picked up the fudge jar, placed it in the refrigerator and closed the door with unnecessary effort. She made a mental note that the sauce required refrigeration, turned on the television and began to eat as she flipped through the channels.

She was well acquainted with the sayings that time crawled or flew, but she'd never experienced such tedium as she did that day. When she was convinced that it surely must be seven or eight o'clock at night, it was actually only noon. By the time 8:00 p.m. arrived, she was ready to walk out into the snow and scream. She wanted—no, *needed* to do something, go somewhere, hear a friendly voice. The tension inside the cabin was so intense the walls fairly vibrated with it, and it built a pressure in her head that made her yearn for release.

In the middle of yet another movie, she decided she could take no more. The night was still, and a full moon shone brightly on the snow. Swinging her feet to the floor, she sat on the edge of the couch, put on her socks and boots, then took her coat from the row of hooks behind the door.

"Where are you going?" Tyler sounded as pressured as she felt.

"For a walk."

"Now there's a bright idea. Have you noticed how deep the snow is?"

She refused to even glance at the windows. "I've been in snow before. My family has a winter place in the Alps where we've skied every winter since I was an infant."

"You skied as an infant," he repeated disbelievingly.

Ignoring him, she did up the buttons on her coat, then tied the belt tightly around her middle, wrapped her scarf around her hair and pulled on her gloves. She was in the process of unlocking and opening the door when abruptly his hand appeared above her head and slammed it again.

"You can't go out."

"Of course I can." Deliberately she wrapped her fingers around his wrist, and she imagined she felt the pulse there increase erratically as she pulled his hand away. He let her do so more to avoid contact with her, she suspected, than for any other reason.

She opened the door and for a moment stood motionless. She *hadn't* noticed how deep the snow was—in a word, *very*. There was no sign of the wood floor of the porch that fronted the cabin, no indication of the steps that led to the ground, certainly no hint of the ground. On the near side of the vehicle, the snow reached halfway up the door. On the opposite side, she could see, it had drifted practically to the roof.

Behind her the sound of Tyler's breathing was slow, steady, shallow. She glanced over her shoulder in his direction but was careful to not actually look at him, and dryly said, "Perhaps it will be a short walk." Then she stepped across the threshold and closed the door.

The night was still and bright. The snow turned the everyday mundane aspects of the world into strange shapes and rounded forms. It was breathtaking in its beauty, though she all too easily understood that it was also tedious and quickly wore out its welcome. If she'd ever attained her goal of becoming a fairy, she would have used her magic to melt it all away—poof!—in an instant. A sprinkling of her fairy dust, and the harsh winter landscape, barren and brown, would return.

And she would take her leave of Tyler and go back to where she belonged.

Feeling homesick and heart-sore, she walked to the top of the steps, marked by the railing frosted with thick snow, and gazed out. Was Lucas somewhere around Garden City, looking out on the same snow, also wishing it away? She felt guilty that she had all but forgotten him in the past twenty-four hours. She was a bad sister, selfish and spoiled, just as Tyler had accused.

She wasn't surprised when the door behind her opened, or when Tyler, bundled in his coat and gloves, came to stand at the opposite side of the steps. She tried vainly to think of something to say—something neutral and impersonal, something with which he couldn't possibly take offense. All she came up with was hopelessly silly.

"Do you know snow provides such good insulation that you can build a cave in deep snow and heat it to a comfortable temperature with nothing more than a small candle?"

"Yeah. We did our survival training at your winter place in the Alps."

Of course they had. And they practiced covert landings on the beaches of Montebello and honed their helicopter insertion and extraction techniques in the island's interior. In his brief time with the organization, he'd learned more and done more than most men ever dreamed of. He'd found the career he wanted, and he held it much more dear than any spoiled little princess.

More than *this* spoiled little princess.

And what did it matter? she philosophically asked herself. So no man had ever kissed her the way he did. No man had ever made her feel the way he did. No man had ever tempted her. Another man would. Someone, somewhere, would kiss her and make her forget Tyler Ramsey existed.

Someday.

"Have you reported to your superiors that you're snowbound?"

"No. They track the weather. They'll know."

"I must remember to ask my sister if it also snowed in Billings. It wouldn't do to ruin a perfectly good lie with such a small detail as the weather. Then the truth would come out, and what might that do to your career?" She tried her genuine best to keep the bitterness from creeping into her voice in those last words, but it managed anyway. At best, he would ignore it. At worst, he might get angry.

Oh, well, again, what did it matter? Soon he would be gone from her life. Not soon enough, in her estimation, but soon.

Tyler's jaw throbbed from clenching it too often and too hard throughout the day. An ache had settled behind his eyes that wasn't going away no matter how many aspirin tablets he took, and his muscles felt as taut as when his training had pushed him past the point of fatigue. He felt lousy as hell, and the last thing he needed was Anna's subtle digs.

The first thing he needed was to get Annie back. She looked

just like the royal brat, except she smiled a lot, clung to him, and was incredibly kissable, and while her dark eyes showed plenty of emotions, pain wasn't one of them.

But he couldn't have her back. The sooner he accepted that, the better.

Staring grimly across the snow, he finally responded to her question. "It would end my career. You would like that, wouldn't you?"

"No," she said quietly. "Not at all."

He wondered if he could believe her. Wondered if he could ask her to give him a chance—first to prove himself to his father, and then to her. If he could ask her to wait, to put her life on hold, to have no boyfriends and for damn sure no lovers until he'd earned his father's and his brothers' approval and respect, and then give him a chance to show himself worthy of her.

Oh, sure, why not? She was twenty-five years old, beautiful, a freakin' princess and a virgin. Hell, she'd probably be happy to lock herself away in the palace and mark off the days on the calendar until he accomplished something that, honesty forced him to admit, he might not be able to accomplish. What if he never succeeded? What if the only thing he proved was his unworthiness to be his father's son? And what if he did succeed and this thing between him and Anna turned out to be nothing more than hormones on her part? The princess amusing herself with the hired help. The virgin looking for an appropriate candidate to relieve her of her virginity.

My father has princes, nobility and sheiks asking for my hand in marriage, she'd said the night before. *They offer power, riches, influence and alliances that could strengthen Montebello well into the next century. What could the Ramsey family joke offer that could possibly compare?*

At least she'd spared him the humiliation of answering her own question: *Nothing.* He couldn't offer her anything except himself, and he knew too well that, at the moment, he was no prize, and might never be.

After another moment of awkward silence in a day filled with nearly a thousand of them, he leaned one shoulder against the post supporting the porch roof and made a simple request. "Tell me about Prince Lucas."

Anna took so long to answer that he thought she might refuse.

Debating whether to cooperate with him? Weighing his request for information against her desire to keep him at a distance? Finally, though, she did answer. "He's ten years older than me—old enough that he didn't mind having me around as our sisters often did. He was my favorite, and I was his. I couldn't have asked for a better brother."

"How did he feel about the fact that one day he would become king?"

"How should he feel?" she asked with an elegant shrug. "How did your brother, Kyle, feel knowing that one day he was expected to take over your father's business?"

"You can't compare being CEO of an airplane parts manufacturing company to being king of a sovereign nation. Besides, Kyle had the option of walking away, which he did. Lucas doesn't have that option." Though he did have the option of disappearing, "forgetting" who he was and living life like a regular Joe for a time. Not that Tyler believed that was what the prince had done. It was just a possibility that had to be considered.

"It wasn't anything about which to have feelings," she replied. "I knew from the time I was small that I would grow up and become a woman. You knew you would grow up and become a man. Lucas knew he would become king. It was natural. Merely one more aspect of his life."

"And he never rebelled? Never wanted to be just a normal man living a normal life?" As he'd done in Colorado for the past year.

"You can't judge the normalcy, or lack thereof, of Lucas's life by your own. His life *is* normal, for *him.* Most young boys don't grow up to become mercenaries, but for you, with your background, it's a perfectly normal thing to be. For a young prince, growing up to become king is also perfectly normal."

"I'm not really a mercenary."

"No?" She raised one brow. "You're a soldier for hire. Is that not the very definition of a mercenary?"

"Mercenaries work for the highest bidder. They'll do anything for anyone as long as the price is right. They show no loyalty to anyone, they care about no one but themselves, and they kill without conscience."

"And you, of course, are different."

The skepticism faintly underlying her words struck a nerve. Damn right he was different, and she should know it by now. Still, he reined in his defensiveness and answered calmly. "There are a lot of people out there with more money than your father ever dreamed of, but I would never work for them. And I don't hire out my services. I work for an organization that contracts with certain governments or groups to provide security, investigative and counter-terrorism measures. But the Noble Men live up to their name. We're not hired killers."

Finally she looked at him, her dark gaze steady. "Have you ever killed anyone?"

"No."

"Could you?"

His mouth thinned. "Yes. Under the right circumstances. To save my life. To save someone else's life." Most definitely to save *her* life.

She gave a small nod before gazing out again. There wasn't much to see besides the snow—a few lights in the direction of the lodge office, a few plumes of smoke drifting up from chimneys in the same direction, a bright moon and a sea of stars in a vast sky. "My brother may not appear to take his responsibilities seriously. He likes to party. He enjoys life. He adores women. But once he becomes king, all that will change. Tremendous responsibilities will be thrust upon him, and he'll lose much of the freedom he now has. No one in the palace blames him for enjoying life to the fullest while he can, but also no one doubts he'll settle down and discharge every one of those responsibilities to the fullest when the time comes."

It must be nice to know your family had such faith in you, Tyler thought. He wouldn't want to be king for anything, but he wouldn't mind having just a taste of that unwavering family support.

After another uncomfortable silence, the princess moved forward, brushed the snow from the stair railing, then gripped it as she took a tentative step, sinking through the snow until her foot made contact with the second step. "When I was a small child, I often wished to see Montebello in snow. On stars, on birthday candles, on Christmas lists, I asked for merely a small bit of snow—a few feet for a few days. I was never greedy. I must have been approximately nine when my tutor explained in no uncertain terms that the island had never had snow, would never have snow and, because of its location, *could* never have snow. I quit wishing then.''

She moved to the next step, and the snow rose to mid-calf. At the bottom of the steps, the railing ended, and she carefully released it, then struggled a few steps away through snow that reached well above her knees.

''So you were a poor little princess, deprived of being a fairy, having snow on your tropical beach or making wishes.''

Looking over her shoulder, she threw a feigned scowl his way. ''It's a good thing you didn't grow up on Montebello,'' she said airily. ''If you had, I would have had no choice but to have you thrown into the dungeon.''

''I've been all through the palace, Princess. There *is* no dungeon.''

''Of course it's not a part of the palace. The royal family have no wish to be disturbed by the wretched cries of their wayward subjects who find themselves in need of redirection.''

Though careful that she couldn't hear it, Tyler gave a heavy sigh of relief. Dealing with the Anna who could tease was no big deal, as long as he remembered to keep his hands to himself. This Anna was tempting, no doubt, and made him want far more than he could have, but all he needed was frequent reminders to keep his distance, and he could do it. He swore he could.

''And you think I need redirection?''

''Your sarcasm speaks for itself. You lack proper respect for my station in life. You fail to grasp the first and simplest rule of being a loyal subject.''

''Which is?''

''If the royals aren't happy, then their subjects are unhappy as well.''

Moving as cautiously as she had, he started down the steps. ''*I* lack proper respect? Who flashed her pearly whites within minutes of boarding the plane in San Sebastian and decreed that I should call you Anna? Who insisted on acting like a regular person?'' Except when her feelings were hurt, which she tried to hide behind the cool, aloof facade of exalted princess. ''Who didn't think twice about lying, sneaking off and deceiving her entire family about her activities, and then dragging me into her deception, too?''

As he approached her, she retreated, though she made very slow progress through the deep snow. "I gave my plans a great deal of thought," she disagreed earnestly. "From the moment I heard the news from Colorado that Lucas was still alive, I thought of little else but his rescue and what I could do to assist. And I thought more than twice about your part in it. I even regretted that it might reflect badly on you...at least, until I got to know you."

Her wicked smile took the sting out of her last words, and he was about to respond similarly when she slipped and, seemingly in slow motion, started to fall. He reached forward to catch hold of her hand, but she'd fallen back too far and he was too off-balance to counter it.

She sank through the snow, landing on her back, and he fell on top of her. Silhouette-shaped walls of snow towered over them, sending little avalanches of icy flakes down on them, coating their clothes, dotting her dark curls, drifting over his collar onto his too-warm skin. Her first response was to laugh, but the humor disappeared soon enough—about the time she became aware of his erection, he figured—and instead she stared up at him, her brown eyes rounded and hazy, her lips slightly parted, her body soft and unnaturally warm for the circumstances. That was fair enough, though, since he was hot enough to melt ice.

The cold, the snow and the fact that he was most definitely *not* keeping his distance faded from his mind as he stared at her. There was a hopeful look in her eyes, and he wondered what it was she hoped for. That he would kiss her? Or that he wouldn't?

Bracing himself on his elbow, he removed one glove, then brushed a few flakes of snow from her cheek. Though her face was flushed beneath her natural tan, her skin was cold and smooth as ice beneath his fingers. As he watched her watch him, his simple action became something more—a lingering touch, a much-needed caress—and he saw clearly the answer to his earlier question. She wanted him to kiss her, nearly as much as he wanted to. His mouth went dry at the prospect, and his blood turned so hot he swore he could feel steam rising.

When his fingers wandered close to her mouth, she turned her head just enough to bring her lips in contact with them for one brief moment. Then she smiled, and her expression turned so incredibly sad that raw pain throbbed straight through him. "We mustn't do this, Tyler," she gently reminded him. "Nothing has changed."

She was right. Nothing *had* changed. She wanted him, and he wanted her more. She was the king's treasured virgin daughter, and the biggest obstacle he faced in completing this job successfully. Making love to her might seem like the most important thing in his life at this moment, but it could cost him his career, his relationship with his family and his own self-respect. It could endanger or even destroy the organization's working relationship with King Marcus, which was of utmost importance. It could destroy him.

She could destroy him. And how much harm could he bring to her?

Pushing away from her took more willpower than he'd known he possessed. He struggled to his feet, then pulled her up. The scarf that had covered her hair fell, draping around her neck in a soft black cloud, and her curls tempted him to slide his fingers through them just once. He was reaching up to do just that when he forced his hands back to his side. This wasn't the time to give in to even the smallest of temptations, because if he did it once, it would be easier to do again. Besides, he was a weak man. If he filled his hands with her curls, it would be too easy to tilt her head back, to lean close, to brush his mouth across hers, to slide his tongue inside her mouth, to slide his hands inside her clothing and his...

Biting back a groan, he turned back toward the porch but reached behind him for her hand. She clasped his hand with both of hers and let him pull her through the snow to the porch. He kicked most of the snow from the steps, then hustled her up and to the door. There she stopped to brush the snow from her coat and jeans, to stomp it from her boots, while he did the same.

When she started to turn the doorknob, he laid his hand over hers. "I'm sorry, Annie. I wish...I wish things were different."

She smiled faintly. "You say I'm young, and yet I learned a lesson at nine years of age that you haven't yet learned at twenty plus that. Wishes are a waste of time, energy and imagination, Tyler. They certainly don't come true."

Still wearing that bittersweet smile, she pulled away, opened the door and went inside. He stood there in the cold, wishing he could be the one to prove her wrong, wishing he could be the man to make every wish she'd never thought to make come true. But the sad fact was, once again she was right.

Wishes didn't come true.

At least, not for them.

Chapter 7

Sunday passed harmlessly enough. While Tyler spent the entire day with his nose in a book, Anna worked her way through the video library. She watched classic old westerns that Roberto loved, comedies, a love story—but only one—and several action thrillers. She was so very tired of movies by the time she went to bed that night that she feared she might never sit willingly through another.

On Monday, snow fell again for a few dreary hours and cabin fever set in in earnest. She attempted to read but couldn't concentrate. She did manage to write a few postcards to friends, nap, listen to music and contemplate taking another stab at a walk in the snow. Considering how the last such excursion had ended, though, she decided it would be in her best interests to stay inside and go quietly insane.

By Tuesday afternoon, she wasn't content to do *anything* quietly. There were so many places she wanted to go, so many things she needed to do, and the inactivity was quickly approaching unbearable. The situation with Tyler was no longer so tense—they were able to make small talk—but both of them were on their guard constantly to keep things from becoming more intimate than was good for them.

Rather, than was good for *him.* She couldn't think of a single thing in the world that could be better for her than becoming intimate with Tyler Ramsey.

It had occurred to her that, if she were as experienced as people presumed her to be, she could attempt to seduce the man. But she wasn't experienced, and she found the idea of coercing him into making love to her against his better judgment reprehensible at best—though if she left the choice completely up to him, it would probably never happen at all. But that was a possibility—a probability—she very well might have to live with.

She was in the midst of surfing through the satellite channels once again available to them when the cell phone rang. Scrambling to her feet, she located it on the table where it had been silently plugged into the charger ever since their arrival at the lodge. Delightedly, she pressed the send button and answered the call.

She'd expected Christina, but it was her mother's voice at the other end. "How is your vacation?" Gwendolyn asked after dispensing with the greetings.

"I'm having a wonderful time," Anna lied. "Montana is a wonderful place, though it's very cold. I believe next time I shall come in the summer, when it surely must be more hospitable."

"And are you enjoying your visit with Christina?"

"Oh, yes." Two falsehoods in less than two minutes. She probably hadn't told her mother more than ten lies in her entire life, and now she couldn't seem to tell the truth.

As she settled on the sofa again, she saw Tyler glance up from his book across the room, one eyebrow raised in silent question. He must have realized right away that it wasn't Christina and probably worried it was Papa instead. Tucking her feet underneath her, she answered his question indirectly. "Oh, Mama, you should see her home. It's lovely—set in the woods, with windows everywhere—and she's so happy. She seems so...American." At least that was true. After so many years in Montana, Christina had acquired an American accent, an American style of dress, and most assuredly an American sense of independence. No one who saw her driving her truck, wearing her jeans and behaving so competently and capably would ever guess she was a princess.

Her mother chuckled. "We all tend to adapt to our situations. Not long after I came here from England, I'm certain I seemed so...Montebellan."

"Sometimes I forget you aren't." Would she ever become something else? Anna wondered, and her gaze crept against her will to Tyler. Arizonan, perhaps? And what exactly was required to be an Arizonan?

To start with, the cooperation of a man who was most uncooperative.

"So, sweetheart, tell me what you've done," Gwendolyn requested.

"I've eaten buffalo," Anna replied, injecting a note of enthusiasm into her voice, "and it really was quite delicious. And I've met some very nice people and seen some lovely scenery. Do you know they have mountains here called Castle Mountains? And a town named Buckingham and another range called the Crazy Mountains? And Montana is one of only fifty states, but it's much, much bigger than the entire kingdom of Montebello. But did I mention that it's very cold?"

"Yes, you did. I suppose having lived all your life in San Sebastian, the Montana winter must be quite a shock to you. Christina said you were...how did she put it? Like a child at Christmas when the snow started. Do you recall, when you were little, that was often all you ever asked for for Christmas? You never quite understood how your father could be the king and yet lack the power to make it snow for you."

"Yes, I remember." And if she were still that same little girl, at this very moment she would be begging her father to make the snow go away so *she* could go away. "How is Papa?"

"He's fine, as always. He's sitting right here, waiting for me to hand him the phone. Give Christina a hug for me, sweetheart, and enjoy your vacation. I love you."

"I love you, too, Mama," she murmured, then a moment later her father's voice came over the line. "Hello, Papa. Have you heard anything new about Lucas?"

"Nothing yet, *bambina,* but don't worry. We'll find him. Your mother tells me you ate buffalo. Roberto will be jealous."

"I know. You really should have let him come with me, Papa.

He would love Montana." And not once in her entire life had she ever been tempted to kiss him, or any of her other body-guards.

"I'm sure he would, but why bother sending two men when one can get the job done?" A curious note entered her father's voice. "What did you think of Tyler?"

She glanced at him guiltily, stretched out in an easy chair, a book in his hands but his attention openly on her. "He—he is a most polite young man."

"Yes, and…?"

"And…he has a great fondness for books."

"Such important perceptions," Marcus chided. "You flew six thousand miles with him, and that's all you learned?"

"What is this, Papa? A performance evaluation? Very well. He was quiet. He didn't want to chat." Except with Mareta. "He was polite and professional, and he refused to call me Anna, even though Roberto and the others always do when we're alone."

"So he didn't indulge and pander to you as Roberto and the others always do."

"No." But he'd given her a kiss that could have curled her hair if nature hadn't beaten him to it. And he made her feel safe in a way that none of her other bodyguards ever had.

"So…would you welcome him as your escort on future trips?"

Feeling her cheeks redden with guilt, she directed her gaze to the ceiling. "No, Papa. I was glad to see the last of him when he dropped me off at Christina's."

Marcus laughed. "Thank you, *mia figlia.* I'll tell his father you gave him a glowing recommendation. Edward will be pleased." Without awaiting a response from her, he changed subjects. "Do you remember Prince Arthur of Cartageña? You met him a few years ago when he attended a reception at the palace."

Anna called to mind the man who had represented the tiny island nation off the coast of Spain at some dreadfully dull event and wrinkled her nose. "My height, no chin, no personality and no interests other than his polo ponies? Yes, I remember him. Why?''

"He's let it be known that he intends to make a formal offer for you.''

With a shiver of distaste, she covered her eyes with one hand. "Oh, Papa, I don't want to marry him. Sitting next to him at one palace dinner is the extent of my tolerance for him. He bored me to tears.''

"But he can provide well for you.''

"I'd rather get a job and provide for myself.''

"From what I gather, he's really quite intelligent.''

"Intelligent and deadly dull. He's unable to converse on any subject but horses, and he lacks manners. He gave me a short lesson on the benefits of artificial insemination over the main course. Besides, Papa, I'm not an object up for sale. Prince Arthur doesn't even know me. How presumptuous of him to think he can 'make an offer' and gain a wife with no more effort than that.''

"Very well, *bambina*. I'll add him to the list of those who tried and failed. But you know, sweetheart, you're not getting any younger.''

"Christina was twenty-nine when she married Jack, and Julia was thirty and pregnant before she married Rashid. I'm only twenty-five.''

"Twenty-five, and you've turned down every man who's dared look your way. You're getting a reputation for being finicky.''

"If accepting a marriage proposal isn't the time to be finicky, such a time doesn't exist. I won't be married to someone who sees me as part of a business arrangement.''

"And you won't be married to any of the young men you've dated. Before you know it, you'll be an old maid," her father gently teased.

Anna swallowed over the lump in her throat. "Better an old maid than an unhappy wife or a bitter ex-wife.''

"You know I only want to see you settled and content.''

But she didn't want to be *content!* she silently protested. She wanted to be deliriously happy and in love, like her sisters, like her parents. She wanted a husband who owned her heart and shared her soul—a husband who loved her as much as she loved him, whose life was incomplete without her in it, whose commitment to her far and away exceeded his commitments to anyone or anything else.

She wanted a man who felt about her the way Tyler felt about his job.

"I am settled, Papa, and I am content." Two lies, to match the two she'd told her mother. "I have no need of a husband for that. In fact, Julia getting pregnant the way she did made me realize I have no need of a husband for anything." She paused a moment to let that sink in, then forced a cheerfulness she didn't feel into her voice and changed the subject. "Now tell me, Papa, what shall I bring you as a souvenir from Montana?"

Another cold Colorado Thursday found Ursula standing at the sliding glass door that led from her tiny apartment to a laughably tiny balcony, listening to the soft murmur of voices coming from the closet-sized space that passed as a guest room. Gretchen was in there with Jessica, doing whatever it was midwives did with their patients. In the parking lot Gretchen's goofy brother, Gerald, was shifting his weight from foot to foot and watching the kids play in what was left of the snow. If they invited him to join them, he wouldn't hesitate to jump right in, despite the fact he was thirty-three years old and topped six feet. Of course, mentally, he probably wasn't much more than six or eight anyway.

He was Gretchen's cross to bear. He'd lived the last sixteen years with her and had brought her nothing but hardship and grief. It wasn't easy having a life of your own when you were responsible for a kid in a man's body. It sure wasn't easy having a love life. Single mothers thought they had a hard time finding a man who didn't mind their "baggage." They didn't know hard until they tried to find a man who wouldn't mind taking on a wife and a feebleminded adult who would be an anchor around their necks for the rest of his life. Even Gretchen's fiancé, who'd sworn to love her dearly, had bailed out rather than take on responsibility for Gerald, too.

At least Ursula's sister was relatively competent. Oh, she was hardheaded as hell and determined to obstruct Ursula's plans for the future, but she could live alone. She'd never needed anything from Ursula beyond a little comforting after their parents' deaths, and a little comforting over Joe.

The guest room door opened, and in the glass reflection Ursula saw Gretchen come out, followed by Jessica. Truth was, Jessica wasn't real thrilled with the idea of using a midwife, but big sister Ursula had pointed out that there were few alternatives. The nearest doctor was miles away over treacherous mountain roads, and first babies often came so quickly. Of course, Jessica could move closer to the doctor, but how in the world would Joe find her if he came back looking for her? And Gretchen was a perfectly good midwife. She'd delivered half the babies in the county and hadn't lost a patient yet.

Of course, Ursula thought with a faint smile, there was a first time for everything.

Broadening the smile, she turned to face them. "So how's the little mother?"

"Mom and baby are fine," Gretchen said. "Don't forget to take your prenatal vitamins every day, Jessica—and eat. No matter how upset you are, you're not your primary concern anymore. You've got to take good care of your baby, and the way to do that is to take good care of yourself."

"I will," Jessica said, letting her hand slide down to rest on her belly. It was such a sweet maternal gesture, and it left Ursula cold.

"I'll walk out with you, Gretchen," she said as her friend started pulling on her coat. She took a short sable jacket from the closet, uncaring how silly it looked with her jeans and T-shirt, and followed Gretchen from the apartment.

Neither of them spoke until they reached the parking lot, where they stood for a moment next to Gretchen's old clunker. Gerald had gotten his invitation to join the kids and was now rolling in the snow, making a mess and giggling with the youngest of them. Just the sight of him made Gretchen's mouth tighten—made her turn away as if she couldn't bear to watch him. Instead she stared at the mountains off in the distance. "Do you think there might be enough money for me to put Gerald in a home with other people like him, and to leave here?''

Ursula resisted the urge to smile triumphantly. "I'm sure of it.''

"It's not that I don't love him. I do. It's just…''

"He's a major responsibility.''

"I've done the best I can, but…''

"You deserve a life, too.''

"It's not as if he wouldn't be just as happy with other people as he is with me. And I wouldn't be abandoning him. Just living my own life.''

"Letting someone else share the burden,'' Ursula agreed sympathetically.

"It would have to be a *good* home. And for the rest of his life. And maybe some money—just a little—to buy me a new start.''

"Absolutely.''

Gretchen continued to stare at the mountains for a moment. Feeling the cold seep into her bones, Ursula ignored her discomfort and waited patiently.

On the snow-covered lawn, the kids' play had become a snowball fight. "You missed him, you missed him, now you gotta kiss him.'' The singsong voice and the giggles that followed came from Gerald and made his sister's face turn even harder.

"Gerald!'' his sister called, her voice sharper than usual. "Come on! We've got to go!''

"But, Gretchen—''

"*Now,* Gerald. Get in the car.'' Once he'd obeyed, she opened her door, then her determined gaze met Ursula's. "All right. I'll help you.''

"Thank you, Gretchen. You won't regret it.''

Living in a mansion in paradise, on a first-name basis with the king and queen and all the royal family, favorite aunt and friend to the future king…neither would she.

Tyler awakened Friday morning to the steady drip of water from the cabin's eaves and the bright welcome glare of sunlight, absent too long. He rose from the couch, aware of the aches and stiffness that seemed to worsen every night he slept on the damned thing, threw a couple logs on the fire and went to the front window. The thermometer that was nailed to one porch post showed that the temperature was already two degrees above freezing, and over in front of the lodge office, snowplows were making good progress through the parking lot.

Thank God, they would be able to get out of the cabin today.

After gathering a change of clothes, he headed upstairs. Anna usually got the bathroom before him—a simple enough inconvenience...except that days of staying away from her made every minute he spent in the steamy room redolent of her various fragrances nothing less than torture. Perversely, though, when he locked the door behind him and brushed his teeth, then stripped for his shower, he found he missed all those fragrances. Without them, the bathroom was just another utilitarian room in a place where he didn't live.

He showered, shaved, then dressed in jeans and a crew-neck sweater. As he left the bathroom with the sweats and T-shirt he'd slept in rolled under his arm, Anna removed the pillow that covered her head, wrapped her arms around it and snuggled in close, then murmured, "You left the water running."

"No, it's off."

With a cranky expression marring her features, she rolled over, opened one eye, then flung her arm over both eyes. "Turn off that light."

"That's the sun, Your Highness, and the dripping is the snow melting. It's nine-fifteen and already thirty-four degrees."

In an instant, she transformed from drowsy and crabby to wide-awake. "The sun? You mean we might be able to leave this horrid cabin today?"

Before he could respond, she threw back the covers and slid from the opposite side of the bed to the floor. He'd spent plenty of hours on the lumpy sofa downstairs wondering what she slept in—a frilly gown, a T-shirt, pajamas—and now he knew. Her gown was some shiny fabric, probably satin, and the deep crimson flattered her dark skin. Tiny straps held it up, and it molded itself to her breasts, her narrow waist and the curve of her hips before ending about halfway down her thigh. It was a plain, simple gown, and just looking at her in it gave him a hard-on of impressive proportions, if he said so himself.

He held his crumpled clothes in front of him for camouflage as she rubbed the condensation from one window, then another, so she could look out. After a quick glance, she spun around, her curls bouncing, the hem of her gown fluttering almost indecently high. He was disappointed when it settled back where it belonged.

"Can we go to the mine today?"

He coughed the huskiness from his voice. "I don't know. We'll have to see what's been cleared."

"I'll shower quickly so we can go. I'm so glad we can leave! It's a nice little cabin, but I've come to hate it."

She swept past him and into the bathroom. The instant the door closed, he shut his eyes and breathed deeply of exotic flowers and subtle spices. The sheets and pillows on the queen-size bed would carry the same scents, and if he'd been weak enough—or was it wise enough?—to seduce her the way they'd both wanted, *he* would smell that way, too.

Clamping his jaw tightly shut, he went downstairs, put on his shoes and socks, and coat and gloves, then went outside. The porch steps were clean of snow for the first time in a week, and the drifts around the SUV had subsided to manageable proportions. He got a combination ice scraper/brush from the back cargo area and got started cleaning snow and ice from the windows. Next door, in front of Number 12, the father was doing the same job on his truck while his kids played in the snow. After a few minutes, though, he put down his scraper to play with them, and Tyler found himself standing motionless, watching them.

When Anna laid her small hand on his forearm, it startled him. He blinked, then gazed down at her. Had he wasted so much time, or had she taken the quickest shower on record? The latter, he'd bet. She wore little makeup, and didn't need what she wore, and rather than wait for her hair to dry naturally, she'd blown it dry and tamed the curls in the process. In her black trousers, emerald-green shirt and rust-colored down vest, with her sleek hair, green ear muffs and gloves to match, she could pass for any young American girl. If he took her to the nearest college campus, she could lose him in the crowd without even trying.

She glanced at their neighbors, then back at him. "Did you play with your father like that often?"

The question was the wake-up call he needed to quit staring and get back to work. "My old man was never around to play with. The first nine or ten years of my life, he was still in the air force and was always busy. Then he retired and started the business, and that took most of his time for the next nine or ten years. By the time he was ready to slow down and make time for snowmen or a game of catch, I was going off to college."

She moved to the opposite side of the truck to avoid the snow that showered off as he swept the brush from side to side. "He did important things."

"Yes, he did. And raising his family wasn't one of them. But I didn't really miss him. Jake did some, and Kyle did, but I had both of them, so it was no big deal."

"And you had your mother."

"Yeah," he agreed, then grinned wryly. "But there are some things a boy just shouldn't have to do with his mother, like sizing his first athletic cup or finding out where babies come from or buying his first box of condoms. There were a lot of times when it would have helped to have a father we could talk to, but he had more important things to do."

"You don't sound bitter."

"I'm not." No, the bitterness had been left to Kyle, for a long time, at least. And that was understandable, because it had been Kyle who'd taken on many of their father's responsibilities, who hadn't gotten to be merely the oldest son and big brother, but had been forced into the role of father figure for Jake and Tyler. "I just wish things could have been different. I think Dad wishes that, too. He realizes that he missed out on some things that'll never come around again."

"And when you have children of your own, you won't repeat his mistakes."

He glanced again at the father and children next door. "I

never really thought about having kids. That would mean growing up, and that was something I resisted for a long time. And having kids means getting married, and that means being committed and stable and doing a job every day, whether you like it or not. Since I couldn't find a job I could face doing every day, I never thought that far ahead.''

But lately…yeah, he could see himself settling down sometime in the not-too-distant future and having kids. Kyle had done it, and he seemed more satisfied than he'd ever been before. There were things Tyler needed to accomplish before he gave marriage any serious consideration—like ensuring that he could hold on to this job he wanted to do every day—but, yeah, someday he would get married and have kids, and he would make damn sure he was there for them.

"What about you?'' he asked as he swept piles of snow from the SUV's roof. "Do all prissy little princesses grow up to become royal wives and mothers?''

"I suppose they do. I adore children. I'm a wonderful aunt to my nephew, Omar, and I assume I shall have several of my own, regardless of whether I marry.''

Tyler felt the muscle in his jaw start to twitch as he squinted at her against the glare off the snow. "Well, that must make King Marcus happy.'' It damn well didn't do much for *him*.

"My sister, Julia, was already pregnant when she married Rashid.''

"But she did marry him.''

"That was her choice,'' she said with a shrug. "But if she'd decided against it, Mama and Papa would have been no less thrilled with their grandbaby.''

"Of course not. But they would have been just a little less thrilled with their daughter.''

"There's no shame in choosing motherhood without marriage. Is it fair that a woman who cannot find a suitable husband should be denied the opportunity to be a mother because of it?''

"You bragged just the other night that a lot of men want to marry you.''

"I wasn't bragging. I was simply stating a fact. And they don't want to marry *me*. They want to marry one of the few princesses available these days. Most of them don't even know me.''

"I could have guessed that. They wouldn't be so eager to marry you if they did.''

She lifted her chin and fixed her haughtiest gaze on him. "I don't see women lining up, clamoring to be your wife.''

He finished clearing the SUV, knocked the snow off the scraper, then returned it to the cargo area before circling the truck to face her. "One of these days you'll marry one of those men,'' he said flatly. "Maybe not Prince Arthur—''

"Never Prince Arthur,'' she declared.

"—but one of them, and you'll fill the royal nursery with little princes and princesses and leave them to be raised by the royal nannies while you're off fulfilling your royal duties. Maybe, if you're finicky enough, one of your princes will become king, and then instead of a mere princess, you'll be Anna, Queen of—''

A snowball smacked into his face, dusting his lashes, sifting into his mouth, stunning him into utter stillness for a moment. Finally, he raised one hand, cleared one eye, then the other, then wiped his face. "I don't believe you— You're gonna pay for that, Princess.''

He started toward her, and with a giggle, she spun around and begun running, heading in a zigzag around the cabin. She was quick, making it to the backyard, but he was quicker, taking her to the ground in a sliding tackle. Shrieking with laughter, she tried to wiggle free, but he flipped her onto her back, straddled her hips to keep her from escaping, then scooped up two big handfuls of snow, patting them together into a snowball of monstrous proportions.

She tried to regain her composure, but her laughter interfered. "You don't dare throw that at me,'' she decreed, her tone seesawing between breathless amusement and princessly hauteur.

"You're right, I don't.'' He held up the snowball, almost too soft to hold its shape, then grinned at her. "However, I do intend to put it someplace where it will have an even greater impact than if I threw it.'' He let his gaze slide down her body, from the collar of her vest to the soft curves of her breasts, straining the buttons that secured her shirt, to the narrow triangle of skin exposed at her waist where the two halves of the shirt had fallen to either side, and he grinned deviously.

"Oh, no, you don't," she warned, her brown eyes growing huge even as a smile twitched the corners of her mouth. "You wouldn't dare— I'll apologize for throwing the snowball at you. I'll tell my father. I'll tell *your* father. Tyler—*Tyler*—"

He let a bit of snow drift down onto that narrow triangle of warm brown skin, and she shrieked again. "You'll apologize, huh?"

She bobbed her head.

"Nicely? Sincerely?"

Another eager nod.

"Hmm. A proper apology from a princess or a snowball inside her clothes. Which would be more satisfying?" While he pretended to consider it, he vaguely noted that the cold was seeping through his jeans, that the heat where her hips cradled his was nothing less than amazing and that they were playing a dangerous game. He was naturally, inevitably getting turned on again, and he suspected she was, too, judging by the hazy warmth in her dark eyes. It was dangerous and reckless and foolish, and at the moment, he didn't give a damn. He didn't want to stop. Didn't want to get up. Didn't want to do the right thing and walk away.

"It will be a very sweet apology," she said with a very sweet smile. "And trust me—it will be *very* satisfying. Just give me a chance to show you—"

Too late he realized that while he'd been watching her eyes and her incredible mouth, she'd dug her own hands into the snow. She began shoveling it up at him by the handfuls, leaving him no choice but to dump his own snow inside her shirt. With another shriek, she renewed her efforts to escape, but he held her, his hands still under her shirt, his body stretched partly over hers, and somehow as she laughed and writhed, his hands moved slowly, purely by accident, farther beneath the shirt until they covered her breasts, and suddenly they both went still.

Silently he cursed the gloves that prevented him from feeling anything more than soft mounds and the small hard crests of her nipples. He wanted to know the texture of her skin and whether it was chilled by the snow or warmed by the internal heat they were so good at creating. If she was chilled, he wanted to warm her, and if she was warm, he wanted to make her burn. He wanted to stroke her, kiss her, taste her, suckle her, until they were both weak. He wanted everything.

And he shouldn't have a damn thing. Couldn't have.

He started to pull his hands free, but she grasped his wrists, holding them where they were, and she delicately arched her back, pressing her breasts harder against him. "Please, Tyler," she whispered. "I need you, and I think…you…need…"

His voice came out harsh and guttural. "Annie, I can't."

"I won't tell anyone, I swear. Your father, your superiors— no one will ever know."

"No."

"Tyler, please…I may be inexperienced, but I know you want this, and I—" She raised one hand to his face, cupping his cheek, gently stroking it. "I've never asked any man to make love to me, but I'm asking you."

For one endless moment, he closed his eyes and leaned against her palm. Then he jerked free of her and got to his feet. He couldn't look at her, lying there, looking at him with shameless desire, so he turned his back to her. "No, Annie. It would be wrong. My job— Your father—"

"No one need know, Tyler. It would be our secret."

"*I* would know!" he shouted in frustration, then turned in time to see her flinch. "I won't be your *secret,* Annie, and you won't be my mistake."

He stared at her a long time, letting the hurt in her eyes seep hot and deep inside him, then he pivoted on his heel. "Come inside and get cleaned up," he muttered as he stalked toward the cabin. "We've got a lot of ground to cover today."

It sounded like a line from one of the hokey country and western songs Roberto was so fond of—*I won't be your secret, and you won't be my mistake*—but Anna didn't feel the slightest inclination to sing along. A mistake. She was quite certain no one in her life had ever considered her a mistake. At least Tyler Ramsey was the first at something. Just not what she'd wanted.

She stood up, brushed away the snow and blotted the melt with her shirt, then returned to the cabin with, hopefully, some measure of her dignity intact. When she reached the front door, she hesitated, fingers wrapped tightly around the knob. For just a moment, she wished she was nobody special—just any twenty-something trying to juggle life, career and love all at the same time. Then she could indulge in her emotions—have a pity party, pig out on ice cream and chocolate or get drunk, and find some other guy to make her forget this particular guy. But if she were just any twenty-something, she wouldn't have any need to indulge her emotions, because Tyler wouldn't be walking away from her all the time. She wouldn't have any impact on his career, and he wouldn't have any excuse to keep his distance.

Instead, she was Princess Anna of Montebello, whose lessons in proper deportment had begun while she was still in nappies.

Head high, expression cool and polite, she entered the cabin, removed her vest and started up the steps. "It won't take me but a moment to get ready," she called to Tyler, who stood at the kitchen counter, his back to her. "Will we be eating breakfast while we're out, or should I snack on something before we go?"

After a moment, he shrugged and mumbled, "We can get something while we're out."

"Very well. I believe I would like a pecan waffle and hash brown potatoes. Doesn't that sound like a very American breakfast?" Without awaiting his response, she removed her shirt and hung it on the doorknob to dry, then took a pullover from the dresser. "I fear I need to experience another common American practice—that of doing laundry—or I shall soon be reduced to wearing my bedclothes and nothing else."

An odd choking sound came from downstairs, muffled by the top she was pulling over her head, then Tyler said, "There's a laundry room over by the office. We can do that tonight."

In the bathroom, she combed her hair, sprayed it generously with extra-hold hair spray, then added a bit more makeup before studying her reflection in the mirror. Only someone who knew her well—her sisters or her friend, Serena—would detect that her emotions were in turmoil. Anyone else would attribute the color in her cheeks and the brightness in her eyes to high spirits or, perhaps, sheer relief at being freed from a week's imprisonment, and she fully intended to get through these next few days without anyone discovering otherwise.

When she returned downstairs, Tyler was waiting near the door for her. She put on her vest, ear muffs and gloves and slung her handbag bandolier-style across her chest, then preceded him outside.

The interior of the vehicle was unusually frigid, so much that it seemed the leather seat would crack each time she shifted her weight. But the big, heavy vehicle had no problem negotiating the partially cleared parking lot and streets. While Tyler pointedly ignored her, she rummaged through her bag for a pair of dark glasses, slid them into place, then pulled out the photograph of Lucas and studied it. As if his rank alone weren't enough to draw women to him, with his dark brown hair and amazingly blue eyes, he was one of the handsomest men she'd ever seen. It was affectionately said in the palace that he hadn't yet met the woman who could tell him no—not his mother, his nanny, his tutors, his sisters, and certainly not the myriad girlfriends he'd possessed. He was charming, kind, a bit of a flirt, and he had a reckless streak that their father claimed had turned his dark hair prematurely white, and even though Anna saw him more rarely than she would like, she missed him terribly. She couldn't imagine living in a world without Lucas in it.

Slowly she realized that Tyler had parked in front of an establishment called Betty Jo's. On the plate-glass window was painted a buxom blonde spilling out of a waitress's uniform— Betty Jo herself, according to the name tag—as well as the promise of The Best Breakfast in Town! Without glancing at Tyler, Anna returned the photo to her bag, then climbed out of the vehicle.

The restaurant was crowded with people who, like her, were practically delirious with their newly-returned ability to resume their lives. There was much talking, laughing, and teasing all through the dining room…except at the table she shared with Tyler. When the waitress arrived with a steaming pot of coffee,

Anna felt almost as if she'd run into a treasured old friend. "You're Betty Jo," she said in greeting. "You look just like your picture on the window."

The rounded, artificially blond woman laughed heartily. "Why, bless your heart, honey, that'll earn you a free cup of coffee. I haven't looked that good since I was twenty-five, and, darlin', I am a *long* way from twenty-five." She filled their cups and distributed menus. "You folks just stopping by or have you been holed up at one of the motels?"

"We've been holed up at the lodge over near the Thrifty Warehouse," Anna replied. "And I think you look very good no matter how far you are from twenty-five. Who is the artist?"

"My boyfriend, Duane. He says that's how I looked when we met. He was traveling on the rodeo circuit, and I had just opened the place. He stopped for coffee and stayed for—well, it's been twenty years and counting. Say—" Betty Jo's brow wrinkled, and she cocked her head to one side. "Do I know you?"

"I don't believe that's possible. I've been in Garden City only one week, and all but an hour or two of that has been spent in our cabin at the lodge."

"Huh. You look awfully familiar. Of course, you sound awfully foreign, and I don't believe I know any foreigners other than a few rodeo cowboys from Canada. Where you from, hon?"

As Anna opened her mouth to answer, Tyler bumped her leg under the table. "Arkansas," she replied, giving him a frown.

The gentleman at the next table over laughed. "You must be slippin', Betty Jo, to mistake an Arkie for some foreigner."

She waved a dish towel in his direction. "Hey, she doesn't sound like no Arkie I've ever met." Once more she studied Anna. "You just look so familiar...maybe not like someone I know, but just someone I've seen. Oh, well, I'll figure it out sooner or later. You know how things just come to you when you're in the middle of doing dishes or reading *People* magazine or trying to fall asleep, and just out of the blue, there it is. Of course, you'll be back in Arkansas by then, won't you, hon?"

she asked with a wink and a nudge. "Let me put your order in and we'll get your food out right away."

Anna watched her walk toward the kitchen, as did Tyler and the gentleman next door. "Don't worry," he said, duplicating Betty Jo's wink. "She'll be back."

About the time she reached the swinging door, Betty Jo did turn and come back, her expression comical. "I didn't *take* your order, did I?"

Anna shook her head. Once the woman remedied that and left again, Tyler scowled at her. "Has your picture ever been in *People* magazine?"

"I'm a princess, I'm single, my brother's gone missing, and my sister's recently married the eldest son of a sheik. Of course it has."

"Anything lately?"

"There was an article a year past about Lucas's plane crash, and another this past summer about Julia's marriage to Rashid. I believe both included some mention of me. Then there was the New Year's party on Montebello. There were so many press on the island then that I have no idea who all of them worked for." She sweetened her coffee, then, merely to annoy him, she added, "Photographs of me have also appeared in *Time, Newsweek,* and *Vanity Fair,* as well as *National Geographic* and various European publications."

Tyler made a disgruntled sound, then his expression took on an air of disapproval. "You've got to quit telling people you're from Arkansas. It doesn't fly. You don't sound like you're from there, and sooner or later someone's going to ask you *where* in Arkansas. Then what are you going to say?"

"Little Rock," she said with a smug smile, well aware he didn't expect her to know the name of even one single town in the state. "Perhaps the next time someone asks me a question, I shall answer truthfully. Or perhaps I should direct all inquiries to you—as if that wouldn't arouse suspicion—speak only when spoken to and walk five paces behind you with my head bowed. Perhaps I should even consider taking up the practice of veiling myself when I appear in public."

He made another sound, this one rude, as if he didn't believe she was capable of being subservient. He was absolutely correct.

Betty Jo returned with their food, setting a giant waffle and hash brown potatoes with fried onions and peppers in front of Anna. Her eyes wide, she spread soft butter across the waffle, drenched it with maple syrup and took a bite that made her sigh. "Oh, this is wonderful. My compliments to you, Betty Jo."

"Oh, I just serve it, hon. I didn't make it," the woman said modestly.

"Perhaps not, but you hired the person who did."

"Gave birth to her, is more like it. My daughter's the head cook these days." She took condiments from a nearby table—tomato catsup, hot pepper sauce and steak sauce, for Tyler's morning hunk of meat—and set them down, then planted both hands on her hips. "Are you on TV, hon?"

"You mean, an actress? I fear I have no talent for performing."

"Pretty as you are, talent doesn't always matter. A singer?" Anna shook her head.

"Are you married to someone rich and famous?"

Once more she shook her head. "I'm afraid not. Just to him."

Betty Jo looked at Tyler, then grinned. "Pretty as *he* is, fame and fortune don't always matter, either. Oh, well, like I said, I'll think of it one of these days."

Once they were alone again, Tyler quietly asked, "Have you been on TV?"

"I'm a princess, I'm single—"

"Yeah, yeah. I should have left you at the cabin. The last thing we need is for some celebrity watcher to recognize you and make a fuss."

"You didn't worry about it in Billings or Clarkston."

"How long were we together in Billings? Forty-five minutes? An hour?"

She gave him a sickly sweet smile. "And it seemed so very much longer."

He merely scowled and continued to eat.

She ate every bite of the hash brown potatoes and approximately half of the waffle before admitting defeat. While Tyler finished his meal, she said, "I believe we should conduct our interviews separately today. We've lost nearly an entire week due to the weather, and I feel it would be best if we move more quickly."

She fully expected him to disagree with her, to remind her that he was the trained investigator while she was merely along for the ride. Instead, after he pushed his plate away, then withdrew money from his wallet, he surprised her. "I agree. But you don't ask any questions in here."

"Why not? Betty Jo likes me, while she merely thinks you're pretty."

"At the moment, she may never connect you with Princess Anna of Montebello, especially with your hair like that. But if you stick a picture of Prince Lucas in her face, she just might remember everything."

"And that would be bad because…?"

"Because your brother is out there somewhere. He may be injured, he might have amnesia, or he could be in some sort of trouble. If the wrong person figures out who he is and finds him before we do, he might decide he deserves a reward for the prince's safe return."

And once he had the reward, he might not return her brother safely, or at all. Though their parents had strived to give them the most normal lives a prince and princesses could have, there had always been a heightened awareness among the family and about the palace regarding the dangers of kidnapping. She knew well it could happen, and the results could be disastrous.

"Very well," she agreed.

"And if you're asked, stick with *my* story. We're up here from Arizona, looking for a man who's gone missing. As far as we know, he's not in trouble, but his family wants to make certain he's all right. Understand?"

She fixed her gaze on him, wishing for the moment that her mother's lessons about not swearing hadn't taken so well. There were a number of things she would very much like to say to him at the moment. But she settled for the simplest and least offensive as she slid her chair away from the table and stood up.

"Very well."

Chapter 8

She stood up as she did everything, Tyler thought. Gracefully. Regally. She never slouched, never darted shy little looks around. She acted like it had never occurred to her that there could be one single place in this world where she didn't belong.

With him came at the top of the list.

In spite of her request that morning in the snow.

He got to his feet and followed her to the cash register. There she took a mint from a tall glass bowl with Betty Jo's twenty-five-year-old figure etched into it, unwrapped it and popped it in her mouth. "I'll start on the opposite side of the street and work my way back toward the lodge."

Of course now that he'd agreed to her plan, he was having second thoughts about it. He was responsible for her safety. What if someone gave her a hard time or, worse, recognized her and grabbed her? What if some nutcase snatched her off the street without the slightest interest in the fortune the king would pay for her return? What if—

He forced himself to take a deep breath. Garden City was a regular small town in a regular state. The people were friendly, the crime rate was low, and women walked the streets safely day or night. The odds of anything happening to Anna were minimal, and even if someone did give her a hard time, there were plenty of decent people around to come to her aid. Her sister ran about free and easy in the big city of Billings, and there was no excessive concern for her safety. And, hell, he would be just across the street at all times.

"Stay on this street," he said at last. "And don't wander off. If someone wants you to go somewhere, come and get me. If someone has information on Lucas, come and get me. If—"

"Oh, please," she interrupted. "You remind me of Miss Ilsa, my nanny when I was four. I'm quite capable, Tyler. I can be trusted to walk into businesses and ask a few questions. And I haven't wandered off with a stranger since…well, since I left the mine in Clarkston with you last week." She smiled pointedly. "See you later."

He watched her go, tracking her progress as she crossed the street, then entered the dry cleaners' and tailor shop at the end of the block. Even when she was out of sight, he continued to watch, until Betty Jo spoke behind him.

"She's a pretty one. How long have you two been together?"

"We're not—" He broke off the absentminded answer and faced the woman. "We're not together, exactly. We—we work together."

"Uh-huh. Well, I've got news for you, hon—a couple looks at each other the way you two was looking at each other…you're together. You may as well accept it now and make the best of it."

His face grew warm as his cheeks turned red. Awkwardly, he shoved the tab across the counter to her, then handed her a twenty. "Do you happen to know if the road to the mine is passable yet?"

"Yes, sir, it is. You have business out there?"

"I have business everywhere." He accepted his change, then pulled the prince's photograph from his inside jacket pocket. "Have you seen this man?"

She held it at arm's length, studied it for a moment, then nodded. "Yes, I have…but not around here." Her narrowed gaze shifted toward the street outside and the path Anna had taken to the dry cleaners', then slowly came back to him as she lowered her voice. "I've seen him on TV, in *People* magazine,

in the newspapers, but no, not around here. Do you think he's
been in this area?''

Tyler shifted uncomfortably. "He was working on a ranch
down in Colorado. Supposedly he headed up this way to work
in one of the mines. He answers to the name of Joe.''

She shook her head vigorously, then handed the picture back
to him. "You can ask around, but I'm telling you, he hasn't
been here.''

"How can you be so sure?''

"You ever see the movie *Casablanca?* With Bogart and Berg-
man? There's a line in it about how everyone goes to Rick's
place. Well, around here, everyone who comes to Garden City
comes to Betty Jo's. We really do have the best breakfast in
town—to say nothing of the fact that my daughter the cook looks
even better than I did in my heyday. Besides, Garden City's a
small town. New people get noticed—and talked about. A new
guy who looked like that—'' she nodded in the direction of the
photograph he'd just put up "—would be fresh out of secrets
within twenty-four hours of arriving here.''

"Thanks,'' Tyler said. He was halfway to the door when she
spoke again.

"So there was a reason she looked so familiar.'' She flashed
a grin. "Don't worry. I won't tell anyone…at least, not until
you've left town. Tell her getting rid of those curls was a good
idea. I would've known her right away if the straight hair hadn't
thrown me.''

Tyler nodded in acknowledgment, then stepped outside. At
the bank down the street, a lighted sign declared the temperature
was thirty-seven degrees. Most of the time he would think that
was pretty damn cold, but after the week they'd had, it felt like
a regular heat wave.

No one else he spoke to that morning shared Betty Jo's recall
for faces. There were a few curious questions about who Lucas
was and why he was looking for him, but mostly he encountered
a general disinterest. No one was rude about it. They simply
didn't know the prince as Joe, Lucas or anyone else and had
zero information to offer. He was beginning to suspect that going
to the mine would be a waste of time, but he couldn't blow it

off. So Lucas hadn't spent any time in Garden City. That didn't mean he hadn't driven straight through town to the mine, looking for work. It sure didn't mean there wasn't someone at the mine who had told him *Sorry, but we're not hiring,* or *You're not qualified,* or *Can't help you.*

He caught regular glimpses of Anna as she moved from business to shop along the street. Once, when she stood outside the drugstore talking to the pharmacist, she looked up and caught him watching her. He would have given a lot if she'd smiled, but she hadn't. Hell, when was the last time he'd given her a reason to smile?

That morning, a small voice whispered, when she'd laughed uncontrollably as he chased her through the snow. Before she'd asked him to make love to her. Before he'd told her no.

Ever since, she'd been acting as if none of it had happened. Was he seeing firsthand the poise and grace that were bred into her? Or had the incident in the backyard meant so little to her? He preferred to believe the former.

But he couldn't rule out the latter.

He reached the end of the business district on his side of the street, waited for a truck to pass, then crossed to the other side. Just as he stepped onto the curb, Anna came out of the video store, a bag of fresh hot popcorn in her hands. "Oh," she said, as if she hadn't expected to see him. "You're ready."

"Yeah. I don't suppose you found out anything."

"I learned a great many things this morning—none of them, I'm sorry to say, pertaining to Lucas. Popcorn?"

He took a handful and tossed one fluffy kernel into his mouth. "My luck was the same. I guess now we head out to the mine."

She nodded as they turned back toward the SUV, a half-dozen blocks away. They strolled along a snow-packed sidewalk as if it were as clear as the blue sky above them, and she ate her popcorn and spent a lot of time gazing in the display windows of stores she'd already been inside. Finally, because he was tired of the silence, because he wanted to hear her voice, he asked, "So what did you learn this morning?"

"That Garden City was founded in the 1870s and was named by a man who promised his wife back East a lovely home in a charming town with a temperate climate perfectly suited for year-round gardening. She liked the town's name and made the journey out only to discover that her lovely home was a hovel, the charming town was dirty and dangerous, and the temperate climate…well…'' She raised her free hand in a gesture toward the snow.

"I also learned that they produce enough gold and silver here to ensure that none of my favorite Italian jewelers should ever run short of materials to produce baubles. In summer, it's a wonderful place to stay while you visit Yellowstone and the Grand Tetons in Wyoming. The sheriff is a former football star at the University of Nebraska, where they go by the rather odd name of Cornhuskers. And the mayor's two sons are both home for a visit from their jobs in Los Angeles, California, and Washington, D.C., and she was quite certain that either one or both of them would be more than happy to show me a good time this weekend.''

Tyler gave her a sidelong glance. "You don't get to have a good time when you're with me.''

"Tell me something I don't already know,'' she said dryly.

The comment stung, though he knew it shouldn't. He wasn't here to entertain her, keep her laughing or seduce her, and, hell, *she* wasn't supposed to be here at all. But she was, and it was killing him.

"Did you learn anything from Betty Jo?'' Anna asked after a time.

"Yeah. She said to tell you your curls would have given you away in a heartbeat.'' He hesitated, then asked, "How'd you get your hair to do that?''

With a faint smile, she touched her hair. "With a blow dryer, a large brush, various solutions and gels, and super-heavy-duty hair spray. My stylist at the palace says my hair will do anything I want it to do…as long as what I want it to do is curl. Before I gave up on wishes, I wished every night to awaken the next morning to straight hair like my mother's or my sisters'. Eventually I accepted that it was never going to happen—at least, not on a permanent basis.''

"I like your curls.'' Immediately he regretted the words. One of the lessons drummed into him in his training—*Show the enemy a weakness and he'll exploit it*—certainly applied here. Not that Anna was his enemy, by any means, but she was a beautiful, desirable, at least temporarily attainable woman who, for some unknown reason, had decided she wanted him. If she had a clue exactly how much he wanted her, he wouldn't hold out much hope for his holding out.

He didn't have much hope for it anyway. If he had a minute with a calendar, he could count to the day how long it had been since he'd had sex. He didn't need a calendar to know how long it had been since he'd wanted it so damn bad. That answer was with him every time he was around Anna, every time he looked at her, touched her, talked to her, yelled at her, hurt her. *Never.*

He'd never wanted any woman the way he wanted her.

Had never been willing to sacrifice so much for so little.

Had never been so close to sacrificing it all.

Had never had such a weakness.

When they reached the SUV, he helped her inside, then glanced up to see Betty Jo watching them through the window. Something she'd said came back to him as he stood there, the scent of Anna's perfume in every slow breath he dragged in. *I've got news for you, hon—a couple looks at each other the way you two was looking at each other…you're together. You may as well accept it now and make the best of it.*

Grimly he shut the door, circled the truck and slid behind the wheel, then headed out of town for the mine. Maybe he could accept it if he thought there was a *best* to make of it, but basically what they were looking at was an affair that might last a few days, maybe a week or two if they were lucky. Then she would return to Montebello, and he would go wherever in the world the organization chose to send him. Her little adventure would be over, and she would meet another man—probably one of those princes, titled jerks or sheiks—and she would get married, settle down and eventually have her first royal baby. Like her sister, Julia, and her sister, Christina.

Except Christina had done it with a whole other kind of noble man—*his* kind. Jack Dalton didn't have a drop of royal blood, but that hadn't stopped Christina from marrying him, and if the king and queen had objected, it had been privately. They'd been all smiles and joy at the wedding.

But *he* was no Jack Dalton. Dalton, an ex-Navy SEAL, had proven himself a thousand times over. There had never been any question whether he was qualified for or deserving of his position in the Noble Men. Though his father had been one of the founding members, he'd gotten there on his own merits.

While Tyler had gotten in on his family's merits. Dalton had earned his slot in the organization before he'd ever been invited aboard, while Tyler was being given the chance to earn his after the fact.

"What's wrong, Tyler?" Anna asked.

The softness of her voice stabbed through him and made his fingers clutch the steering wheel tighter. "Nothing."

"Then why did we drive past the turn for the mine?"

Glancing in the rearview mirror, he saw a sign with the name of the mine prominently displayed backwards. He hit the brakes, then swung the truck in a tight circle, muttering curses all the time.

"My mother says that swearing is the last resort of people without imagination," Anna said mildly. "Though, frankly, I find your curses quite imaginative. I never would have thought to use those words in that particular combination."

"Your father swears, you know."

"Not in front of my mother, he doesn't."

"Well, I'm not your father, and you're not my—" Abruptly, he broke off, the final word—*wife*—trapped by the knot that choked him. He turned off the highway onto a paved road that led to the mine, acutely aware of her watching him, of the tension that made him hot and robbed him of the air he needed desperately. He couldn't manage a breath until he'd parked in front of the office and climbed out, letting the cold air wash over him.

Water dripped steadily from the roof of the building and ran in rivulets around his boots as he opened the passenger door. When Anna made no move to release her seat belt, he asked, "Are you coming in?"

She smiled politely. "No, thank you. I shall wait here."

"You sure?"

When she nodded, he closed the door and took the steps two at a time to the double-glass doors painted with the mine's name and that of its parent company. A week ago he'd been furious to find her in Clarkston, and now it felt strange going into the office alone. What the hell was wrong with him?

Just before opening the door, he spun around and returned to the truck, opening her door once again. "Does it bother you?"

"Does what bother me?"

"My swearing. Because I don't do it in front of most people. I don't have to do it in front of you."

Once more she smiled, though this time there was none of that aloof, regal princess crap about it. It was an honest-to-God, natural, genuinely amused smile, like the one she'd given him that morning just before she'd thrown the snow in his face, just before he'd dumped his own snow on her and found himself fondling her—

Just the memory made a groan rise from deep inside, and he had to clamp down hard to stop it from escaping.

"No, it doesn't bother me at all."

"Are you sure? Because I could stop."

"That easily?"

"Yeah. That easily." More or less.

She shook her head, and he wished for the curls that normally shimmered and bounced every time she moved her head. "It doesn't bother me," she repeated. Then the dark brown of her eyes softened and warmed, and her smile somehow turned secretive and innocently wicked. "However, perhaps I can think of something you do that does bother me, so you can give me a demonstration of this phenomenal control of yours."

His body reacted to her words and that smile in all the right ways—or wrong ways, he guessed, depending on your point of view—and he sucked in a lungful of frigid air to lessen the heat. "Sweetheart, you've been living with the best example for a week now and haven't even noticed," he mumbled as he closed the door and retraced his steps to the glass doors.

As he walked inside the office, he glanced back at her, sitting all prim and proper in the passenger seat, and experienced an-

other spurt of desire, building, getting harder and edgier. Maybe
the princess couldn't truly appreciate his phenomenal control
until he lost it…and at that very moment, he was getting pretty
damn close to that point.

God help them both.

After a fruitless visit to the mine, Tyler and Anna returned to
the cabin, gathered their laundry and crossed the narrow drive
to the lodge's laundry room. It consisted of three washers, three
dryers and one long table opposite them, and had that steamy
fabric-softener smell that Tyler had always associated with laundry day when he was a kid. The mesh laundry bag he carried,
marked "Ramsey" in permanent black ink, was stuffed to the
gills, and Anna carried the grocery sack that contained the detergent, bleach and fabric softener they'd bought at the Thrifty
Warehouse, along with a bottle of liquid detergent for their
sweaters.

"What do we do first?" Anna asked as he dropped the heavy
laundry bag on the table, then emptied it.

"Sort the clothes."

"Into yours and mine? Types? Colors? Styles?"

He glanced at her. "You've never done laundry before, have
you?"

She shook her head.

"Okay. I sort the clothes and you sit down."

There was one orange vinyl chair at each end of the room.
She moved one closer to the table and watched as he began
making piles all around. After a moment, she sniffed. "That's
not so very difficult."

"I never said it was, Your Highness."

With one slender hand, she pointed out various piles. "White
clothes, dark clothes that can be dried, dark clothes that
shouldn't, light clothes that can be dried and light ones that
shouldn't, towels and sheets and—"

The pile that stopped her was her own clothing—unmention-
ables in delicate fabrics and even more delicate shades. Small
bras and tiny panties. Lace and ribbon, satin and silk, sexy little
see-through bits of nothing, in the palest of pastels. He wasn't

surprised they left her at a loss for words. He pretty much felt that way, too.

He got the first three loads started, then glanced at his watch. "Do you mind if I go back to the cabin for a minute? I need to check in with Kyle."

"I shall be quite safe here, I'm certain."

He was about to walk out the door that faced their cabin, twenty yards away, when she spoke again.

"Tyler? Have I thanked you for not telling anyone I'm here?"

He thought back to the shabby motel in Clarkston, when he'd lied to her about calling her father. She'd thanked him, sworn he wouldn't regret it and promised he wouldn't even know she was there—yeah, right—and then she'd kissed him. He should have run away as far and as fast as he could...or tendered his resignation and spent the next ninety-six hours in bed with her.

"Yeah," he said with a grim smile. "You thanked me." She'd trusted him, he'd betrayed her trust, and she'd thanked him for it.

Shoving his hands into his pockets, he returned to the cabin, took off his coat and picked up the phone. While waiting for his brother to answer, he settled at the front window, where he could watch the laundry room door. Not that he thought Anna might be in any danger there. He figured she was almost as safe there as she would have been at her sister's house in Billings. He just wanted to...watch.

"What's up, little brother?" Kyle's voice drew his attention back to the call, though his gaze remained across the way.

"Little brother? I'm as tall as you are and ten pounds heavier."

"Yeah, but you'll always be the baby. How's Montana? I heard you got snowed in."

"Let's just say I've had better experiences being snowed in."

"When you weren't alone, you mean."

"Who says I was alone this time? We had plenty of warning that the snow was coming."

"You telling me that on your first solo job, you went out and picked up a girl to keep you company?"

"No," Tyler admitted.

"Well, damn, what's wrong with you?" After a laugh, Kyle went on. "Have you had a chance to ask around about Lucas?"

"Yeah, today. Nobody's seen him in town, and he never showed up at the mine looking for work, so it's a fair bet he's never been here at all. Any news on your end?"

"Nothing. This guy Joe seems to have appeared out of nowhere and disappeared the same way. Whether he's the prince or not, apparently he doesn't want to be found. Kinda makes you wonder why, doesn't it? I mean, if he is the prince, and he's got amnesia, why did he take off like that? And if he doesn't have amnesia, why did he take off like that? And if he's not the prince and really is just some drifter…"

"Yeah, I know. And why would he take off to work in a mine? That would be about as likely for Lucas as you waking up in the morning wanting Jake's job." Kyle had fought so hard against running the family business that it was doubtful anything in the world could make him give it a shot. "You know, I've gotta wonder if this guy Joe really is Lucas, or if we're on a wild-goose chase. If the weather holds, we—" Tyler mouthed a silent curse before continuing "—I'm leaving for Golden in the morning. If I don't find any sign of him there, I think I'll go to Colorado and talk to this Ursula Chambers myself. Is that okay?"

"Sure, no problem. While you're there, can you stop by the sheriff's office and see if they've found out anything about the man Lorenzo caught breaking into the Chambers house?"

"Will do. How's Joanna and the baby?"

"They're fine. I'll be seeing them in a few days."

The background noise on the line increased to a hum during their momentary silence, then Tyler cleared his throat. "Can I ask you something?"

"Sure. You can ask anything," Kyle said, quoting one of their father's favorite sayings. Tyler finished it in unison with him. "But whether I'll answer is the real question."

"When you met Joanna…how did you know she was the one you wanted to marry?"

Kyle's laughter boomed over the line. "Jeez, you really are young, aren't you? When I met Joanna, I knew two things—she was a beautiful woman, and I was horny as hell. It was a while before marriage and love entered into it.''

Though most people would reverse the order of those two—love and marriage—Tyler knew Kyle had put the words in the order he'd meant. Joanna had gotten pregnant their first night together, and when Kyle had found out some three months later, he'd automatically assumed she would return to the States with him, marry him and provide for their child together. Love had come into the picture after the proposal but before the actual marriage.

"Let me guess... You met some woman up there in Montana, and you're trying to decide if it's okay to have sex with her merely for the sake of the sex itself or if you have to *commit* to her. You know, Ty, sometimes purely recreational sex is exactly what the doctor ordered. You don't have to have a relationship with every single woman you go to bed with. You don't have to offer them a future or even see them again after the sun comes up tomorrow. You're single and unattached, and you're free to have single, unattached sex, no commitments required. Just a good supply of condoms.''

Tyler didn't even have that...but he was sure the kindly pharmacist who had seemed so taken with Anna would be more than happy to sell them to him.

But he also didn't have Kyle's former appreciation for uncommitted sex.

"You know what your problem is, Ty?'' Kyle went on. "You expect too much. I bet you've never had sex with a woman you didn't have some sort of relationship with, have you? You think every date should lead to a relationship and every relationship should at least have the potential for marriage, and that's just not the case. Some women are meant to be in your life for a night or a week and then gone. You don't have to beat yourself up because you had great sex with a woman you're never gonna love.''

"So you had great sex with Joanna, then didn't see her again for more than three months, and even that was dumb luck. And if you hadn't seen her again, that would have been all right with you.''

"The hell it would. But Joanna was meant to be."

"How did you know?" More importantly, *when* did he know? Because Tyler was pretty damn sure he couldn't stop wanting more than Kyle seemed to think he should. He didn't *want* to sleep with a woman for the sole purpose of having great sex. He wanted to *know* who he was making love to. To borrow a line from Anna, he wanted it to mean something.

"I— Jeez, you couldn't have called Joanna about this, could you? I'm sure she's got lots more answers than I do."

"I can call her now," Tyler offered. "I'll tell her that you're talking up the advantages of indiscriminate recreational sex and that I wanted to get her opinion on the subject." For all Kyle's talk, Tyler knew Joanna made him toe the line. He also knew his brother loved her dearly and never looked twice at other women.

"Well, of course everything I say applies solely to you," Kyle teased. "Being a very happily married man, I have no interest in the dating and mating game beyond giving advice to my kid brother, who never takes it anyway."

"I always take your advice."

"Sure you do. You gonna take it this time? You gonna sleep with this woman?"

With his free hand, Tyler rubbed the weariness from his eyes. "I'm doing my best not to."

"Why not?" Kyle asked, then immediately continued. "Never mind. I forgot I was talking to the only man I know who's incapable of enjoying casual sex. Most men would be afraid she might think it meant something. You'd be concerned that she *wouldn't* think it meant something. Okay, so she obviously means something to you—I mean, hell, this *is* you we're talking about. What's the problem?"

Tyler had so many answers he didn't know where to start. She was a virgin. She was a princess. He was working for her father. He couldn't not see her again after the night was over— and wouldn't want the sex if he could. She meant a hell of a lot to him, but not as much as his job did…or did she? And was he anything to her other than part of the good time she was having while supposedly on the lam from the royal life?

"I just don't see much sense in pursuing a relationship that's destined to go nowhere." He didn't want to hurt anyone, and he damn sure didn't want to get hurt himself. And if anyone could hurt him, it was Anna. Without much more than a cool smile and a regal blow-off, she could break his heart.

That was the problem. She could break his heart. He was already way past the casual sex stage, and she...he didn't know what she wanted, besides to have a little freedom, experience life as a normal person and lose her virginity. He didn't even know if she cared who helped her with the last. Had Rusty back in Clarkston been in the running? If Tyler convinced her that he really wasn't going to give in, would someone else do just as well? Maybe one of the mayor's sons?

Over his dead body.

"You're an overachiever, you know that?" Kyle said.

"Oh, yeah, right. I've screwed up practically everything I've ever tried. The old man wonders how in hell I could have his blood flowing through my veins and still be such a major failure."

"What the hell are you talking about?"

"How many jobs has Dad held in his lifetime? Three—the air force, the parts business, and this other stuff. How about you? Two. And Jake? One. And then there's me. I've had twelve, maybe fifteen, jobs in the past thirteen years. I never held on to any of them longer than eight or ten months. Hell, I couldn't even make it in the family business."

"So what? You took a lot of jobs that *nobody* would willingly hold on to longer than eight or ten months. And it's not like you were lying around, living off Mom and Dad in between jobs. Whenever you quit or got fired, you always found another job right away—maybe not one you particularly liked or wanted to keep, but one that paid the bills until something better came along." Kyle swore. "Jeez, Tyler, where's the achievement in sticking with a job you hate for forty years? All that shows is you're a glutton for punishment. It's not behavior to aspire to— more like something to be pitied. Besides, if the old man thought you were a screwup, do you think he *ever* would have brought you into the organization? You know how much this bunch means to him. He never would have let either of us get within a million miles of 'em if he didn't believe we had something to offer them.''

"But…every time I changed jobs, he made bets on how long I'd last at the new job, and whether I would quit or get fired. He always acted like it was a joke, but he always had this look in his eyes, like…'' Tyler broke off. There was a limit to how much of his guts he was going to spill to his brother, and admitting that their father had always been disappointed in him exceeded that limit.

"The old man joked,'' Kyle said quietly. "He's not real good with emotions, you know? And he wasn't around often enough when we were growing up to get any better with them. If he was worried, he joked. If he wasn't worried, he joked. But he wasn't disappointed in you. He was probably bewildered that anyone as smart as you didn't know what he wanted to do, especially since he'd always known for himself. But he didn't have any problem with the fact that it took you a while to figure it out. If he did, he never would have gotten you in with the Noble Men.''

"Maybe. But he did have to get me in. I couldn't have done it on my own.''

"Well, hell, Ty, we *all* got help from our fathers. This isn't a job where any joker off the street can put in an application and get hired. This party's by invitation only, and you gotta know somebody to get your name on the guest list.''

That was true. Even Jack Dalton—hotshot former Navy SEAL—had been brought into the organization by his father. Somehow Tyler had forgotten about that.

"Listen, little brother, do yourself a favor. Quit thinking so much, take this girl out to a nice dinner, maybe go dancing and spend a wild night with her. Don't expect it to change your life, and don't be disappointed if you wake up in the morning and you're not in love with her, and don't feel like you could be, should be, would be, if you just tried a little harder. What's that saying—'Sometimes a cigar is just a cigar'? Well, no matter how much you try to pretty it up, sometimes lust is just lust.

It's not a failure, and it doesn't make you a screwup. It just means you're a human being.''

How quickly would his brother's advice change if he knew the girl in question was King Marcus's youngest, most sheltered, most pampered daughter? In a heartbeat, he'd bet. "Thanks, Kyle. Listen, I've gotta go. I'll check in with you later.''

Hanging up, he grabbed his jacket and headed for the laundry room again. In spite of all the water everywhere, there was still plenty of snow on the ground, and as the sun set and the temperatures started to drop, it was going to be joined by ice. He wouldn't mind a hell of a lot if the weather kept them in Garden City another day or so, though that would almost certainly seal his fate. He was beginning to think his fate was already sealed, anyway.

Anna was standing at the laundry room table, singing softly to herself as she folded a pile of damp clothes that couldn't be run through the dryers. The dryers were running, as were the washers, and the piles of dirty clothes were all gone.

She paused when she saw him. "The washing machines stopped while you were gone, so I put the clothes in the dryer, and I added one sheet of fabric softener to each load. Then I started the washing machines again, and I selected the temperatures from the chart on the back of the detergent box and added detergent in the amount indicated on the box, plus bleach for the sheets and towels in the amount indicated on the bottle, and put the clothes in.'' She smiled happily. "There's really not so very much to this laundry business, you know?''

She looked so beautiful, and so damn pleased with herself for managing to figure out the mysteries of dirty laundry, that Tyler knew he'd guessed right on the walk from the cabin. His fate *was* sealed.

Now it was just a question of whether he would survive the choices that had been made for him.

Chapter 9

Perhaps it was too mundane for most people, as well as an indication of how incredibly spoiled her life had been, but Anna had truly enjoyed doing laundry that afternoon. She had liked taking the clothing from the dryers, hot and fresh-scented, and learning to fold the bath towels in half, then thirds, then in half again, in pairing socks and smoothing wrinkles from jeans. Granted, it wasn't a job she would want to do every day of her life, but at least now she knew how, and that made her feel more competent. More like a real person.

She finished hanging the last of her undergarments over the shower curtain rod in the bathroom. The rest dangled from the railing in her loft bedroom, as well as from doorknobs and hooks. The sweaters were already neatly laid out over furniture protected by still-warm towels, and the rest of the laundry was put away where it belonged.

Now it was dinnertime.

She took the stairs two at a time, then went into the kitchen, where Tyler was marinating two thick steaks in a blend of bourbon and spices. He'd already scrubbed two potatoes and placed them in the oven. Now she was going to help him make a salad and cook mushrooms and onions to go with the beef.

"You're rather a handy man to have around," she remarked as she washed, then dried her hands. "You cook and do laundry, you dance quite well—" a fact she knew, sadly, from watching him with Cindy at the Silver Spur and not from personal experience "—and you're handy with various weapons. Oh, and you kiss quite well, too." Not that she'd had enough of his kisses or, frankly, had had so very many others to compare against. But she could endure kisses from a million men only to prove what she'd already learned with Tyler—you couldn't improve on perfection.

"Why, it's a wonder some woman hasn't taken me off the market and set me up in a home of my own," he said dryly.

"Well, there are a few rather prickly personality issues," she replied, automatically reaching for the mushrooms to clean. "You're a bit on the bossy side. You're as stubborn as any man I've ever known. You tend to be a little smug and arrogant at times. You're exceedingly polite, and you suffer at times from a one-track mind."

The smile he gave her was thin and sarcastic. "Gee, thank you, Your Highness. Would it be a little arrogant for me to point out that you might have chosen a better time to deliver such a personality assessment than when I'm cooking your dinner?"

"Only a little." She grinned. "But there are cookbooks on the bookshelf over there. If I can learn to do laundry from the back of a detergent box, then I'm quite certain I can learn to grill steaks from a cookbook. Except...if I may ask, where is the grill?"

He pointed to the stove, then, when she remained unenlightened, lifted the center portion. Underneath, running from front to back, was a gas grill.

"How convenient. You Americans do love your barbecuing, don't you?" Circling to the other side of the counter, she sat down on a stool and began tearing lettuce into a bowl. "When you spoke to your brother this afternoon, did he have any news of my brother?"

"Afraid not. If we don't find anything in Golden, I'm going to Colorado to talk to Ursula Chambers again. Maybe she's remembered something else."

Though she didn't look up from her task, she'd noticed his choice of pronouns. *If we don't find anything in Golden, I'm going to Colorado.* What did he intend to do with her? Send her back to Christina in Billings? Or arrange for Lorenzo to send the Gulfstream to the airport nearest Golden and send her all the way back to Montebello?

So, unless they found themselves snowbound again, she had another two, perhaps even three or four, days with him, and then he intended to send her, one way or another, back to her family. And then…how many weeks or months would pass before she saw him again, and how would he behave when he did see her? Would he keep his distance, as he'd always done before? Or would he perhaps become a more frequent visitor at the palace? Would she see him on occasion in San Sebastian's nightclubs, speaking with other women, charming them, dancing with them, leaving with them?

Feeling a hot quiver of jealousy vibrate through her, she wished she had turned down his suggestion for a quiet dinner in the cabin. She wished she had told the mayor to have one or both of her sons pick her up for dinner out this evening. Then, instead of brooding over the prospect of Tyler with another woman, perhaps he would brood over the prospect of her with another man.

And perhaps it would be only his sense of duty as a temporary bodyguard that would make him pay even the slightest attention.

"Do you mind a suggestion, Your Highness?"

It took a moment for his voice to penetrate her thoughts, then she blinked and focused on him. "About what?"

"An easier way to do that." He gestured toward the green onion she was cutting for the salad. He'd entrusted her with a small knife, its blade only four inches and none too terribly sharp—though sharp enough, honesty forced her to admit—while he used a large knife, its blade approximately a foot long and sharp enough to cut through hot-house tomatoes without a hitch. "Line up the onions on the cutting board—" he did so "—then cut off the ends all at once." Folding his fingers around hers on the knife handle, he demonstrated once more. "Then cut through them all at once." Still holding her hand—and the knife—he made two cuts, then released her.

Slowly, or so it seemed.

Her fingers tingled, her chest grew tight and her face warmed. Clearing her throat, she pretended she couldn't still feel the pressure of his large hand over hers. "Th—that's most efficient. Thank you."

"Your sister, Christina, seems to be extremely self-sufficient for a princess," he remarked as he removed a mass of tomato chunks from his own cutting board to the salad bowl. "It must have been a shock to your parents—their daughter wanting to leave the palace and live alone in another country. No housekeeper, no cook, no staff, no bodyguards."

Anna shrugged. "They had concerns. But tell me your mother didn't worry about your undergoing training for a dangerous job in another country."

He shrugged, also.

"Papa granted Christina a great deal of independence, but there were requirements on his part, also—the house, the security system, the bodyguard when threats arose."

"The bodyguard she later married. That must have made the king happy."

"And why would it not?"

"His daughter married to a mercenary and living in Montana? No royal son-in-law, no power, no riches, no alliances that would benefit Montebello? He must have been disappointed."

"Jack's not really a mercenary," she said, repeating his own denial back to him. "And, no, Papa wasn't disappointed in the least. He knew Christina loved Jack, and Jack loved her in return, and that was all that mattered."

"And yet he tries to marry you off to strangers."

She scraped the onions into the salad, then picked up a long, fat cucumber. Though she may not have ever made a salad, she knew the tough, waxy skin would add nothing to it, so she concentrated for a moment on peeling it. When she had a clean cucumber with minimal waste, she smiled, then laid it down to chop. "Papa would never marry me off to anyone I didn't want to marry. He simply passes on the offers he receives in case there's something he's unaware of—someone to whom I might say yes. Also, considering the odds of my running into these men at some event or another, it's only polite if I know that I've rejected them.''

''Would you ever marry a stranger?''

A few weeks ago her answer would have been an emphatic, unequivocal *no!* Marriage was too significant an undertaking—and too difficult—to attempt without love. In the morose mood that had come over her since learning that he intended to send her on her way in a few days, she could reverse herself and say that marriage was too significant and difficult to attempt *with* love. Emotion clouded the mind, while dispassion would serve to clear it. Business arrangements were often far more successful than marriages for just that reason.

''Perhaps I would,'' she remarked thoughtfully. ''There would be many advantages to such an arrangement.''

Tyler scowled at her. ''Such as?''

''If you have no feelings for a person, then you have no feelings to get hurt. A marriage entered into calmly, rationally and with detachment would be made quite stable by the very lack of emotional involvement. Like any good business arrangement, it would be based on the mutual benefits each partner would derive from the union. Decisions would be handled logically, and there would be little reason for arguments, disagreements or dissatisfaction. All in all, it could be a quite comfortable arrangement.''

His green eyes were dark and stormy, and the muscle in his jaw twitched as he carefully set the knife down, flattened both palms on the counter and leaned toward her. ''That's a load of garbage.''

She blinked. ''Pardon me?''

''A marriage is not an arrangement. If there's no emotional involvement, there's no point.''

''The point,'' she patiently explained, ''is the mutual benefits each partner receives. For example, if I married Prince Arthur—'' she managed to contain the shudder the mere thought sent through her ''—his country is small and none too forward-thinking. They've lived under an absolute monarchy for generations, which, for them, translates to a luxurious lifestyle for the royal family and relative poverty for their subjects. The current king is working toward creating a democracy instead, which is something with which Papa could assist them. He would provide advisors to help the king achieve his goals, as well as keep Arthur in line both prior to and following his ascension to the throne. Frankly, Arthur's capable of neither running an absolute monarchy nor heading a democracy, even in name only. All he cares about is his polo ponies, which are quite an expensive hobby, you know. In effect, in marrying me, Arthur would gain the expertise—albeit in the form of others—to run his country."

"And what would you gain besides an idiot for a husband?"

"I would eventually become queen—" not that she'd ever harbored any such desire "—and I would have children." Perhaps. Much as she treasured her maternal urges, the idea of intimacy with Arthur left her feeling a bit queasy. And as for allowing him to provide half the genetic material necessary to create children... It would be so unfair to the poor babes. Perhaps they could rise above having an idiot for a father, but perhaps they couldn't. And perhaps she could love them in spite of their having an idiot for a father...but perhaps she couldn't.

"In case I didn't make my opinion clear earlier..." Tyler leaned a few inches closer. "That's a load of garbage." Then he offered her a sarcastic smile. "Oh, pardon me. That's a load of garbage, Your Highness."

"And you've formed that opinion based upon what?"

"How about the fact that I've spent more time with you than any other man in the world, excluding your father and your brother? That I know you better than any other man in the world?"

"You think so?" she asked casually. "Did I mention that you tend to be quite arrogant at times?"

"It comes so naturally with you that I don't even have to work at it."

She carelessly scraped the cucumber pieces into the bowl, laid the knife and cutting board aside and folded her hands together to hide the tremble she couldn't control. "In this instance, you're quite right. I've never slept even one night, let alone seven, with any other man in my quarters, no matter how innocently. No other man has ever kissed me the way you did. Certainly no other man has ever…touched me the way you did this morning.'' The mere thought of it made her throat tighten and sent an ache through her. ''Most certainly I've never asked any other man to make love to me…though you did refuse.''

Though she knew it was quite impossible, for an instant it seemed that time stopped. She could no longer smell the potatoes baking or the pungent spices in the marinade, could no longer hear the soft music coming from the stereo or feel the heat from the fireplace. Instead she heard the ragged rhythm of her own breathing, and the uneven beat of her heart. She smelled the spicy musk of Tyler's cologne and felt the heat emanating from him, from her, from the very air between them.

For that timeless moment, he stared at her, his green eyes darkly intense, and she stared back, barely breathing, barely thinking, overwhelmed by feeling. Then he spoke, his voice husky and thick. ''Ask me again.''

She attempted to smile but couldn't, to reach for him but couldn't do that, either. What if this was nothing more than a very cruel joke—his way of ensuring she would never again try to seduce him? But there was no humor, cruel or otherwise, in his expression. His cheeks were flushed, his jaw taut, but the telltale muscle there was still. His entire body had gone tense, his hands pushing so hard against the counter that the pressure points had turned white.

This was no joke.

Tension drained from her body, leaving warmth and easiness in its place. She disentangled her hands and raised one to tentatively, then gently, touch his cheek. ''Will you make love to me, Tyler?''

''Yes.''

''Why?''

''Does it matter?''

She reflected on that. Tomorrow morning, possibly it would. In a few days, when she'd returned to her family, she was quite certain it would. But tonight, at that very moment… With a small smile, she shook her head, and then she slid to her feet and awkwardly shifted her weight. ''I presume… Shall we…? What do we do now?''

He drew a deep breath, then grinned, and everything seemed normal again. But how could it ever be normal again when he'd finally agreed to make love to her? How could *she* be normal again when he was soon going to make her heart whole...or break it beyond repair?

"Now we finish cooking dinner," he said. "There's no hurry, Annie. We've got all night."

All night. That sounded most promising.

Though she found it more difficult than he to return to their mundane tasks, eventually she managed...but all the while, her thoughts were on him, them and what they would soon be doing. Wanting, needing, anticipating. Ah, yes, anticipating.

While she tossed the salad, then set the table, he sauteed the mushrooms and onions in a skillet with butter, then finished them off with wine. He tossed the steaks on the grill, sending a lovely, mouth-watering aroma through the cabin, and before long he dished them onto their dinner plates.

In a brief moment of panic she wished she could call Christina for advice, but her sister would surely be shocked that they hadn't passed this hurdle days ago. Then Anna would have no choice but to admit that she'd lied about her relationship with Tyler, and she sincerely didn't want to admit any such thing.

But it would be all right. Tyler would provide the only guidance she required.

She was tense when they sat down to eat, but he soon talked her out of it. It was as if the decision he'd struggled against had released his own tension and given him a natural easiness she'd rarely seen. He engaged her in conversation, made her smile and even laugh and, put simply, charmed her all the way through the meal.

When he complimented her on her part in the dinner, she glanced at her plate, surprised to see that it was as empty as his. The salad, while merely a salad, had been tasty, the baked potatoes delicious with butter and sour cream, the steaks grilled to perfection and the mushrooms and onions caramelized and richly flavored. "We make quite good partners," she said, thinking of their joint laundry operation as well as the jointly-prepared dinner. Upon hearing the words aloud, though, she realized how easily he might misinterpret them and think she was already expecting some sort of commitment from him. Granted, she wasn't overly experienced at this man-woman business, but she was quite certain asking for a commitment was a good way to scare a man away.

Tyler's only reaction was a brief moment of stillness, however, followed by a shrug. "We work well together," he agreed.

She smiled with relief. "Yes, that's what I meant. Shall we demonstrate it once more in cleaning the kitchen?"

"No. We can do that later." Sliding his chair back, he stood up and extended his hand to her. "Come and dance with me, Annie."

Placing her hand in his, she allowed him to draw her gratefully, nervously, into his embrace. The music on the radio was soothing—jazz, all horns and lazy rhythms, easy to dance to, even easier to pretend to dance to. She trembled in his arms but couldn't help it. When he lowered his head and nuzzled her hair from her ear in order to kiss it, she gave a soft groan of pleasure.

"You're a beautiful woman, Annie," he murmured, holding her body close to his, "and I've wanted you from the first time I got close to you. I tried so damn hard to deny it, but I can't..."

Somewhere in there, he stopped moving and slid one hand to her bottom, lifting her hard against his arousal. The other hand he slid into her hair, tilting her head back so he might kiss her. She sensed he aimed for restraint, but there was nothing restrained about his kiss. It was hot, greedy, demanding, and it turned her muscles weak. She welcomed his tongue into her mouth and sucked at it hard, finding that the harder, the more demanding his kiss, the harder and more demanding she wanted it. Fever spread through her, robbed her of rational thought, of self-control and fear and everything except need. Passion. Hunger.

"Tyler," she whispered. Whimpered. "Please..."

He leaned against the back of the sofa and her legs opened instinctively when he lifted her. With his tongue deep in her mouth and his hands on her hips, he thrust against her, hard and hot, stimulating but oh, so unsatisfying. She wanted more—his naked swollen flesh against her naked moist flesh. She wanted his kisses on her breasts and his caresses everywhere. She wanted him inside her.

She needed him inside her.

Abruptly, he ended the kiss with a savage curse, and when she would have pulled him back for more, he held her a frustrating few inches away. His eyes were opened wide, and his breathing was rough and uneven as he stared at her.

"What's wrong?" she asked, suddenly feeling awkward and unsure. He still wanted her—his erection was quite powerful between her thighs—but he looked…stricken.

"I just need—" she shifted position, and he closed his eyes, groaned hoarsely, then looked at her again "—a little control. I don't want to hurt you, Annie, I don't want—"

She pressed a small kiss to his forehead. "Wanting you and not having you hurts, Tyler. Feeling you so close—" she moved again and succeeded in making them both groan "—but not where I need you hurts. Please…I don't want control." Trusting him to support her weight when she let go, she unbuttoned her shirt, shrugged it off, then undid the front clasp of her bra and shrugged it away, too. After sliding one arm around his neck, she brought his hand to her breast, shaping his large calloused palm to fit, sliding it side to side so it scraped her nipple and made her breath catch in a gasp.

"I want you, Tyler," she whispered. "All of you."

Please…

The loft was warm, dimly lit by the lamps below, and smelled of Anna's perfume, shampoo, lotions. Tyler stood beside the bed, gazing down at her, as she slid her delicate little hands under the hem of his sweater. She tugged the garment higher, over his ribs, his chest and finally his head, then tossed it aside. "Now we are even," she said with a nervous smile, then her smile faded as she ran her hands over his chest before pressing a kiss somewhere above his heart.

He threaded his fingers through her hair, gently forcing her head back so he could look into her eyes. "Are you sure about this, Annie? Have you thought it through?"

"I'm very sure." She spoke quietly, with complete confidence, but he pushed for more.

"What will your Prince Arthur say when he discovers you lost your virginity with a red-blooded American commoner?"

"He's not *my* Prince Arthur and he never will be, so it's none of his business."

"But if you marry him…"

"I'll never marry him."

What were the chances she might marry *him?* Tyler wondered. But he couldn't find the courage to ask. Not yet. Maybe not ever.

Hooking his finger in the waistband of her slacks, he pulled her close for a kiss, painfully aware of her breasts flattened against his chest, of her fingers stroking through his hair, of her other hand toying with his own waistband. He felt a slight tug and thought it might be the button on his jeans, heard a faint rasp and realized it was his own zipper gliding down, and then her hand was inside the tight denim. With one gentle caress, she robbed the air from his lungs, made his vision go black and caused him to break out in a cold sweat. Her touch created an exquisite mix of pleasure, pain, satisfaction and torment that made his knees go weak and could too easily reduce him to begging.

To counter it, he carefully guided her hand free, then lowered her to the bed, following her onto the mattress. Immediately she reached once more for his groin, but he pushed her hands away, holding them at her sides while he bent to take her nipple in his mouth. He suckled them both, drawing long and hard on first one, then the other, making her tremble and groan with need. At the same time he undid the zipper on her pants and slid his hand inside, stroking the soft bare skin above the elastic band of her tiny panties.

After a time, he raised his head and gazed down at her as he continued the not-so-innocent caresses across her stomach. Her features wore a fiercely strained look—woman in the throes of passion, he thought with a little of the smugness she'd taken him to task for. Her face was pale, with color high on her cheekbones, and her amazingly kissable lips were swollen and slightly parted, tempting him to kiss her once more. Her nipple puckered as he brushed his mouth across it, and her smooth dark skin rippled enticingly every time he stroked her.

"You know," he murmured as he lazily pushed her pants lower on her hips, "I've never made love to a princess before. Or a virgin."

She lifted her hips and helped him shove the garment lower, then kicked them off before opening her eyes and smiling dazedly, sensuously, at him. "It can't be very different. I'm just like every other woman you've ever been with."

Except he'd never loved any of the others. He'd liked all of them, and had even thought he might love some of them, but he knew now he hadn't. What he'd felt then couldn't compete with what he was feeling now. He wanted to stay right there with Anna forever. He wanted to take her fiercely, savagely, so thoroughly that no other man could ever touch her, and yet he wanted to love her so delicately, with such care. He wanted to teach her everything she would ever know about love and sex and satisfaction, to protect her and keep her safe, to have babies with her and live together forever.

When, truth was, their forever might last only a few days.

He couldn't think about that now. He put it out of his mind and grinned at her instead. "Annie, darlin', I don't believe you're like *any* woman I've ever known. You're one of a kind."

"Thank you," she said with a giggle. She looked so damned tempting, stretched out in the center of the bed, wearing nothing but a scrap of pale green panties. Her waist was narrow, her hips rounded, her legs surprisingly well-muscled, and she was that same warm brown shade all over. Incredibly soft warm brown. Apparently, she was well aware of how she looked as she raised her arms above her head in a lazy stretch that arched her back, brought her breasts an inch closer to him, made the muscles all down her body quiver, then relax, and raised the temperature of the air surrounding him about twenty degrees.

"Darlin', you're gonna pay for that," he murmured hoarsely. She smiled sweetly. "Promises, promises."

With his own smile, he returned to kissing her breasts, but this time his hands were busy, too. His fingers stroked across her nipples, down her midriff to her flat belly, slipping between her thighs for an innocent caress. Automatically she brought her legs together, but he merely wedged one knee between hers, pushed them apart, then even wider, and continued to stroke her through the soft, slick fabric of her panties. After a few touches, the satin was damp with her arousal. A few more touches, and the muscles in her thighs quivered and her hips began to move in an unsteady rhythm, rising to meet his fingers. Her eyes were closed, her hair tangled about her head. Her breathing came quick and shallow, and her nipples were hard and straining for his attention.

Finally, when a low whimper rose in her throat, he slid his hand underneath the satin, gliding over damp curls and hot flesh, sliding one finger inside her. Her body clamped hard and tight on it, and the knowledge that before long she would be clenching *him* like that was damn near enough to bring a whimper from him.

"Your body's ready for me, Annie," he said, his voice thick and taut. "Can you feel how hot and wet you are? Do you want me now?"

"Yes, p-please," she whispered.

He removed her panties, then stood up to strip off the rest of his clothes. "And you say I'm too polite. You don't have to say please, darlin'. That's exactly what I intend to do." Opening the nightstand drawer, he removed the box of condoms he'd picked up at the grocery store when they'd bought the steaks for dinner and took one out.

"Oh, my."

The small words drew his attention to the bed, where Anna was openly looking at him. Her face was flushed, and her expression was dubious, to say the least. He tossed the plastic packet on the mattress, then sat down beside her. "Surely you've seen naked men before."

"Of—of course. In films and—and magazines. But I wasn't intending to—to be intimate with them. Besides, I thought…the camera makes everything look bigger, you know." She scrambled to sit up, hugging her knees to her chest. "I, um, don't think that will f-f-fit."

Tyler was perplexed. He hadn't expected this. Yes, she was a virgin, and yes, it was perfectly normal for her to be nervous—after all, even he knew it was supposed to be more pain than pleasure her first time—but he hadn't expected her to try to hide away after getting her first look at his erection. On the other hand, it was a nice stroke to his male ego that she thought he was too big. No matter what anyone said, size always mattered.

He just hadn't thought it would matter *this* way.

"Trust me, babe, it'll fit perfectly," he assured her as he peeled one arm from around her legs. He set her hand on the sheet next to her hip, then pulled the other arm loose, placing it similarly. "I won't lie to you—this first time might hurt. I don't know how little or how much. I'm kinda new to this virgin stuff, too. I can promise you this, though—it'll be worth it. I swear on my life." He pressed a kiss to her knee as he wrapped his fingers around her ankle, then pulled her leg out straight. "I swear on *your* life, which I'm sworn to protect with my life." He did the same with her other leg, then stretched out on the bed beside her, leaving wet kisses along her hip to her narrow waist.

She giggled as she slowly slid down to lie beside him. "Papa made you swear?"

"No."

"The Noble Men did?"

"No. This has nothing to do with them. It has nothing to do with a mission or an assignment. It's just you and me, Annie—" he kissed her shoulder "—and I will risk anything to keep you safe—" and the tender skin where her breast just started to swell "—and to protect you from harm—" and the pulse beginning to beat harder at the base of her throat "—and to make you happy." He kissed the full curve of her pouty bottom lip, then thrust his tongue inside her mouth.

Her response was instantaneous and fiery. She sucked hard at his tongue as her hands roamed his body, stroking over his arms, down his back, rubbing his erection with both delicate hands. She rolled onto her back and pulled him with her, positioned him between her thighs and thrust her hips in short, needy strokes against his shaft, taking the tip of him inside, each time taking him deeper. The muscles in his arms tightened as he kissed her with all the force he couldn't use elsewhere, and sweat popped out on his forehead as he shifted his weight to his left hand, then used his right to silently coax her into lifting her legs, wrapping them around his hips, holding her there as he prepared for the one thrust that would accomplish the deed.

"I'm sorry," he whispered against her mouth before pushing hard into her, tearing past the tight flesh and filling her completely. Her muscles spasmed where her body gloved his, and a choked cry made it past her clenched teeth. He held himself utterly still and kissed away two solitary tears that seeped from her eyes. "It'll never hurt again, baby, I swear. I'm sorry...I'm sorry...I'm sorry..."

Later, still buried deep inside Anna's soft, hot, pliant body, Tyler drew the first breath of substance in what seemed like forever and smelled her perfume, his cologne, their sex. His muscles were fatigued from too much restraint and still twitched in protest at odd moments, and he thought he might have to stay exactly where he was forever, or at least until morning. That was only another... Lifting his head from her shoulder, he squinted at the clock on the nightstand but saw the box of condoms instead.

Aw, hell. He'd gone to the trouble of buying the condoms without Anna knowing, had taken one out of the box, had fully intended to use it...until she'd started moving against him, taking him when *he* was supposed to be taking *her,* and all he'd been able to think about was getting inside her, feeling her so tight and hot around him, making love to her... He'd totally forgotten the condom.

Never, since his first time eleven years ago, had he *ever* forgotten. It was a lesson Kyle and Jake had drummed into him from the time he was fourteen. Always remember, never forget... And he'd forgotten.

It might have been the second smartest thing he'd ever done.

Anna had paid little enough attention to the tub in the bathroom in the week they'd been guests at the lodge. Though she preferred showers, the tub was serviceable—larger than usual, with whirlpool jets evenly spaced around the sides. Late that Friday evening, she decided long, lazy soaks in the tub held tremendous advantages over quick showers...particularly when shared with Tyler.

He was behind her, leaning back against the high, sloped surface of the tub, and she lay on top of him, her head on his shoulder, her back to his chest, his unflagging arousal against her bottom. The only light in the room came from candles on the counter—utilitarian white candles in tin holders, borrowed from the cabin's emergency stash—and the air was steamy and redolent with the scent of jasmine-scented bubbles.

As usual, Tyler had been right, she thought drowsily. The first time had hurt, though not terribly so. And it had been worth it. And he had fitted perfectly. As if they'd been designed, one for the other.

She couldn't wait to experience the second time.

"Annie?"

"Hmm."

"I, uh...I need to tell you... You need to know..." He took a breath that lifted her a few millimeters in the water, then blew it out again. "I forgot to use a condom." His tone was guarded, giving away nothing of how he felt about his oversight. Was he regretful, disappointed, sorry?

She needn't know to understand her own feelings. She was glad. And she didn't feel the least bit guilty about the fact that she'd thrown the plastic-wrapped square from the bed to the floor when he was distracted by their kiss. "So you did," she murmured.

His hands slid lower until they cupped her stomach. "You understand what that means?"

"I was a virgin, Tyler. Not an idiot. It means I could get pregnant."

"And then you would have to marry me."

Her smile faded, along with a bit of the lazy comfort that had seeped through her. Marriage for the sake of a child—could she do that? On occasion she'd considered the prospect of marriage for the sake of an alliance, to support the royal house of Sebastiani, and it had all seemed very cool, logical and—pardon the pun—conceivable. But to marry a man she adored, whom she very well might love, and know that he'd agreed to it only for the sake of his child.... She wasn't at all certain she could bear that. Better to marry a complete stranger than a man she might love who didn't love her in return.

"Your parents would forbid your brother, Jake, from ever traveling to Montebello," she said mildly, thinking of Joanna, several months pregnant when she married Kyle.

"They'd think those Montebello women are as fertile as they are beautiful," he replied, brushing his mouth over her ear.

"Perhaps the truth would be that those Ramsey men are as virile as they are handsome." She stretched and felt his erection rub enticingly against her. "Can we do it again?"

His chuckle was deep, sweet, charming. "You're a greedy little thing, aren't you?"

She turned so she could see him. "What we had was very nice and exceeded my highest expectations, but...I know there's more. You were holding back, I presume to avoid causing me further discomfort. I want it sweet and gentle and hard and demanding. I want it all."

"It's up to you, babe." Guiding her legs apart, he stroked between them, making her shudder, then eased one finger inside her and probed deeply. "Does that feel good?"

"Oh, yes," she whispered, her entire body suddenly limp, all her sensation centered on that one intimate touch.

"Is it tender?"

She wanted to lie and say no, wanted him to continue until it felt so good she cried with it, but she couldn't help but wince a time or two. "Just a bit," she admitted. "But you can make me forget. You did before."

Sadly for her, he withdrew his hand and wrapped his arms around her. "Let's take our time, Annie. We'll see how you feel in the morning, okay?"

How she felt in the morning was fine, a bit sore but brimming with energy. She awakened before the sun had cleared the eastern horizon and found herself relegated to the smallest portion of the queen-size bed, with Tyler snuggled close behind her, his arm firmly around her waist. She simply lay there for a time, listening to the steady sound of his breathing, wondering if there was anything she might do to influence his feelings for her. Was there some sensual secret to use in bed, or some little hint for outside bed, that might sway him toward an emotional commitment to her?

She rather doubted it, else some enterprising and wise woman would have already packaged it for sale and made a fortune. She would have to win Tyler's affection on her own, and risk heartache if she failed.

The mere thought turned her morning blue.

Slipping from the bed, she completed her morning routine, including a hasty shower, then went downstairs. A few logs on the smoldering coals brought the fire back to life, and the temperature on the lower level began to rise accordingly. In the kitchen she loaded the previous evening's dishes into the dishwasher, as she'd watched Tyler do every day for a week, then measured out soap from the box under the sink, started the machine and congratulated herself when neither excess water nor suds poured out. Next she made herself a cup of gourmet instant cocoa, tossed in a few tiny marshmallows, then carried it into the living room to sip in front of the crackling fire.

It was truly ironic that a mere week and a half ago, she'd fed her sister a story about how she and Tyler wanted a chance to develop this relationship between them when no such relationship had existed. And now…now she was worried about broken hearts and being pregnant—or, rather, not being pregnant. She would be delighted to discover in a few weeks' time that she carried his babe, regardless of whether he demanded to marry her—which, of course, he would. He was that kind of man. Responsible. Driven by duty.

But, God help her, she didn't want to be his duty. She wanted to be his love, his life, his wife.

But, given no other choice, she might settle for duty.

She became aware of him an instant before the stair near the bottom creaked under his weight, but she didn't turn, needing the few additional seconds to clear the melancholy from her expression. He stopped behind the couch, bent and kissed her forehead, then slid his hand from her shoulder inside her robe and gave her breast a fleeting caress. She tilted her head back so she could smile at him, then, utterly shameless, she loosened the belt on her robe and exposed her breast to more of his teasing touches.

"You certainly know how to get a man's blood pumping," he murmured, bending lower to kiss her nipple, then holding her head for a deep, hungry, upside-down kiss. "Did you sleep well?"

"Incredibly so."

"Me, too. Want to wear me out again?"

"Close the blinds and have your way with me, or teach me to have my way with you."

His green gaze glittered wickedly as he secured the blinds on the front and side windows, then approached the couch. Already, his arousal tented his boxer shorts, and already she felt the moisture collecting between her thighs in anticipation of feeling him there.

As shameless as she, he removed his boxers, then sat naked on the couch, lifting her onto his lap and giving her another long, lazy kiss. It took him less than a moment to discover that she was utterly naked under the robe, and his response was quite gratifying.

After they kissed and petted and fondled for a time, she shrugged out of the heavy terry robe and thrust her hips against his. "Come inside me, *tesoro mio.*" My darling.

"The condoms are upstairs. Let me go—"

Bracing her hands on the back of the sofa, she refused to be set aside. "Forget the condoms."

"But—"

"I want *you*, Tyler. I want to *feel* you. *All* of you."

"And if you get pregnant?"

With or without him in her life, she would be deliriously happy. She'd always intended to be a mother, and to be mother to his child would be the second best possible future. Best, of course, would be raising his children together with him as husband and wife. Family. "Ah, can you imagine the child with your dedication and arrogance and my stubbornness and determination?''

"God help anyone who crosses him," he said with a laugh.

She smiled, shifted her hips, and rubbed against him. "Please come inside me now, Tyler, and teach me to be wicked with you."

He positioned himself, lifted her hips and ever so slowly lowered her, filling her, stretching her, sending a flood of heat and need racing through her. When she'd taken all of him, she flexed the muscles deep in her belly, tightening them around him, and made him turn pale and swear with great imagination. She liked the response.

He showed her how to move her hips, to thrust, then withdraw, then take him even deeper again, and she learned how to create friction and pressure, to ease it, then double it. "So lovemaking is all about power," she murmured, bracing her palms on his broad shoulders.

"About shared power," he replied in a ragged voice. "Right now you're...ah, jeez, Annie, you're killing me...but as easily as you can make me beg, I can make you weep."

"I would like that," she whispered, bending to drag her tongue across his nipple. "After I make you beg, you can make me weep with sheer pleasure."

And she did.

And so did he.

Chapter 10

Ursula Chambers hated snow, she hated cold, and she most emphatically, absolutely, undeniably hated winter!

That made clear, she maneuvered her sister's pickup truck through the ranch gate and over bumps that might have been a cattle guard or could have been the frozen carcasses of every man who'd ever let her down, for all she cared. She was tired of fighting the beat-up old Ford on frozen roads all the way from town, of dealing with her pathetic whiny sister, of waiting impatiently for her ticket to paradise to arrive so she could get out of this miserable existence. The images of the wonderful life that awaited her in a Mediterranean kingdom were the only thing keeping her going through these awful months of waiting.

For a moment, she closed her eyes, tilted her face to the Sunday afternoon sun and imagined herself living in the royal palace, the doting aunt to the future king of Montebello. There would be servants at her beck and call, and handsome, wealthy men lining up at her door, preening and pleading for just a bit of her attention. She would open *People* and *In Style* to find her own beautiful self smiling up regally, happily from the glossy pages, and she would be the desire of men, and the envy of women, everywhere.

Her every wish would come true.

And all she had to do was see that her sister's every wish died…along with Jessica herself.

The all-too-familiar slide of the wheels made Ursula's eyes jerk open, and she filled the frigid air with curses. The damn sun offered glare but no heat, and the landscape around her was as far from paradise as a place could be. Once she was installed in the palace, she would jet around the world with her myriad admirers—and, soon enough, her rich-as-sin infatuated husband—but she would *never* return to Shady Rock, Colorado, or this damn ranch. If anyone ever tried to make her come back, she would press one hand to her forehead, cry prettily and rouse such sympathy, they would never make that mistake again.

By the time the ranch house came into sight, her fingers were numb from gripping the steering wheel, her butt was aching from the inadequate padding in the seat, and she was going to need hours in front of a roaring fire to chase the chill from her bones. She couldn't believe her idiot sister considered this piece of crap adequate transportation. It used motor oil the way an aging movie star used Oil of Olay, it was uncomfortable as all hell, it didn't have air conditioning for Colorado's hot summers and not much heat for the damn cold winters. When the baby was born and Jessica was dealt with, Ursula wasn't even going to bother to sell the junk heap. She intended to just leave it where it sat, a rusting monument to her sister's lunacy.

She slid to a stop near the back door, grabbed her bag and hurried inside. The house was dark and dreary, and opening the curtains did little to help. In her opinion—the only one that counted, after all—it was cramped, plain and no more suitable than her dump of an apartment in town. In New York she'd had such a lovely place, with soaring windows, exposed brick, an expansive floor plan and just a few homey touches to warm up the cool, minimalist effect. Granted, she hadn't paid for it, but why should she have? Gardner had gotten plenty from her in return. For a time she'd thought she had given him the best years of her life.

Now she knew, like the saying said, the best was yet to come.

She'd told Jessica she would make certain the hands were taking care of everything on the ranch. After kicking the furnace up to the tropical zone, she went to the kitchen and gazed out the window over the sink. The outbuildings—barn, sheds, cabins and bunkhouse—stood not too distant, snow coating their roofs like frosting on a gingerbread house. A few shaggy horses were in the corral, but there were no signs of the rest of the horses, the cattle or the hands. They were probably cozied up in their houses, watching TV and storing fat for the rest of the winter. While the boss was away, the hands would play...

All right, everything looked okay, she thought dismissively. Turning away from the window, she wandered down the hall toward the living room, turning on lights as she went, then stopped when she reached the mirror near the front door. Never one to pass up an opportunity, she tilted her head this way, then that, critically inspecting her reflection. After a long, intense study, she smiled. As usual, she was perfect.

Her hair was perfectly coiffed, her makeup perfectly applied. Her skin was as smooth as daily pampering and regular chemical peels could accomplish, her teeth bleached to a blinding white, her lips improved upon—though only slight improvement had been needed—with an injection of collagen. Her cheekbones were strikingly high, the look in her eyes astonishingly innocent when she wanted it to be, and her mousy hair had been lightened to the absolutely perfect shade of honeyed blond.

She was beautiful.

And she would look even more beautiful on the arm of a powerful and wealthy duke, prince or king. Queen Ursula, she thought dreamily, and imagined herself accepting curtsies and bows from all her loyal subjects. They would love her dearly, and she would bask daily in their adoration. She might even—

A knock at the door startled her from her reverie, rousing her irritation. It had better not be one of those dreary little ranch hands of Jessica's, come to intrude on her plans. If it was, she would fire him on the spot.

She unfastened the locks and jerked open the door, then stared. This was no lowly ranch hand. The man on the porch stood about six feet tall, and he had raven hair, dark eyes and a cleft chin. That alone was enough to make her weak in the knees. On top of that, the whole package came together incredibly nicely. He was breathtakingly handsome, and the first thought to pop into her mind was what beautiful children they could create together...*if* she were the type to sacrifice her figure merely for a brat.

He was dressed mostly in black—boots, slacks, coat, gloves—with a dove gray scarf around his neck. His jacket was unzipped enough to reveal a gray and black patterned sweater underneath, and he looked as if he didn't even notice the dropping temperatures. She knew without touching that the garments were of top quality, without seeing labels that they'd borne price tags exceeding her annual clothing budget.

Handsome, well-dressed and presumably well off. The man of her dreams.

She arranged herself in a more welcoming position, grateful that she'd bypassed the jeans she normally would have worn for a trip to the ranch in favor of mint-green slacks and a sweater in mint green, pale peach and the softest of lavenders. With her honeyed blond hair and her porcelain-fair skin, she knew she looked soft, sweet and good enough to eat—a treat any day, no matter what the temperature.

"Can I help you?" she asked, settling for a demure tone.

"I hope so. I was told I could find lodging for the night—a bed-and-breakfast, I believe—but I seem to have taken a wrong turn somewhere." His voice was elegant, cultured, touched with a bit of an accent and slid over her like raw silk. Oh, yes, he could definitely be the man of her dreams.

Depending on whose side he was on. There was no denying that his accent, faint as it was, was very much the same as Prince Lucas's, and he certainly had the coloring she associated with the Mediterranean region, as well as the bearing she associated with royalty. She didn't believe she could be fortunate enough to find an honest-to-God royal on her doorstep, but someone with ties to the royal family just might be good enough.

Someone who could help fulfill her goals would be perfect.

"Apparently you did." She glanced at the sun, sinking lower on the horizon. "Come in, please, and I'll see if I can help you find your way."

Once inside, he removed his coat and scarf, and she hung

them on the quaint coat tree in the corner behind the door, then led him into the living room. She wished she'd had advance notice so she could have turned on lights, built a fire, lit some candles and generally made the place more appealing, but her visitor hardly seemed to notice. Instead, he stopped in the middle of the room and watched her with a warm, appreciative look that notched up her body heat ten degrees or so.

"I'm Ursula Chambers. And you are...?"

"Pardon my lack of manners. I have no excuse except that your beauty took me by surprise. Desmond Caruso."

She offered her hand, but instead of shaking it, he lifted it to his mouth, leaving the lightest of kisses on her fingertips. A shiver chased down her spine. "I'm so very glad to meet you," she all but purred. "Can I get you some coffee to chase away the chill...or maybe something stronger?"

"I'm not chilled," he replied in a low, smooth voice, "but a drink would be much appreciated. It's been a long day and I could use a little help unwinding."

"Wait here." More than a bit dazed, she headed for the kitchen, and realized that she was no longer chilled, either. One long look from his incredibly dark eyes, one touch of his amazingly sensuous mouth, and she was damn near warm enough to steam.

In the kitchen, she started the coffeemaker, then searched the cabinets for the bottle of rum she'd given Jessica for her last birthday. Even though her sister wasn't much of a drinker and didn't appreciate that the bottle was the best Gardner's money could buy, naturally she had kept it, just in case it might come in handy someday. Well, someday had arrived.

"You have a charming home," Desmond Caruso said from behind her, startling her as she found the bottle on the top shelf in the pantry.

It was on the tip of her tongue to deny that she would deliberately live in such a rundown place—not that her apartment in town was any better—but just in time she caught herself. "Why, thank you. Personally, I think of it more as...rustic. Primitive. What brings you to Colorado, Mr. Caruso?"

"Please call me Desmond. I'm merely doing some traveling."

"Really?" She knew from the slight narrowing of his gaze that the skepticism that barely colored her response hit its target. "You know, I've never heard of a bed-and-breakfast in this area, and yet strangely enough, you're the third person in recent weeks who's stopped here searching for one."

"Really." He rested one hand on the counter and the other on his hip. He wasn't as tall as she normally liked her men, but he appeared every bit as muscular as any well-oiled Hollywood hunk. She had such a weakness for muscles that she could easily overlook height, or lack of.

"The first two were a couple—a redhaired woman, a man with brown hair and green eyes. And what a coincidence—he spoke with the same accent you have. Said they were newly-weds, but..." She let a hint of naughty wickedness creep into her voice and her smile. "They didn't act like any newlyweds I'd ever seen."

"And did you help them find their way, too?" he asked silkily.

The coffeemaker gurgled and burped as the last of the water drained out of the reservoir. She drew her attention from him long enough to fill both cups, slid the heavily spiked one to him, then held her own in both hands as she leaned against the counter. "I don't know if I did. Mostly, it seems, we talked about the ranch, my sister and one of her hands—a man named Joe. A drifter. He just wandered in a year or so ago, and wandered off again last month. You'd think newlyweds would be more interested in each other than a no-account stranger, but not those two."

"So this no-account drifter named Joe intrigued them."

"Intrigued," she repeated. "Yes, that's a good way of putting it. They asked a lot of questions about him. Too bad I didn't have a lot of answers to give them." Tilting her head to one side, she studied him a moment, then asked, "Where exactly is this bed-and-breakfast you're looking for? Perhaps I can make a few calls and get directions for you."

"I don't believe that will be necessary. I'm really not the bed-and-breakfast type, I'm afraid."

"No, you don't look it," she agreed. "But you do look the

hungry type. Can I persuade you to stay for dinner?" Not that food was what he hungered for. Having a great many yearnings of her own, she prided herself in being able to recognize them in others.

"You're beautiful and you cook, too."

"Not if I can avoid it. But the freezer is well stocked. I'm sure I can find something." Without waiting for a response from him, she opened the freezer and rummaged through its contents. Desmond Caruso, whoever he was, was looking for the prince. She would bet the farm on it—or, in this case, the ranch. But did he want to return Lucas to the bosom of his loving family, or keep him away? *That* was the important question.

By the time dinner was ready—frozen beef stew heated until bubbling hot—Desmond had begun asking his own questions about Joe, but she coyly avoided answering them. While she carried the dishes, drinks and utensils into the living room, he built a fire, then they settled on the floor in front of the fireplace to eat. It was warm, cozy, and a perfect scene for seduction. Her killer instincts told her it was a toss-up who would make the first move.

"With Joe gone, you must be shorthanded," Desmond remarked.

She shrugged. "Work slows down in the dead of winter. The other hands can take up the slack without any problem."

"Don't you think it's odd that he would just pick up and leave like that?"

She held her wineglass to the flames, turning the deep red liquid the color of fire, then took a sip. "I think it's odd that cowboy Joe has the same accent as two handsome, elegant, sophisticated foreigners. I think it's odd that those same two foreigners are so interested in—pardon me, so *intrigued* by—a supposedly no-account drifter. And I think it's very odd that all this intrigue stirred up about the time the authorities resumed their search for that missing prince from Montebello, who, as luck would have it, looks amazingly like the missing Joe."

Of all the things she'd said, he responded to the one she'd least expected. "Do you think I'm handsome?"

Her laughter was sudden and unexpected, too. "As if you don't know the answer to that, Desmond."

"I know most people's answer. I'm asking for yours."

She set her empty soup bowl away, brushed cracker crumbs from her sweater, then leaned against the stone hearth. "I think you're incredibly handsome. I also think you've come here under false pretenses, and I know that I'd rather hear the truth from you than lies."

Any other man might have taken offense at that lies comment, but not Desmond. He reclined on the floor, his weight resting on his left arm, one knee bent, and he studied her a moment before nodding. "Very well. I have reason to believe—as you do, too—that your drifter, Joe, is, in reality, Prince Lucas of Montebello."

"And you've come to take him home, right? I imagine the king would pay quite a pretty penny to the person who could do that." Though she watched him closely, the only expression that crossed his face was one of studied indifference. "Of course, first you have to find him, and that's easier said than done, especially if he doesn't *want* to be found. What kind of reward do you think the king would offer?"

He negligently shrugged and named a figure that made her little heart go pitter-patter. But right on the heels of the adrenaline rush came the thought that if Prince Lucas was worth so much to his father alive, how much more would his only child be worth if the prince was dead?

More than she could imagine—and, honey, she could imagine a *lot.*

"So if we found Joe—er, Prince Lucas—and took him home, we would receive a reward big enough to share." Sharing wasn't a concept she'd ever willingly embraced. Her philosophy was What's mine is mine and what's yours just might become mine, too. But in this case she'd be willing to make an effort...or, at least, to pretend.

"Your portion would be so much that you wouldn't know what to do with it."

She subdued the unladylike snort that tried to escape. Obviously he didn't know who he was talking to. All her life she'd wanted and needed great sums of money, and she'd never gotten them, not all she needed, not always when she needed them. Even she wouldn't venture a guess on how much she could spend before she started running out of ideas. A half million? Two, four, maybe even ten times that amount?

So…she could work with Desmond to return the prince and share a reward that was sizable, but not enough. Or she could work with him until they found the prince, then find some way to cut him out of the picture and keep the entire reward for herself. Or she could go along and get along, and gradually sway him to what she considered the best outcome—find the prince, remove him from this life, then show up in Montebello with her poor orphaned nephew. *That* would ensure her a lifetime of riches as the prince and future king's only living maternal relative.

Tough questions…not.

She removed her shoes and set them aside, then stretched out one leg and lazily drew her stockinged foot back and forth over the fine fabric of his trousers that covered his calf. "Tell me, Desmond—are you interested in a partnership?"

His dark gaze started with the delicate waves in her honeyed blond hair, then slowly, moved steadily downward, pausing on the perfect 36 Ds Gardner had paid a small fortune for, sliding over her middle and her perfect hips, the results of hours of aerobics, the StairMaster, *Buns of Steel* and liposuction. When he'd reached her manicured Marvy Mauve toes, he smiled a smile with the potential to make her swoon even if he wasn't handsome, elegant, sophisticated and connected to the Montebellan royal family.

"Always, Ursula." If her question had been asked in a sex-kitten purr, it was answered in a hungry-dangerous-tiger rumble. His long, thin fingers wrapped around her wrist and jerked her to him, and his sensuous mouth hovered a mere inch from hers. "Why don't we finalize the details of this partnership?" he asked, his lips brushing hers with every word. "Then we can talk about finding the prince."

And then he kissed her—hard, greedy, demanding—as he drew her to the floor. As his hands slid under her sweater and freed her breasts from her delicate lavender lace bra, a line from an old song echoed through her mind.

Two tickets to paradise…

According to Tyler's calculations, their late Sunday afternoon trip from Garden City to Golden should have taken two hours and thirty minutes. But his estimate hadn't included an unscheduled stop off an isolated back road or testing the SUV's cargo area for comfort, so they arrived in Golden later than planned. They checked into a motel, went out to dinner, then spent a quiet evening in their room—quiet being relative, of course.

But Monday morning, it was back to business as usual. He was damn tired of showing the prince's picture, asking the same questions time after time and hearing the same answers. Even more than the frustration, he disliked the effect negative response after negative response had on Anna. Though she hadn't been any too cheerful when they left the motel that morning, by late afternoon, when they called it quits, she was downright morose.

When they returned to the motel, she laid her coat across the bed, then sat down at the small round table. After removing his own jacket, he went to stand behind her, rubbing her shoulders with firm, tension-easing strokes. "We're going to find your brother."

She removed the photograph of Lucas from her purse and gazed at it. "Do you think so? Really, honestly?"

"Really." But he lied. Truth was, he didn't know what to think. If this Joe from Colorado really was Prince Lucas, he couldn't have just disappeared. Thanks to the renewed search for him, his face had been in the papers and on the news on a regular basis, so surely someone would have recognized him. Just last night they'd caught a film clip on the evening news of Lucas at some royal event a few years ago. He'd been smiling and charming, escorting *the* most popular Hollywood actress at that time and, at the end of the clip, dancing his youngest sister, Princess Anna, around the ballroom floor. Her hair had been done up in some sleek, sophisticated style that completely obliterated her curls, and she'd worn a gown that sparkled like a million stars, a strapless thing that clung to her breasts, her waist, her hips. She'd looked so glamorous and beautiful that, if Tyler hadn't already been hard, thanks to the very intimate kisses she'd been giving him at the time, he would have become that way instantly.

He hadn't been able to get that image of her out of his mind. She'd looked…well, like a princess.

And he was just an average schmuck from Arizona.

"Why haven't we found even the smallest clue? If he truly came to Montana to find work in one of these mines, why has no one seen him?"

"Maybe because he didn't come here." Maybe Ursula Chambers had been mistaken. Maybe Joe or Lucas or whoever the hell he was had deliberately misled her. Or maybe *she* had deliberately misled Lorenzo.

"But if he's not at the ranch in Colorado, and he didn't come here, then where is he? And how shall we ever find him?"

"We just keep trying, babe. We don't give up."

"You can't ask the people in every town in America if they've seen my brother."

"No," he admitted. "But we'll do what we can."

She let her head fall forward, and for a time the only sound in the room was her soft groans of pleasure as he moved his attention to the taut muscles in her neck. Before long, though, she spoke again. "When you go to Colorado, I'd like to go with you."

His first impulse was to tell her no. Letting her traipse around Montana with him was reckless enough. But how was taking her to the small Colorado town of Shady Rock any more reckless than dragging her around Garden City and Golden? What kind of threat could they possibly run into there that didn't also exist here?

Besides, he intended to leave for Colorado the next afternoon or Wednesday morning. If he didn't let her go, he would have to put her on a plane to Billings, where sooner or later Christina would put her on the Gulfstream back to Montebello. He might not see her again for weeks, even months. When he did see her again, her life would be back to normal. She would once again be Princess Anna, living in the palace, attending royal functions, surrounded by adoring subjects. Her adventure would be over.

Along with whatever she felt for him?

"All right," he agreed selfishly, because he wasn't ready to let her go yet and because she rewarded him with such a pretty smile that he couldn't resist teasing her. "You didn't expect that, did you?"

"Actually, no. I assumed I would have to find some way to outwit you again, as I did in Billings."

"Darlin', you've been outwitting me at every turn. It's because you're so damn beautiful that most of the time around you I'm dazed and confused."

"Hah. You've been most competent. I had begun to doubt my appeal for rugged American men. After all, I'm neither blond nor blue-eyed nor busty."

He studied her a moment, then asked, "Why would you want to be? I'm partial to dark brown curls, brown eyes and small, nicely rounded breasts perfectly sized for my hands." Sliding his hands down her front, he proved that her breasts were, in fact, perfect and, in the process, made her eyes go smoky and dark.

For a moment she let him have his fun. Then she caught his hands, held them away and solemnly gazed up at him. "Tyler, I—" Abruptly she broke off—not as if she couldn't find the words for what she'd wanted to say, but as if she couldn't find the courage. What could make her so serious? Another thank-you for letting her scam everyone and accompany him? Maybe a thank-you for finally giving in and making love to her? How about a reminder that she'd promised him nothing—no future beyond this trip, no possibilities, no love?

Whatever it was, the moment passed. With a sheepish smile, she pressed a kiss to each of his palms, then escaped his hold. "I'd like to freshen up before dinner. It'll take only a minute."

He stood where he was until the bathroom door closed behind her, then forced a lightness into his voice that, according to his reflection in the nearby mirror, he didn't manage in his expression. "Only a minute," he said, loud enough to be heard through the door. "Yeah, like I haven't heard that one before."

The door opened and her balled-up sweater sailed across the room in his direction. He caught it, along with a whiff of her perfume, and his chest tightened. Maybe he should take back his agreement to let her go to Shady Rock with him. If she was going to break his heart, didn't it stand to reason that the sooner it happened, the sooner he would get used to the pain? And if she *wasn't* going to break it—if she intended when she said goodbye to add something like I love you or Please come see me—then the sooner he knew that, the better, right?

Maybe.

He used the remote to turn on the television, then stretched out on the bed. Might as well make himself comfortable while he waited...or as comfortable as a coward could get. What if *she* was waiting for *him* to say something like I love you or I don't want you to go? What if she needed some assurance she wasn't making a fool of herself and risking unbearable hurt?

He was a soldier, trained to protect and defend. He'd undergone rigorous physical as well as mental training. He was prepared to successfully complete his mission, no matter what it took. Death, danger, destruction—all in a day's work. And yet he was afraid of the devastation one slender, impossibly beautiful, delicate little princess could wreak on him.

Jeez, if it was this tough for everybody, it was a surprise anyone risked falling in love.

Eventually she came out of the bathroom again. She'd changed into her University of Montana sweatshirt and, presumably, had done something with her hair and makeup. He wasn't sure. She'd looked gorgeous going in and looked gorgeous coming out.

They walked to a restaurant across the street and down a block. The sign outside advertised home cooking, and the menu supported it. Fried chicken, chicken and dumplings, meat loaf, pork chops and liver and onions topped the menu, and it promised some pretty damn amazing-looking pies for dessert. Anna requested a typical American picnic lunch, then had to explain to the puzzled waitress that meant fried chicken, potato salad and baked beans. Tyler settled on chicken and dumplings that were made the way his mother made them, and when they were done, they each ordered a slice of banana cream pie with mile-high meringue.

The waitress had just delivered the pie when a man approached their booth. Tyler figured the guy was in his early twenties, several inches shorter than him, probably twenty pounds lighter. His hair was blond, his eyes an unlikely blue, and he was just a shade too...*something* for Tyler's liking.

"I understand you two are asking a lot of questions around town about some guy that's missing," the man said, looking from one to the other. "I heard you had a picture and was wondering if I could see it."

Anna automatically reached for her handbag, but Tyler bumped his leg against hers to get her attention, then gave a faint shake of his head. He withdrew his own copy of the same photo from his jacket pocket and wordlessly handed it to the man.

He studied it a moment, then nodded emphatically. "Yeah, that's the guy. I thought it probably was."

"You've seen—"

Once again Tyler signaled for Anna to be quiet, and she immediately closed her mouth. She couldn't contain the hope that flared in her eyes, though. She practically shimmered with it. "I'm Tyler Ramsey," he said, leaning forward to offer his hand. As he did so, his sport coat just happened to fall open, giving the stranger a good look at the shoulder holster he wore.

"Jimmy Drucker." His handshake was weak, his smile phony. "And this beautiful lady is...?"

"None of your concern. So you think you've seen him." Tyler nodded toward the photograph, and once more the man nodded vigorously.

"He called himself Joe. Said he'd been working down in Colorado. Got tired of cowboying and decided to give mining a try."

"Where did you run into him?"

Drucker looked left and right, then said, "I'll have a seat if you don't mind. Don't want to call too much attention to a private conversation."

When he moved as if he meant to slide onto the bench next

to Anna, Tyler planted his size-twelve boot there. "Pull up a chair."

With a sly grin, Drucker grabbed a chair from the nearest table and swung it around backwards, then straddled it. "I get your message, Tyler. You wanna keep the pretty little girl all to yourself. Can't say as I blame you."

"What about Joe?"

"Joe...yeah. There's this little town not far from here—not much to it besides a few bars and a fleabag motel. That's where I met him...oh, not long ago. We kinda hit it off. I'd done some mining off and on, so he asked me a lot of questions, and truth is, I reckon I kinda turned him off of it. He decided there's better ways to earn a living."

As, apparently, had Jimmy Drucker, Tyler thought cynically. If the man made it through five more minutes without mentioning money, Tyler would be surprised. "So Joe went off to find work someplace else. You wouldn't happen to know where, would you?"

Drucker grinned. "As a matter of fact, I'm gettin' to that." But, of course, he didn't. Instead he turned his attention to Anna. "You're sure a pretty little thing. You know...you kinda look like him. Granted, he's older and his eyes are blue, but...yeah, there's a real strong resemblance in your nose and your jaw. He wouldn't happen to be related to you, now would he?"

Tyler leaned forward again and rapped the table for his attention. "Let's get this straight, Drucker. You don't sit beside her. You don't talk to her. In fact, it would probably be in your best interests if you don't even look at her. Your business—if you have any—is with me. Understand?"

The idiot didn't take offense, which roused Tyler's suspicions even more. Instead, he grinned yet again. He was working way too hard to appear friendly and harmless, when Tyler figured he was about as harmless as a snake.

He didn't like snakes.

"You were going to tell us where Joe went to find work," he impatiently reminded the man.

"Well..." For the first time since he'd approached, Drucker's grin disappeared completely and was replaced by a look of chagrin. "I'd like to do just that, but...you know, this has been a tough winter. I got sick, couldn't work, lost my job. Ordinarily, I wouldn't even think of trying to profit from someone else's problems, but...I got some mighty big problems of my own...well, it's customary in cases like this to offer a reward for information."

"Is it, now," Tyler said disinterestedly. "I'll tell you what, Drucker. You tell me something about Joe that isn't common knowledge, and I'll see what I can do about getting you that reward."

"I already told you—"

"Nothing that you couldn't have gotten from any one of the dozens of people we've talked to today."

"But I told you— " Drucker broke off, looked from Tyler to Anna, then back again, then shrugged. "Okay, here's something you haven't been tellin'. That prissy little girl there is Joe's sister, only his name ain't Joe. It's Lucas. Prince Lucas Sebastiani. One of these days soon that's gonna be King Lucas. And he's worth a fortune."

"And you figure you should have part of it because...?"

Drucker's grin returned. "You help an important man find his way back home, you ought to get something for your effort. Considering Prince Lucas is a *real* important man, I'd expect something worthy of his importance."

As Tyler cynically studied him, memories of childhood visits to his grandparents crept into his mind. Because his father's air force career had kept them moving, he and his brothers hadn't seen their grandparents as often as most kids, but they'd spent weeks with them every summer. In general, the visits had been great—long, hot days, fishing and swimming, Grandma's lemonade on the porch swing. But, being the Ramsey boys, sooner or later one of them would screw up, and their grandfather would invite him out back for a come-to-Jesus meeting. The meetings had generally been short, and when they were over, that boy had seen the error of his ways, hallelujah!

He would give almost anything to invite Jimmy Drucker out back for his own come-to-Jesus meeting, but doing so would mean leaving Anna alone in the restaurant. Maybe she would be safe. Maybe Drucker was working alone, or was the only one who'd figured out who she and the missing Joe were.

But maybe he wasn't. And while it was most likely that he knew nothing about Prince Lucas's whereabouts, there was no doubt he knew exactly where Princess Anna was and had a pretty good idea how much the king would pay to get her back.

As Tyler was considering how best to keep Anna safe, yet still make certain that Drucker was nothing more than a con artist, the solution to his problem appeared in the doorway across the room. He signaled the waitress, leaned over to whisper in her ear, then sat back. "Okay, Drucker, so you recognized the prince. You still haven't told me anything that suggests you've had any personal contact with him. Where is this little town where you met him? When was it? Who else knows about it? With nothing more than a few bars and a fleabag motel, surely someone else saw him, too. Maybe you were the only one to recognize him, but I can't believe you were the only one to even see him."

Drucker shrugged elaborately. "Well, now, I'm pretty much a stranger in that town myself. I can't give you any names, but yeah, I'm sure the waitress at the bar remembers—" As a hand clamped on his shoulder, he broke off and looked up, a friendly smile at the ready, but it faded quickly enough when he saw the sheriff.

"Mr. Ramsey. Ma'am." Sheriff Ray Mitchell, whom they'd met earlier that afternoon, nodded in Anna's direction, then turned his cold gaze toward Drucker. "What're you doing here, Jimmy?"

"Uh, n-nothing. J-j-just having a bit of friendly conversation is all." He tried to stand up and made it a few inches off the chair before the sheriff pushed him down again.

"What's the problem, Mr. Ramsey?" Mitchell asked, then added, "'Cause when Jimmy's involved, there's always a problem."

"Now, that's not fair. We were just havin' a conversation," Drucker said, a whine entering his voice.

"He claims to have information about the man we're looking

for," Tyler said. "But he wants money—and a lot of it—before he shares it."

The sheriff scowled. "Jimmy, if you spent near as much time working as you do coming up with these schemes of yours, you'd be a rich man. What're you telling 'em about that fellow?" He gestured toward the photo on the table.

"Nothin'," Drucker said sullenly.

Tyler took that opportunity to speak up. "He says he ran into him at a bar in a small town near here, and he claims he knows where he was headed when he left."

Sheriff Mitchell glared down at Drucker, who refused to raise his gaze from the tabletop. "Is that so?" Still holding on to him with one hand, Mitchell pulled up another chair and sat down close. "Why don't you tell your Uncle Ray all about it, Jimmy?"

Tyler winced inwardly. So Jimmy Drucker, scam artist, was nephew to Ray Mitchell, respected lawman. That must provide for some interesting family dynamics.

"You ever see that man, other than on television or in the papers?" Mitchell asked.

Looking as if he was trying to make himself too small to notice, Drucker grudgingly answered, "No."

"So you intended to... What? Weasel some money out of them, set up a meeting that was never gonna happen, then disappear until they was gone?" Mitchell cuffed Drucker on the back of the head, then pointed at Tyler. "That man works for a *king,* for God's sake. Do you think he'd be stupid enough to pay you for information without some proof that you knew what the hell you were talking about?"

Finally Drucker lifted his gaze to his uncle's face and said defensively, "I wasn't lookin' for a lot. I figured I'd ask for fifty thousand and maybe get five hundred of it up-front. Even a couple hundred would've been plenty for my trouble."

Mitchell cuffed him again, then gave him a shove. "Go on. Get out of here. Get your scrawny butt home and stay there. We aren't finished with this yet."

Red-faced and grumbling under his breath, Drucker left the booth and the restaurant, then Mitchell gave a sigh. "I apologize for Jimmy. His mama's raised him without a daddy, and she was way too easy on him. I've done what I can, but…''

"You have nothing to apologize for, Sheriff," Anna said politely.

"Do you think he told you the truth?" Tyler asked. "Is there any possibility at all that he really did run into the prince?"

"Nah. Not Jimmy. He's never kept his mouth shut about anything in his life. He's just always looking for an easy mark and thought he found one here." Rising, the sheriff returned the two chairs to their table, then gave them a curt nod. "Again, I apologize, and I promise, he won't bother you again."

After he left, Tyler returned the photograph to his pocket, then pushed his pie away. He didn't have much of an appetite left. Anna did the same as he took out enough money to pay the bill, then they headed for the cash register at the door.

The silence as they returned to the motel was awkward and strained. He wanted to say something to chase the melancholy look from Anna's eyes, to give her hope and make her feel better, but he didn't have any magic words. All he knew to do was hold her close, and this wasn't the time for that.

Once they reached their room, she took off her coat and immediately turned on the television. He took off his coat, moved his suitcase to the bed and began packing the few items he'd unpacked.

"What are you doing?"

"We're leaving. We'll drive into Butte tonight, and leave for Shady Rock in the morning."

She shut off the TV again and began gathering her own stuff even as she asked, "Why don't we spend the night, then go to Butte in the morning?"

"Because maybe the sheriff is right and Jimmy won't bother us again. Maybe he's as harmless as a kitten without claws. Or maybe he'll get the idea that if he can't scam some money for Lucas, he might be able to collect some for you."

Without acknowledging the threat he'd alluded to, she quickly finished packing, put on her coat and gloves, then waited patiently while he loaded the luggage in the SUV right outside.

When he returned to escort her to the truck, she smiled faintly. "I didn't feel the least bit threatened by him."

"Honestly, Princess, I don't think he is a threat. But I'm not going to take any chances." He gestured for her to leave, but she gently placed her gloved hand against his cheek.

"Even if he were dangerous, I still wouldn't feel threatened, because of you. I know you'll protect me."

He pressed a kiss to her glove. "With my life."

With another small smile, she turned, walked into the night and climbed into the waiting vehicle. Before he could close the door, though, she held out one hand and her smile turned to a grin. "Just as I would protect you, *tesoro mio*. With my life."

Chapter 11

Tuesday morning found Anna and Tyler waiting at the airport in Butte for their early flight to Denver. There, she knew, they would rent a vehicle at the airport and make the several-hours' drive to Shady Rock, where he would question Ursula Chambers, and if they discovered another clue, he would…

Truthfully, she wasn't certain what he would do, besides report it to his superiors. Would he be assigned the task of investigating it himself, and if he was, would he be willing to take her along? Or would he think it time at last to send her back home where he thought she belonged?

He wasn't offering answers, and frankly she wasn't quite up to asking for them, for fear she might not like whatever she heard.

When their flight was announced, they joined the other passengers in line and she turned to embrace Tyler. For practically the first time since they'd left San Sebastian, his shoulder holster was absent, as he'd had no choice but to lock his weapons in their checked bags. Remembering how sexy she'd thought the holster was on their first day, she smiled. These days she found him quite sexy without it. In fact, she found him sexiest wearing nothing at all.

"Wouldn't it be lovely if we found that Lucas had returned to the Chambers ranch?"

"Lovely," he agreed dryly. "But don't get your hopes up. If he had, I feel fairly certain we would have heard from Ursula Chambers."

"Most likely so." She watched as he gave the gate attendants their tickets, then they strolled down the jetway to the waiting aircraft. "What do you know about her?"

"Not much. She's in her mid-thirties, a little taller than you." He grinned. "According to Lorenzo, she's blond-haired, blue-eyed and busty."

Anna debated whether to scowl or smile confidently. She chose the bright smile. "It's a good thing then that you're partial to dark brown curls, brown eyes and breasts perfectly sized for your hands, because you wouldn't appreciate living in the dungeon. Take my word for it."

"Where is that dungeon again?"

"Oh, there are several, depending upon which crime you commit. Coveting busty blondes would put you in the deepest, darkest, dankest of them all."

He located their seats and stepped ahead so she could take the window seat. She fastened her seat belt, tucked her bag between her hip and the outside wall of the plane, then wiggled about a bit. "You know, Papa's planes are much roomier than this."

Tyler burst into laughter as he settled beside her. There was barely enough room between rows for his legs, and his shoulders filled the width of the space he was allotted. "Yes, Your Highness, your father's fleet of high-dollar private jets *are* roomier than a commuter airliner. Welcome to the real world."

"It wasn't a complaint. Simply a comment." She elevated the armrest between them and leaned close to him, and his arm just naturally wrapped around her shoulders. "I'm not spoiled… except for you."

He pressed a kiss to her forehead and murmured a response she was quite certain he didn't intend her to hear. "Good."

Despite the cramped surroundings, Anna found the experience interesting. She'd never been on a commercial jetliner, and she listened avidly to the flight attendant's address on safety features, though she appeared to be the only one doing so, as well as the pilot's brief welcoming speech. They were really very polite and accommodating. Perhaps she would recommend to Mareta that she seek a job in commercial aviation. She certainly wasn't going to fly with Anna anymore.

Of course, once airborne, there were more similarities to her previous experiences flying. The engines droned. The ever-cheery attendants served drinks and snacks. Her restlessness began building. After a time, she rested her head on Tyler's shoulder, closed her eyes and entertained herself with a few favorite fantasies—finding Lucas, safe and sound, and taking him home. Seeing the pure joy on Papa's and Mama's faces when they embraced their son for the first time in months. Introducing them to Tyler, not as one of the Noble Men or Edward Ramsey's son, but as the man she loved and would soon marry. They would hold the wedding on Montebello, with not quite the pomp and circumstance that had surrounded Julia's wedding but more than the quiet ceremony Christina had chosen. Papa would send the Gulfstream—two or three of them if necessary—to bring Tyler's family to the island, and there would be parties and celebrations and stolen moments and long walks on the private beach and quiet nights in her apartment and—

Gradually she became aware that the plane was descending into Denver. Before long they were on the ground, where they collected their luggage and their rental vehicle, another black SUV, and set out for Shady Rock.

"Colorado doesn't appear very different from Montana," she remarked after a time. "What is your favorite state?"

Tyler spared her a glance. "Oh, gee, why don't you ask a tough question? There's only fifty of 'em to choose from."

"Which one? And why?"

"Montana. Because that's where I got to know you."

"Seriously," she commanded.

"The Arizona desert is special," he said at last. "And for mountains, you can't beat the Colorado Rockies...unless your preference runs to the Blue Ridge Mountains in North Carolina. Louisiana's got New Orleans, which is hard to top...but so is the ocean in Oregon or Maine. The rolling green hills of eastern

Oklahoma are nice, and Texas—hell, it's got it all. Then of course—"

She slapped his arm. "I get your point. You can stop now."

"You want me to stop?" he asked innocently. "You get a sudden desire to check out the cargo space back there?"

"There's nothing sudden about my desire for you," she pointed out, then grew serious. "This has been the best adventure of my life. Thank you, Tyler. I'll never forget even one minute of it."

Her words seemed to make him uncomfortable. His jaw tightened, and the amusement that had lightened his emerald gaze seeped away. Inexplicably her own mood darkened as well. She shifted in her seat and directed her gaze out the side window instead.

Truthfully, there was nothing inexplicable about her mood change. Though she hadn't intended it, her words had sounded very much like a prelude to goodbye, and he hadn't made any comment. She didn't require much. A simple "It's not over yet" would have sufficed.

But perhaps, for all practical purposes, it *was* over. Her charade couldn't continue forever, and he hadn't given even the faintest hint that he would like to see her when it was ended.

After a stop for lunch, they reached Shady Rock, then followed Lorenzo's directions to the Chambers ranch. It seemed the nearer they got to the ranch, the worse the roads had deteriorated. When they made the final turn, onto a narrow lane that led directly to the ranch, she gave a small sigh of relief.

The ranch house, along with its buildings, was set in a clearing with forest and pasture all around. There was snow on the ground, a fact she'd begun to take for granted, and smoke curled from the chimney into the clear blue sky. An old dilapidated pickup truck was parked near the rear entrance, and beside it stood a fairly new SUV with the same rental agency sticker on its bumper as the SUV they drove. It appeared it was Ursula Chambers's day for company.

"Can you see your brother living and working here for nearly a year?"

Those were the first words Tyler had spoken in far too long.

She glanced at him and shrugged. "Certainly Lucas has a fine appreciation for the creature comforts," she said. "But if he has amnesia and doesn't remember that...I suppose he could be happy anywhere."

"And could you be happy anywhere?"

"What matters isn't where you are, Tyler, but the people with whom you find yourself. I would imagine even heaven to be a dreary place if you were missing those you love."

For one long moment he simply gazed at her, as if weighing the truth or the sincerity of her answer. Because the look made her uncomfortable, she opened the vehicle door and slid to the ground.

Silently they trekked through the snow to the front porch, where they cleaned their boots, then Tyler knocked. A moment later the door swung open, but it was no busty, blue-eyed blonde who greeted them. Anna stared at her cousin, Desmond, who stared back guiltily, as if he'd been caught with his hand where it didn't belong. Swiftly he attempted to cover his momentary shock, offering them a warm friendly smile that, despite best efforts, was neither warm nor friendly.

"Anna. Ramsey. What a surprise meeting you here."

"I should think so," she replied, since she was supposed to be with Christina in Billings and Tyler, last Desmond would have known, was in Montana. Certainly Tyler's side trip to Colorado had been approved by his superiors, and almost certainly her father and Lorenzo had been so informed, but Desmond wasn't privy to all of the king's business—a fact he'd found annoying in the past. "What are you doing here?"

Before he could answer, a throaty feminine voice came from around the corner, and an instant later the busty blue-eyed blonde appeared. "Who is it, Des?"

Ursula Chambers, Anna presumed. While the blue eyes might be natural, the blond hair had received help from a colorist's chemicals and the bust...definitely chemicals of another sort. A great deal of them. If Anna carried such weight on her chest, she would surely suffer from back aches, but Ursula seemed to have no problem whatsoever navigating.

"I'm Tyler Ramsey, and this is Anna. Can we come in?"

"Of course," Ursula said. "Please, come in and warm up by the fire."

Clearly she didn't recognize Anna's name or face. Though she'd found it a pleasant change to go unrecognized these past few weeks, Anna found herself wanting to give the woman the full royal treatment. More than that, though, she wanted to know what Desmond was doing there and why he seemed so cozy with the Chambers woman, and she especially wanted to know why all the tiny hairs on the back of her neck were standing on end.

With a nudge from Tyler, she stepped across the threshold, then followed Ursula into the living room. Desmond was left to close the door, then bring up the rear.

"What can I help you folks with?" Ursula asked, perching on the arm of an overstuffed chair.

The fire on the grate was little more than coals. A faded quilt provided a splash of color on the braided rug in front of the fireplace, and it nearly hid the lacy crimson bra half under it. Anna glanced from Ursula to Desmond, standing across the room from the woman. Did he appear a bit hastily-put-together? Was his hair in need of combing, and was that faint color across his jaw lipstick? Had he and the woman—

Heat warmed Anna's cheeks. She now knew more about him and his activities than she wanted to know. It made her voice taut as she repeated her earlier question. "Why are you here, Desmond?"

Once again Ursula interrupted before he could answer. "You know these people, Des?"

His smile was taut. "Anna is my cousin, and Ramsey is working for her father."

Anna felt an odd need to deny his words, but the truth was, he was as much her cousin as Lorenzo and his older brother, Max. After all, it was their fathers' blood that connected them, so what did it matter that Desmond didn't share a mother with Lorenzo and Max?

What mattered, she admitted, was that he was here in Colorado when he shouldn't have been, and that look of guilt when he'd seen them at the door. What especially mattered was that he had become intimately involved with the woman who appeared to be their best chance for finding Lucas.

Most of all, it mattered that instinct told her there was something not quite right here.

"I could ask you the same question, Anna," Desmond said at last. "Uncle Marcus seems to be under the impression that you're in Billings visiting your sister. I'm sure he would be very curious as to how you wound up in Colorado with Ramsey."

She refused to be intimidated. She could handle Papa—it was a skill with which she'd been born—and any concerns he might have about her time with Tyler would surely be alleviated when she told him she loved Tyler. Whether he loved her back, whether he chose to never see her again, she would always love him.

"You could ask the same question, Desmond," she said coolly, "but I am under no obligation to answer your questions. You, unfortunately, cannot say the same about *my* questions."

Anger turned Desmond's blood hot, but he kept it well-hidden. Eighteen years of being *almost* a royal but not quite, *almost* a fully accepted part of the family but not quite, had given him plenty of practice. Feeling nothing but derision and hatred for his worthless little cousin, he reached deep inside himself to find calm. "Ursula, would you be so kind as to give us a moment alone?"

"Of course. I'll fix some coffee." She scrambled to her feet and left the room.

Hands behind his back, he strolled to the hall door to make certain that she had, in fact, gone to the kitchen. He wouldn't put it past the little bitch to hang outside the door and eavesdrop. But the hallway was empty, and the sounds of water running and cabinets opening came from the kitchen.

Standing there where he could see, Desmond faced their guests and prepared to lie. "How could I not come, Anna?" he asked smoothly. "This ranch is the only substantive clue to Lucas's whereabouts. Your father has done all he can, such as sending people—" he gestured toward Ramsey "—to search for Lucas. Total strangers as well as friends are looking for him. Lorenzo has gotten involved. Even you have. How could I stay home in San Sebastian and do nothing? Your papa is so anxious for news. It broke my heart to watch him face each day with less and less hope. He's not a young man, and as much as he loves his girls, his son holds a special place in his heart. It's killing him to watch and wait and hear nothing. And so I came. Perhaps I can't truly help, but on the other hand, perhaps the others have missed something that I, who have known Lucas so many years, might catch.''

Of course, knowing Lucas all those years didn't count for much when the two of them had never even remotely resembled friends. Though there had never been any question of his rightful place in the Sebastiani family, Desmond had known from the beginning that Lucas neither liked him nor wanted him around. For a time he'd written it off to the similarity in their ages— Lucas was only a year younger, an immature boy who might not want to share his attention with anyone else—but eventually he'd realized his cousin didn't trust him.

And as it turned out, Lucas had been right to distrust him, he thought, keeping back his sardonic smile through force of will.

That boy's going to be the death of you, his stepfather used to warn his mother. The old bastard had been partially right. Desmond *was* going to be the death of somebody.

His dear cousin Lucas.

The future king would be dead.

Long live the new king, his dear half brother Lorenzo.

Tyler wouldn't claim to actually know Desmond Caruso. Their paths had passed a number of times on Montebello—in town, in clubs, at palace functions. He knew enough about Caruso to know he didn't want to know him better, and finding him there with Ursula Chambers just reinforced that notion. He was a little too smooth, too cagey, too...hell, Tyler didn't know exactly. He just knew he didn't trust him.

As far as that went, he didn't trust Ursula Chambers, either. There was a gleam in her eyes that set all of Tyler's senses on alert. She was an ambitious woman, and he was damn sure something about this whole search had set her highest ambitions in motion.

They were sitting at the kitchen table, four untouched cups of coffee between them. "Ms. Chambers—"

"Oh, please..." She laughed. "Call me Ursula." But the laugh was a touch too phony, the graciousness a degree overdone.

"I understand you had a hand working here at the ranch by the name of Joe, who disappeared not long ago. Have you heard anything from him?" Though he suspected Desmond had told the woman that they believed Joe was the missing prince, he wasn't going to be the one to let the cat out of the bag if Desmond hadn't.

"No, I'm afraid I haven't. I do hope everything's all right. He was a bit on the odd side, I admit—very private, kept to himself, very much a loner—but...cowboys tend to be on the odd side, if you ask me. I think it's the job—the hours and the work and the isolation. I love being out here in the middle of nowhere, but it takes a special breed to fully appreciate it."

Funny. Tyler would have bet next year's salary that she was happiest in the middle of a big bustling city. She didn't strike him as the type able to endure solitude or her own company for long.

"You know, Tyler—may I call you Tyler?" She laid her hand over his on the table and batted her big baby blues. When he nodded, she gave his hand a squeeze before releasing it. "You know, Tyler, a person never would have guessed from talking to Joe that so many people would be so interested in him. I mean, according to him, he was pretty much alone in the world—didn't have any family or any past that he wanted to talk about, at least. In the whole time he was here, no one paid him any mind, and then he leaves—which cowboys tend to do, you know—and suddenly people care. Why is that?"

"I'd like to think that *somebody* would care about all of us if we disappeared," he replied easily. "What about your other employees? Any of them friends with Joe?"

She shook her head. "I only have three other hands, and they're all married. Two of them live in those little cabins out back. The third one has a place a few miles from here."

"And where did Joe live?"

"In the bunkhouse. He was a hard worker. I hated to lose him. But like I said, cowboys tend to move on down the road."

Granted, Tyler hadn't conducted too many interviews, and he was probably missing some of the subtler nuances, but he would have to be deaf and blind to not know that something didn't add up. Maybe it was finding Desmond there, shacked up with the woman, or maybe it had more to do with the fact that he couldn't shake the feeling he was watching an actress rehearse her latest role. Ursula was playing Friendly Female Rancher for all she was worth, but it didn't quite ring true. It played more like Friendly Female Rancher as written by someone who'd never actually met one.

Tyler was no expert on the role, but he was pretty damn sure that a woman who kept a place like this afloat, even with help, would have done more than her share of hard work and would show a fair amount of wear and tear. Ursula's skin was too smooth to have spent any time at all in the elements, she was too comfortable in clothes too expensive for the role, there wasn't one callus on her hands, and he doubted those long red fake nails would last long at all when working cattle or horses.

"What about women?" Anna asked abruptly. She'd been coolly silent since her conversation with Desmond—which, co-incidentally, had also felt like a play. Concerned Cousin and Nephew wasn't a role Desmond could pull off with great success, since his sincerity was as phony as Ursula's warmth.

For whatever reason, the question momentarily stumped Ursula. She gave the princess a blank look, blinked slowly and asked, "What do you mean?"

Anna shrugged. "Did he have a girlfriend? Was there anyone special in town? Did he date?"

Good question. Lucas was a ladies' man. He probably hadn't been without female companionship for longer than a week or two since he turned sixteen. He loved women, and they loved him in return.

Ursula's gaze flickered to Desmond—*Why?* Tyler wondered—then she gave a helpless little smile and shrug. "Not that I know of. He spent his working hours here, and most of his free hours, too. He rarely went into town."

Truth or lie? If they accepted it as truth, they might miss any number of people who knew Lucas better than his boss. On the other hand, maybe he'd had no reason to go into town to look for companionship. Lucas had always had a special weakness for busty blondes, and Ursula obviously had had no qualms about jumping into the sack with Desmond. Presumably a woman got as lonely out here as a man did.

"You don't know how much I wish I could tell you something that would help you locate Joe," Ursula said. "I do worry about him so. I considered him a good friend and I hate to think of him out there on his own and maybe in trouble somewhere."

Once again she took Tyler's hand. Across the table, Anna's gaze narrowed, and on her right, so did Desmond's. Wisely Tyler pulled away from her and laced his fingers together. "You wouldn't mind if we talk to your other employees and have a look around the bunkhouse, would you?"

Again her gaze went to Desmond before she answered. "Of course I wouldn't mind, except there's no one here to talk to today. I saw both hands and their wives drive off a few hours ago, and the third one left as soon as his work was done this morning. They were all going into the city for a rodeo, and they won't be back until late."

"Oh. Well, how about the bunkhouse?"

Her agreement came so quickly that Tyler knew there would be nothing to find. "Sure—though, of course, that was one of the first things I did after Joe left. Let me get the key for you."

While she rummaged through a drawer, Anna returned to the living room to get their coats. About the time he finished zipping his, Ursula held up the key with a triumphant smile. "I hope you won't mind if I wait here," she said. "I'm recovering from a nasty flu, and I'm trying to avoid unnecessary time in the cold."

"Want to come along, Desmond?" Tyler asked.

The other man shook his head. "I believe I'll wait here as well."

So the two of them could compare notes and share suggestions?

Tyler took the key, then followed Anna outside. They'd made it halfway to the bunkhouse when she finally spoke. "Liars."

His opinion exactly.

"I wouldn't trust her as far as I could throw her. Fortunately for her, if she landed on her front, she would bounce."

Certain they were being watched from the kitchen window, Tyler used the unsure footing as an excuse to take her arm. "Oh, come on, Princess. Have you never wanted to be top-heavy or have your chest enter a room two minutes before you did?"

She gave a haughty sniff. "Only a man could appreciate such excess."

"Ursula apparently likes it."

"She did it for the men who like it."

He feigned surprise. "You mean, they're not real?"

"About as real as Desmond's concern for my brother," she muttered as they carefully climbed the three steps to the bunkhouse door. As soon as they stepped inside and closed the door, the feeling of hostile gazes boring into Tyler's back passed.

The bunkhouse consisted of one large room and a bathroom, and it was damn near as cold inside as it was out. It lived up to its name, with three rows of rickety bunks lined up along the walls, along with a wood-burning stove, three ancient army surplus trunks and a row of wall lockers. One corner of the room served as living space, with a sofa, a couple of chairs and a low table that had once held a TV, judging from the rabbit-ears antenna discarded on its dust-covered surface. Another table held a couple issues of outdated magazines, and that was it. All the contents of the room in seventy-five words or less.

Only one of the six bunks was made, the one nearest the stove, with worn sheets and a couple of wool army blankets. The pillow was the only thing that wasn't way beyond its prime. He would guess it had been purchased relatively recently and hadn't seen much use. Because the bunk's intended occupant had been spending his nights elsewhere?

While he checked out the magazines, Anna went to the sleeping area. She opened trunks and wall lockers, got down on her knees and looked under each of the three bunks, then began unmaking the bed. He left her to it while he went into the bathroom—small, drab and offering nothing but dust.

"Tyler!"

Quickly he returned to the main room, where he found her standing next to the torn-up bed, clutching a bit of blue something or other to her chest. When he approached, she offered it for his inspection. Her hands trembled, and her lashes were wet with tears. "Look, Tyler! It's Lucas's cap! I know it is—I've never seen another like it! See the logo? And the blue? We teased him that no one could ever miss seeing him coming when he wore this on the slopes. Oh, Tyler, Joe *is* my brother, and he was here, alive and well! He's alive, Tyler!"

He took the ski cap from her and examined it. It was black, with a wide electric-blue band, and in the center of the band was a complex geometric shape using every blindingly bright color in the spectrum. He didn't doubt her identification for an instant. God knows, he'd spent more than his share of time on the slopes, and he'd never seen another like it.

"Oh, Tyler…" Anna touched it tenderly. "For the past year, I've told myself that Lucas wasn't dead. I convinced myself that I would somehow *feel* it if he were. Even when the authorities seemed to be working as hard to take away our hope as we were to hold on to it, I *knew* he was alive. But…" Her voice softened to little more than a whisper. "There were times I doubted. I thought perhaps I simply wanted it to be true so desperately that I was refusing to accept the facts. I thought…maybe he *was* dead, and that explained why no one had ever seen him, why he'd never contacted us, why he was still missing after more than a year. But he's *alive!* My brother is out there somewhere alive, and we have to find him! We have to bring him home!"

Clutching the cap, Tyler wrapped his arms around her, pressed her head to his chest and stroked her hair. "We're gonna do that, Annie. I swear, we are. Now that we know for sure, the king will put more men on the case and, I promise, we'll find him."

He held her a long time, until the trembling stopped and her breathing calmed—held her and considered the next step in the search. It had been simple enough before they'd come to the

Chambers ranch, and finding Desmond there had made it even simpler. But he hated it all the same.

"So what do we do now?" she asked at last, her voice muffled against his jacket.

He squeezed his eyes shut for a moment, breathed deeply of all her scents, then put her away from him. Gently he dried the tears from her cheeks, then tucked a curl behind her ear before finding the courage to say, "Now we send you back to San Sebastian."

"*No!* Tyler, you can't—"

He gave her a look that stopped her protest before it got much of a start. "Do you trust me, Annie?"

"With my heart and my life."

"Then trust me on this, please." He seated her on the bunk that had belonged to her brother, nudged the mattress back into place, then sat down facing her. "I know he's family, but...I don't trust Desmond. His being here doesn't make sense. This search has been going on to some degree for more than a year. He's never been a part of it and never shown any interest in being part of it. Why now? Why all this sudden concern for Lucas now that it appears he's alive?"

"They've never been close," she replied softly. "But Desmond *is* close to Papa, and has become even more so since Lucas's disappearance."

Maybe, Tyler thought. Frankly, he found it difficult to imagine anyone developing a real closeness with Caruso. The man reminded him of a cold-blooded snake. He was too smooth, too charming, too...surface. If forced to venture a guess, he would say no one on Montebello truly knew Caruso, not even Lorenzo, his half brother and best friend.

"Whatever's going on with Desmond, the bottom line is he *shouldn't* be here, and he damn well shouldn't be shacking up with Ursula Chambers."

Despite her serious mood, Anna smiled faintly. "Shacking up? Is that what we've been doing these weeks past?"

Heat filled Tyler's cheeks as he scowled. "No, it isn't. Well...sort of. But it's different between us." At the very least, she was fond of him, and as for him…hell, he loved her. Plain and simple.

Maybe enough to give up his job and his best shot at earning his family's respect for her.

Maybe even enough to risk finding out that she *didn't* love him.

"So that's another of your English slang phrases that I shouldn't be wearing on a T-shirt, yes?"

"Yes, Your Highness, it is," he said dryly. "Now stop trying to distract me. We were talking about sending you home."

"But I don't want to go."

"I want you to. I need you to."

She gave a shake of her head that made her curls bounce. "I can help you. After all, it was I who thought to look under the mattress and subsequently found the cap."

"Yes, you can help. And you can help most by going home…and asking, commanding or ordering Desmond to escort you there."

He knew from her expression that she'd grasped his point immediately. If Caruso was accompanying her back to Montebello, he couldn't be here in Colorado doing whatever it was he'd come there to do. He couldn't scheme with Ursula or interfere with the search for Lucas in any way. Still, she made a halfhearted effort to be stubborn. "And what if he refuses?"

"He can't refuse, and he knows it. All it would take is one phone call from you to your father, and the king would order him to do as you request. Frankly, I don't think he wants you making that phone call." For whatever reason, Caruso had lied to the king and everyone else about the purpose and the destination of his trip to the States—Tyler was certain of that. If anyone in the palace had known he was going to Colorado, his movements would have been tracked, merely as a matter of record, and Tyler would have been notified.

"So you want me to return home and thus ensure that Desmond is out of the way here."

He grinned. "Exactly."

"Do you think…" Her expression turned troubled, and guilt darkened her eyes. "Do you think he means harm to Lucas?"

Had Caruso gotten too cozy in his newly developed friendship with King Marcus since Lucas's disappearance? Would he protect his position at any cost? Could he possibly be stupid enough, foolish enough, reckless enough, to try to remove any competition for that position—even the king's only son?

It certainly wouldn't be the first time one family member had turned on another, especially when power or wealth was involved. But it was too serious an accusation to make, too dangerous a conclusion to reach, without something more to go on than a feeling that things weren't right.

"I honestly don't know what he's doing, Annie. Maybe I'm being paranoid. Maybe he truly is just trying to help. But we can't take any chances. Getting him away from here and back to San Sebastian seems the best course of action to me."

"And what will you do?"

"I've got to talk to the local sheriff about the man Lorenzo caught trying to break into Ursula's house. That may or may not require some follow-up. Then I'll report in and see what the bosses want me to do."

"So…" Anna gazed at her hands, clasped in her lap. "You may go from here to your next assignment."

He found it easier to look at her hands, too. "Maybe. Or maybe back into training. I don't know."

"You… We… We, uh, might…" After a moment, she drew a deep breath and squared her shoulders. "Very well," she said, looking and sounding every bit the cool, collected princess. "Shall we return to the house and break the news to Desmond that he's cutting his trip short?"

"In a moment. There's one more thing I need to do first." Abruptly he took her in his arms, lowered her to the bed, stretched out with her and kissed her. It was hard, hungry, a desperate attempt to silence the questions echoing in his head. What if this was the last time he could ever hold her? What if his job kept him away from Montebello? What if she didn't want him there? What if he was nothing more to her than a pleasant aspect of her American adventure? What if she forgot him and married one of her princes or kings?

What if he told her he loved her and she didn't love him back?

What if she did?

When finally he released her, somehow he'd wound up on his back and she was lying on top of him. He was hard, and she was soft and hot where her hips rubbed him. Her lips were swollen, giving her a well-kissed look, and her eyes seemed twice their size, filled with a sadness that made him ache inside.

He recognized a goodbye when he saw it.

He released her slowly—his fingers didn't want to let her go any more than his heart did—and she sat up, then stood up, putting the width of the room between them. As he sat up, she combed her fingers through her hair, straightened her coat, avoided looking at him. "We should go."

"Yes," he agreed, even though the last thing he wanted was to walk out that door.

She walked to the door, her back to him, and waited. "Of course we won't tell Desmond and Ms. Chambers about finding the ski cap."

"Of course not." He opened the door for her, then closed and locked it behind him. When he reached to steady her as they descended the snow-covered steps, she none too subtly moved away.

Once again he felt the force of Caruso's and Ursula's gazes as they approached the house. By the time they walked into the kitchen, though, the couple was sitting at the table, as if they'd remained there the entire time.

"Find anything?" Ursula asked idly.

"No, we didn't. We won't impose on you any longer." Tyler turned his attention to Caruso. "Anna has decided to return to Montebello this evening, which naturally requires an escort. You wouldn't mind doing that for her father, now would you?" He said it in a conversational way, as if it were a sure thing, as if Caruso couldn't possibly refuse. And even though suspicion flared momentarily in his dark eyes, it disappeared immediately and was replaced by eagerness.

"I would be honored to escort my charming cousin home," he said, giving her an oily smile. "Between my job and the demands on her time, we spend so little time together. This will give us a chance to talk."

Anna smiled politely. "I'll look forward to it."

"Then why don't we get started?" Tyler asked. "I'll see you to the airport in Denver."

"That won't be necessary," Caruso began, but Tyler cut him off.

"Oh, I think it is. I would be remiss in my duties if I didn't personally put the two of you on a chartered jet headed east." And he knew just who to call—his brother, Jake—to arrange a last-minute international chartered flight. By the time they drove back to Denver International, Jake would have a Dassault Falcon waiting. It was the next best thing to the Gulfstream, and it would have a crew whose loyalty was to the Ramseys, who would make sure Anna's snake of a cousin didn't try anything and would deliver her safely home.

Since he had no choice but to agree, Caruso tried to do so graciously. "Very well, then. Shall I follow you, or vice versa?"

"If you know the way, we'll follow you."

Caruso smiled. "I always know where I'm going. Excuse me while I get my coat."

Tyler, Anna and Ursula stood around the kitchen table, none of them speaking. Anna looked about a million miles distant, and Ursula looked as if she were trying to determine her next move. When Caruso returned wearing his coat and gloves, she offered him her hand.

"Your visit this afternoon was a pleasure, Desmond," she said. "And Tyler, yours, too. I wish you luck in finding Joe. If you have any more questions, feel free to come back and ask them, Anna."

Though the reasonably polite thing to do would be head to the SUV and let Ursula and Caruso say goodbye in private, Tyler wasn't feeling the least bit polite. After all, it was a sure bet he wasn't going to get any time alone with Anna once they reached the airport. The goodbye she'd said in the cabin was going to be all he got for the time being.

Maybe forever.

* * *

Ursula watched from the living room window until the two vehicles were out of sight, then turned away. Thanks to Ramsey and that little twit Anna—what a prissy thing she was!—Desmond had been forced to leave his suitcase behind. It was upstairs in the guest room where they'd spent the better part of the past two days, making wicked love and wickeder plans. She wouldn't waste time searching through it, though—had, in fact, already done that the first night, while he slept. All she'd found was a small fortune in clothing and damn near as many toiletries as she packed when she traveled. Desmond Caruso was a vain man.

Being a vain woman, she didn't hold it against him.

Instead she went down the hall to Jessica's office, sat down at the desk and turned on the computer. Though he'd confided a great deal in her, Desmond had never told her exactly who he was—not that she'd pushed it. Finding out things like that was what the Internet was for.

Of course, she'd kept two rather major secrets of her own. In all their talking and scheming, there'd been no mention of Jessica, or the baby she carried. Desmond's plans involved getting rid of Prince Lucas in order to slip someone else into his place. She didn't believe he would be at all happy to learn that the prince had a child who would be the rightful heir to the throne after his father's death, and she didn't intend to give him advance notice.

That baby had a fabulous future ahead, and she fully intended to be at his side.

Every step of the way.

Just as Jake had promised, the Falcon was waiting at the general aviation terminal when they arrived. Tyler sorted Anna's luggage from his own, but when he started to pick up the bags, she reached for them, too. "You're not my porter," she reminded him, her wan smile an indication of how little she felt like teasing.

"I'll carry your bags, Annie." Gently he removed her hands from the straps. "These guys—" he nodded toward the crew "—are all armed and well trained to take care of you. If Jeff there in the middle isn't the most gracious flight attendant, it's because he's a bodyguard instead. You might want to show Caruso how your weeks in America among the common folk have changed you by inviting Jeff to watch movies with you in the cabin or whatever.''

"I will.''

"I put your brother's cap in this bag.'' He tapped the larger of her suitcases. "See that it gets turned over to Lorenzo and no one else, all right?''

"I will.''

He turned the luggage over to the crew, who stowed it, then returned to the truck, where Anna still waited. His smile was unsteady and kept slipping away no matter how hard he tried "I guess this is goodbye.''

"Thank you for everything. And I'll tell Papa you were a most professional bodyguard.''

This was probably a good time to tell her that she and Christina could quit lying now; Papa knew all about her adventure. But he didn't want his last few minutes with her colored with anger, disappointment or worse, and Desmond was waiting impatiently in the jet's doorway. "I, uh… Thank you.''

"For what?''

He shrugged. He didn't have words for most of what he wanted to say, and didn't have the nerve for half of it. "Be careful.''

"I will.'' She started to turn away, then swung back around and faced him once more. His chest grew tight, and in spite of the frigid temperatures, he felt heat spreading outward through his body. *"Mi manchi. Mi somo inamorata di te.''*

"What does that mean?''

For a moment she simply gazed at him, then translated. "Be careful. Stay safe.''

Disappointment shafted through him. He'd thought… maybe…the way she'd looked so serious…

He forced one of the grins she considered so arrogant. "Always, Your Highness. Always.''

With a haunting smile, she turned away again, this time for good, and boarded the jet without a look back. Tyler tried to make himself get in the SUV and leave—after all, he had a long drive back to Shady Rock, and he was already tired from the traveling he'd done that day, and the very last thing in the world he needed was to watch her fly away out of his life—but he couldn't move. He watched the crew board, close the air stairs and secure the hatch. He watched as they taxied away from the hangar, and he continued to watch until finally, in the distance, the jet appeared, a bright mix of colors, in the sky.

Feeling more lost than he'd ever been, he drove back to Shady Rock, where he talked to the sheriff about the attempted break-in weeks ago at the Chambers ranch. Though Lorenzo had stopped the man from gaining access to the house, in the struggle he'd knocked the guy unconscious and his return to Montebello had prevented him from gaining any further information on him.

There wasn't much more to learn, the sheriff told Tyler. The guy's name was Kevin Weber, he was short, dark and olive-skinned, and no one had seen him since he'd posted bail and disappeared. No one had a clue where he'd come from, where he'd gone or how he'd chosen the Chambers ranch to rob. It was obviously not an overly prosperous place—not many ranches in that area were, what with all their capital tied up in their livestock. Of course, there were always people around who'd rather steal ten dollars than work to earn fifty.

As he stood to leave the sheriff's office, the older man clapped him on the shoulder. "You look like you could use a big thick sirloin and a soft cushy bed."

He was both hungry and tired, Tyler admitted, though who cared about sleeping when you slept alone? "Is there somewhere around here where I can find both?"

"Yep, there's a motel and restaurant side by side, just down the street."

He nodded in acknowledgment, then asked one more question. "I went out to the Chambers place earlier, just to ask a few questions and have a look around. What do you think of her?"

"The ranch has been in the family for years. She loves it and works hard to keep it going—and take my word for it, it's a damn hard job." The sheriff shrugged. "She's well liked and respected around here."

The opinion certainly didn't mesh with his own. Maybe he *was* just paranoid. Maybe the job had already gotten to him. Maybe he was that poorly suited to it, because he damn well wouldn't have suspected any of that about Ursula. Of course, hadn't he thought this afternoon that the role she was playing for them wasn't the real her? Maybe she'd felt intimidated, or had been pretending to be the kind of woman she thought would appeal to Caruso. Either one would explain why he and the sheriff could be talking about two different people.

"Thanks for your time. If you hear anything about Weber..."

"I'll pass it on."

The sun had already set by the time he left the building, and the temperature had dropped with it. Dinner and a room for the night were his first priorities, he decided as he climbed into the truck. *Then* he could sleep.

Maybe.

If Anna let him.

The jangle of the telephone on the nightstand jerked Tyler from a restless sleep. Feeling as if he'd dozed only moments, he flung out one arm to locate it, knocked it off the table, then blindly followed the cord to the phone, then the receiver. "Yeah."

"Rise and shine, little brother. It's afternoon here, which means it's morning there. Too late to be sacked out like some kind of unemployed bum."

"Go to hell," he muttered, then let the phone fall away from his ear. He felt like he'd gone ten rounds with Mohammed Ali and lost every one of them. Nope, forget Ali—he hadn't felt this bad since he'd been knocked on his ass by a bottle of Everclear back when he was in college. He'd been sick as a dog and hung over for a week, and he'd sworn he would never do it again if only God would let him die.

Unfortunately, the phone hadn't fallen so far that Kyle's loudly pitched voice wouldn't carry. "Jeez, Ty, how much sleep do you need to be sociable? You're acting more like our old man than my kid brother.''

It took a supreme effort to get the receiver back up to his ear. ''I was up late driving Monday night. I flew to Denver early Tuesday morning.'' And, thanks to Anna, got precious little sleep in between. ''I drove more than six hours yesterday, and it's—'' he pried open one eye to check the clock on the nightstand, and his voice climbed an octave ''—four in the freaking morning. What do you want?''

''I thought you'd like to know that Princess Anna and Desmond arrived home an hour or two ago, and the king and queen are tickled pink with the ski cap.''

Tyler raised his free hand to rub the ache settling in his chest. *That* was the real reason he felt so damn sick this morning. Not the travel, the lack of sleep or the three—or five—beers he'd had before bed.

Anna.

He missed her, and he wasn't sure he could live without her.

''You there, bud?''

''Yeah, I'm here.'' He pushed himself up higher, then stuffed a pillow behind his back. ''How'd you find me?''

''The princess said you were going to talk to the sheriff in Shady Rock. Since you didn't check in with anyone last night, I called him, and he said he'd sent you to a motel in town. Since there's only one…''

''Damn, you should've been a mercenary,'' Tyler said sarcastically even as he wondered how Anna was. Had she slept at all on the long flight home? Had she missed having him right there at her side? Was she glad to be home and anxious to get back into her royal routine?

Was she eager to put her adventure behind her?

''Have you figured out what the hell Caruso was *really* doing at the ranch with Ursula Chambers?'' he asked to distract himself.

''Not yet. He's sticking to the same story—he wanted to do something because of his great concern for the king.'' There was a moment's silence, then Kyle cautiously went on. ''We haven't quite figured out what the hell Princess Anna was doing there with you, either.''

"Ask the king."

"All this time, we thought she was in Billings with her sister and—"

"*Ask* the king," Tyler repeated, his jaw clenching.

There was another silence, then Kyle spoke again. Damn thing about being the oldest brother—he thought he had a God-given right to stick his nose into everyone else's business. "That woman you met up in Montana...the one you were trying to decide whether it was okay to go to bed with...tell me that wasn't Princess Anna."

Tyler didn't tell him it was none of his damned business— that went without saying. He didn't tell him anything at all. And that was enough.

"Hell, Ty... You do make some amazing choices. What're you gonna do now?"

"That's a good question," he replied, deliberately twisting it. "I've followed orders. Where do I go from here?"

"I meant about Princess An—I guess you knew what I meant, huh?" Kyle cleared his throat, then asked, "What did you find out about the burglar?"

Dutifully Tyler repeated what little the sheriff had been able to pass on about Kevin Weber, then waited.

"Let me talk to Lorenzo about this, then I'll get back to you. Don't go back to sleep. I'll make it as quick as possible."

Tyler agreed, then hung up and stared into the darkness. Kyle had let him off easy this time, but that wouldn't last. He knew how to pester the deepest secrets out of anyone—another oldest-child trick, Tyler thought. He had never known how to keep Kyle from worming out the truth about everything, until now— make the truth so damn painful you think you're gonna die. Then you could keep it to yourself.

The phone rang again less than fifteen minutes later. Kyle skipped the greeting and went straight to the point. "Max Ryker, Lorenzo's brother, is a private investigator in the United States. The king's going to ask him to find this Weber guy and find out what he can tell us. He wants you to stay where you are—

at least in Colorado. You can find a nicer place if you want, as long as you let us know where. And Max will contact you as soon as he gets there."

"Okay. Can I go back to sleep now?"

"One other thing. King Marcus said to extend his sincere gratitude to you for taking such good care of his daughter." Kyle practically snorted. "He doesn't have a clue, does he?"

Tyler ended the conversation the same way it had started. "Go to hell," he said. And then he hung up.

"I thought you would sleep the afternoon away. It's still early morning on Colorado time."

Anna glanced up at her father and smiled. "I slept on the plane. I'm quite rested." She slid to the side, and he joined her on the marble bench where she had a lovely view of the palace and the gardens in one direction and the city and the sea in the other. If pressed, though, she wouldn't be able to answer which direction she'd been looking before Papa had joined her. Inward, perhaps—or outward. All the way to Colorado.

"How was your vacation?"

"Lovely. Montana is a wonderful place. I understand why Christina loves it there."

"You and your sister got caught up on all your visiting?"

Rather than tell an outright lie, she smiled. "Sisters never get completely caught up, Papa."

"She and Jack must have shown you a good time."

"I had an exceptional time."

"Lovely, wonderful, exceptional... For a woman who uses such superlatives so freely, you certainly look down, *figlia mia*." He chucked her under the chin, the way he'd done when she was a small child and climbed onto his lap for hugs. "Is there anything you want to share with your papa?"

Fearing she couldn't say a word without giving in to the tears that burned behind her eyes, she smiled brightly and shook her head.

"Nothing at all? Then perhaps you would like to tell me how you wound up in Colorado with your cousin when I distinctly recall sending you off to Montana to your sister."

His look was so knowing that Anna realized he already possessed at least the basic details of her grand adventure. Had Tyler told him? Christina? Or had he discovered the information from other sources?

Whatever his source, he didn't wait for confirmation from her. "Or perhaps you'll share with me your opinion of your bodyguard. No? Then I'll share with you the news that he's meeting with your cousin, Max, in a day or two. He'll fill Max in on everything that's happened so far, and then Max will take over this part of the investigation."

Anna clenched her jaw to keep from crying out that she didn't care what Max did—cousin or not, she hardly knew him—and from asking about Tyler. Where would he go? What would he do? Would he come and see her, or would he be grateful she was out of his life?

But because she was determined to keep her misery to herself, and her father was waiting for a response, she smiled again, albeit sadly. "That's nice, Papa."

"We will find Lucas, *bambina*."

Of course they would. Tyler had said so, and he wouldn't lie.

He'd also said his job was the most important thing in his life. That he had no time for distractions. That she was a distraction. That a relationship between them was wrong.

And he wouldn't lie.

Turning to her father, she burst into tears. Just as he'd done countless times when she was young, he lifted her onto his lap, wrapped his arms around her and patted her soothingly. "There, there, Anna *bella*, it's all right. Everything will be all right. I am the king, and that makes it so, eh?"

She wept as if her heart were breaking—wept as she'd never wept before. When finally her tears ran out, Papa's shirt was soaked and her eyes were puffy, her nose stuffy.

"Do you love Tyler so very much?" her father asked quietly.

She didn't wonder how he knew—didn't even care. "Yes."

"I shall command his presence—"

"No, Papa! If he comes, it must be because he loves me—not because he was commanded."

Her father's dark eyes lighted with mischief. "Then I shall

command him to love you…though how anyone could *not* love you is beyond me."

"Please…don't do a thing. This must be between Tyler and me."

"I can't bear to see you unhappy."

She wiped her eyes, then sniffed. "I appreciate your concern, Papa, but whether together or apart, Tyler and I must deal with our problems ourselves. We created them. Now we must live with them."

On Wednesday, Tyler moved to a hotel in Denver and restlessly awaited the arrival of the king's nephew on Thursday. He'd never met Max Ryker Sebastiani, but he'd picked up bits of information about him in the course of his training. Max was the middle of three sons produced by King Marcus's younger brother, Antonio. Desmond was the eldest, Lorenzo the youngest. Being the first-born legitimate son meant that Max inherited his father's title upon his death, though it didn't appear to mean much to him. After a stint in the Royal Montebellan Army, he'd dropped the Sebastiani name and come to the U.S., where he'd opened his own private investigations firm. Rumor was, he'd wanted to distance himself from the royal family and had done a damn good job of it.

Ryker had booked a room in the same hotel Tyler was staying at, and they'd arranged to meet in the main bar soon after his arrival. Tyler got there first, choosing a table where he could see the entrance, ordered a beer and waited.

When this assignment was completed, he would have a week off before reporting back to the Middle East for further training. When he'd heard the news, for one moment he'd hoped he would be returning to Montebello. Finding out that he wouldn't had been so damn disappointing that he'd decided he might never hope for anything again.

He hadn't decided yet what he would do with the time off. Maybe visit his parents in Arizona. Maybe see how his only nephew and sister-in-law were doing. Or, hell, maybe he would just stay there in the hotel until it was time to report. At this point, nothing much really mattered.

"Ramsey?"

Shaking himself out of his morose thoughts, Tyler looked up to find an older, tougher version of Lorenzo standing beside the table. With a nod, he shook hands, then gestured toward a chair. "Have a seat."

Ryker wasted no time on small talk, but got right down to business. Within a half hour, Tyler had given him every last piece of information he had on the search for Lucas, Ursula Chambers and Kevin Weber, and they were both ready to call it quits. Tyler had gone so far as to pay his tab and head for the door before he suddenly turned back.

"Do you speak Italian?"

"No more than I have to," Ryker said, then shrugged. "The Sebastiani family has plenty of good Italian blood flowing through their veins. Along with it, we got a love of Italian food and at least a passable command of the language. You have something you need translated?"

"Yeah. My pronunciation may not be the best, but it's something like *Misono inamorata deti.*" He stumbled over the unfamiliar words. "I think it has something to do with being safe."

Ryker laughed. "If someone said those words to *me,* I'd consider them pretty damn dangerous. I guess it depends on your point of view."

"What do they mean?"

"'I love you.'"

Tyler's room key slipped through his fingers and clattered on the table as he stared at him. "No... There must be... That can't..."

"I can't think of anything having to do with being safe that would sound remotely like that. It was a woman who said it, right?"

"Yes, but...she knows I don't speak Italian. Why would she...?"

"Maybe she was afraid you'd run the other way if she said it in English."

And why shouldn't she be afraid? With all his stupid talk about how important his career was, about making mistakes and ruining chances, he'd given her plenty of reasons to believe that nothing serious could ever develop between them, and not one damn reason to believe it could. He'd never told her he loved her. Even when he'd put her on a plane back home, he'd never even hinted that he was going to miss her or that he might want to see her again. He sure as hell hadn't told her he wanted to spend the rest of his life with her.

Abruptly he grabbed the key where it had fallen, spun around and headed for the door.

"Hey, where are you going?" Ryker called.

"To Montebello," Tyler replied. "I have to see the king."

Saturday was another beautiful day in paradise. The sun was shining with a bright, merciless clarity that brought everything into sharp relief, and the breezes off the Mediterranean were cool and refreshing. As they traveled through the garden, Anna caught a mélange of scents and fragrances that couldn't possibly exist in the same mixture anyplace else but here.

For the first time since her return, she felt a sense of peace. She had reached a decision in the early hours of the morning as she'd paced the balcony outside her apartment. She was going to locate Tyler, and one way or another they would find some resolution. Either he would give her hope or take it from her, break her heart or make it whole, but she simply couldn't go on this way. Being weepy and weak and delicate wasn't her nature. Yes, the stakes were high, but wasn't the prize worth it?

She'd been making plans in her quarters when a summons from her father had arrived. She was to meet the king in the gardens, the servant had announced, but he'd offered nothing else. It wasn't a rare request. She often spent much of the weekend with one parent or both, and she loved the time with them. But this particular afternoon, she would prefer to be packing her bags and selecting the best method for discovering where she might find Tyler.

When she spied her father sitting on a bench under an arbor, she couldn't help but smile. He was a handsome man, so distinguished looking and powerful. It was no wonder that her mother loved him even more today than when they'd first met nearly forty years ago—and no secret that he loved her mother dearly, madly, desperately. They were the happiest couple she'd ever known, and she was determined to be just like them.

"Papa." She greeted him with a kiss. "I received your message."

"Obviously, for here you are. Have a seat, my daughter."

She obediently sat on the warm marble bench.

"How are you today?"

"Better."

He studied her a moment, then nodded. "You look better. No more clown nose."

When he tweaked her nose, she playfully slapped his hand away and scolded him. "It's rude to comment unfavorably upon a person's appearance. Hasn't Mama managed to teach you that lesson yet?"

"Your mother has despaired of teaching me anything...such as minding my own business."

Anna stared at him, a sense of dismay growing inside her. "Oh, Papa, what have you done?"

"I haven't done a thing, *bambina.* Besides, you *are* my business. Your mother says this is the wrong time, that I should wait, but as I told her—as I've told you before—you're getting a reputation for being finicky. Men are becoming reluctant to offer for you, knowing that chances are better than even you'll reject them."

She gave a soft relieved sigh. In spite of his desire that she marry, she knew he would never force her into an alliance she didn't make for herself. Though the timing was off, as her mother insisted, if he felt it necessary to pass along another ill-suited offer, then he was welcome to do so.

Just as she was welcome to turn it down.

"Are you saying some brave soul has expressed an interest in marrying me?" she asked, able to tease in spite of the ache in her chest.

"Yes. And I've accepted on your behalf."

Chills racing through her, Anna jumped to her feet as she stared at him. "You *what?* You can't do that, Papa! You can't—! I'm a grown woman! You promised I could choose! You wouldn't—! You can't!"

"Now, Anna *bella,* you've said no to every suitor who's come along. And he's a fine young man who promises to be a good husband to you and a good father to your children." His voice turned coaxing, wheedling. "You know your mother has been longing for more grandchildren since Omar's arrival. This suitor is respectful and respectable, and I do believe he can take care of you as well—no, even better than I. And you'll be happy, if you set your mind to it."

She debated between feeling angry, betrayed or hurt, but settled on rebellious. "I won't do it, Papa! I won't marry some—some damned prince or duke or king, and you can't make me!"

"Such language for a lady."

The soft, chiding voice came from behind her and made her chest tighten until she could barely breathe. She saw her father's broad smile as he rose from the bench, and she realized what she should have known all along—that he'd been teasing. Hope so intense it made her weak rushed through her, leaving tiny trembles in its wake. She squeezed her eyes shut for a moment and summoned the power of all the wishes she hadn't made since she was a small child. *I hope it's Tyler. I hope he loves me. I hope he wants me forever and ever.*

Then she opened her eyes and turned.

He was standing on the shell walkway a dozen feet away, looking so dear and handsome that the sight of him would have made her heart break if it hadn't healed it instead. She stared at him hungrily, wanting to touch him, to kiss him, to throw herself into his arms and never, ever let go. But she stood where she was, not moving, staring, silently rejoicing. The wishes had come true. She could see it in his emerald eyes.

"I know it's arrogant of me to ask the king for his youngest daughter in marriage," he said quietly. "I don't have a kingdom or a title. I can't offer power, riches or influence, and I can't strengthen any alliances. But I can give you these promises—I'll protect you with my life and keep you safe. I'll adore you when you're adorable and even more when you're not. I'll thank God every day for having you in my life. I'll do my best to make your wishes come true. I'll be a better person for you.

And I will always, always love you, Anna *bella*, my beautiful Annie.''

She took a few hesitant steps toward him. "Papa has a kingdom," she said, gesturing in her father's direction, then noticing that he'd gone and left them alone, "and I have my own title. There are many kinds of power, riches and influence, and you have an abundance of the best kinds. The only alliance I care about strengthening is the one between you and me. I couldn't ask for anything more than the promises you've already offered. And just between you and me..." She closed the distance between them and raised one hand to brush her fingertips across his jaw. When she spoke again, her voice had turned husky and soft. "I find your arrogance so very American and so very sexy."

He turned his head to leave a fleeting kiss on her fingers, then caught her hand. "And?"

"And what?"

Using his hold, he backed her toward a small private alcove where a marble statue of a busty nude presided. "Say it, Annie," he commanded.

She felt the solid stone at her back and the tingle of awareness of his body in front, and offered him a sultry smile. "Say what?"

"Tell me you love me. You did it before. I want to hear it again, in words I can understand."

"Can you understand this?" Grasping his shoulders, she pressed her body to his and claimed his mouth in a greedy, needy, desperately longing kiss that made him hard and turned her all soft and warm and achy.

"Words, Annie," he murmured when he freed his mouth. He nuzzled her throat, then left a line of damp kisses along the vee of her blouse, before raising his head and locking gazes with her. "Have pity on me, darlin'. These last few days, thinking it was over with you, have been hell. Don't make me beg. Give me the words, please."

She lifted her chin and smiled. "I love you, Tyler."

"And you'll marry me?" He grinned endearingly. "Say yes, Annie. I've already got the honeymoon all planned out."

He was every dream, every wish and every hope she'd ever had, all combined in one. How could she possibly say anything else?

Sometime later—hours, she thought, or maybe only moments—she raised her head from his chest and drowsily watched until he could feign sleep no more. His lashes fluttered first, then the corners of his mouth twitched, and finally he opened his eyes to look at her.

"You said you had our honeymoon all planned, but you never told me. Where will we go?"

He drew her on top of him, with only the folds of the cool linen sheet between them, and tangled his fingers in her curls. "The only place we possibly could go."

She thought of all the exotic locales throughout the world—sophisticated cities, tropical paradises, resorts of every kind—but none of them held any particular appeal. But, as she'd told him before, it wasn't the place that counted, but with whom you were there. Then, as his grin stirred the heat deep in her belly once again, as they both began tugging the sheet from between them so he could slide slowly, deeply, completely, inside her, she knew exactly where he meant, and the answer brought her a smile of delight.

"When shall we go?"

His hands gripped her thighs, holding her still as he thrust hard into her. "Later, darlin'. Right now I'm in heaven."

All their time together would be heaven, she thought dreamily. But, frankly, she couldn't wait until they were married and making love on their honeymoon.

In Arkansas.

* * * * *

The excitement mounts
next month when
ROMANCING THE CROWN
continues with Max Ryker's romance in
THE DISENCHANTED DUKE
by Marie Ferrarella—
only from Silhouette Intimate Moments!
Turn the page for a sneak preview....

Chapter 1

"You got a strange call in this morning that you might not want to return."

Max Ryker had just walked into the first-floor office that he maintained in Newport Beach's trendy Fashion Island. He paused before closing the outer door, puzzled by the enigmatic sentence his grandfather, Bill Ryker, had just greeted him with.

"Well, seeing as how I just wrapped up a case for Lilah Beaumont," he mentioned the name of the most recent Hollywood star who had availed herself of his well-honed investigative services, "if the call is about taking on a new assignment, strange or not, the odds are I'll be returning it."

"I don't know about that," his grandfather murmured in response as he pivoted his wheelchair to his desk. He picked up a phone message, then spun the chair around 180 degrees.

"Here." Bill held out a yellow piece of paper he'd written a long telephone number on.

Max's smile faded just a shade as he read the message. It was just two words: Please call, and a name, followed by a telephone number.

The number was only vaguely familiar, but the name...the name belonged to a man Max owed his allegiance to. Not as a subject of the man's country, and not even because King Marcus of Montebello was his uncle, but because the monarch was his friend as well. At times, when he was growing up, Max had felt that Marcus was the only friend he had in a country where he'd never quite fit in, despite his royal family name.

Max's full name was Maximillian Ryker Sebastiani, and he was a titled member of the royal ruling house of Montebello, a small, proud country that occupied an island located halfway around the world from the United States. But he'd shed his title and then his last name in what proved to be a semifutile bid for anonymity.

Bill turned his wheelchair around 180 degrees, and headed for the door.

Max crossed to the door, opening it. "You don't need to clear out."

Bill spared him a kindly look. "Figure I'll give you some privacy."

Max closed the door after his grandfather and went back to the desk. Taking a seat, he placed the yellow message down on the blotter and studied it for a long, silent moment before he finally picked up the receiver. Blowing out a breath, he pressed the series of numbers that would connect him with the palace.

It took a while, but finally Max heard his uncle's deep voice say hello on the other end of the line.

"My grandfather said you called with urgent business," Max said once they'd exchanged greetings.

His uncle paused and then replied, "I need a favor."

It was rare that King Marcus asked for anything. Still, time had taught Max to qualify things and not jump in head first, eyes shut. "As long as it doesn't involve returning to Montebello on a permanent basis, you only have to ask."

"It would actually be right up your alley, as you *Americans* say. I hear you're a private investigator these days."

"Yes," Max said.

Marcus laughed. "Talkative as ever, I see." And then his voice became audibly more serious. "All right, Maximillian. I need you to track down a Kevin Weber for me. I'm told he recently—" there was a pause as Marcus hunted for the right words "—jumped bail, I believe it is called. He is wanted for crimes committed in a small town in Colorado."

"That's the expression." Max frowned as he wrote down the name. So far, this wasn't making any sense. "What do you want with a so-called American bail jumper?"

There was another pause, a longer one this time. "Nothing is what it seems, Maximillian, but for now, that is all the information you need. Weber recently was seen in a small town in New Mexico. Tacos or Chaos—"

"Taos?" Max suggested, trying not to laugh.

"Yes," Marcus declared, "that is the place. I need this Weber brought back to Montebello."

"Why?"

"That is on a need-to-know basis, I am afraid. You'll be told when the time comes, Maximillian. You have my word. But until then—" Marcus paused, then said, "These lines are not always secure."

"I understand. But you have to give me more than that to work with."

"I'll send you a fax of what the man looks like, along with a more exact location, but nothing further right now."

Max nodded to himself. "Give me what you can."

Taos, New Mexico
One Week Later

As unobtrusively as possible, Cara Rivers checked the small handgun she carried in the holster strapped to the inside of her thigh. Barely the size of a derringer, the weapon contained a clip with a surprising amount of ammunition. Enough to bring the bail jumping scumbag in the motel room just thirty feet away from her down to his knees.

Cara reviewed everything she'd scoped out about the rundown motel where Kevin Weber was holed up. There were two sets of stairs, one on either side of the second floor where his room was located.

She figured that if she rushed the front door, she could catch Weber before he had a chance to make his way out the back window. That he had a plan of escape she never doubted. She knew that Kevin Weber wasn't stupid. Quite contrary, the man was nothing if not crafty. Luckily she was just as crafty.

Bounty hunting wasn't exactly the kind of vocation most people would have associated with someone who looked the way Cara did, but that was just the kind of advantage she made full use of. Blond, blue-eyed and delicate-boned at five-four, she looked as if her biggest concern in life was how even to get her tan and how long she wanted her bangs to be. Men told secrets to women who looked like her. They let their guard down because they thought her IQ was undoubtedly only slightly higher than her supple bust size. They were always unpleasantly surprised to find out otherwise.

Cautiously, she made her way toward Weber's door from the right stairway. She had tailed the man here from Shady Rock, Colorado, after putting in more than two weeks of following clues and then canvassing the various places he had been known to frequent within the New Mexico area.

A movement on the opposite stairway caught her attention. A tall, somber-faced man walked up the stairs. Dark complexioned with dark brown hair and broad shoulders, he could have been a male model in one of those pricy magazines that catered to the upper crust. But the way he carried his hand in his pocket alerted her.

There was no doubt in her mind that his hand was covering a handgun.

It was another bounty hunter.

Cara would have bet her well-earned reputation on it. She knew a professional when she saw one, even a handsome one. Damn it, there was no way he was going to get her man, not after all the woman hours she'd put in tracking Weber down.

Quickly, Cara cut the distance between herself and Weber's door. By the time the good-looking stranger approached, she was standing in front of the door in question, blocking his access to it. With a triumphant toss of her head, she knocked.

A moment later, a deep voice from within the room growled. "Yeah?"

"Housekeeping," Cara chirped cheerfully, aware that the man at her side was giving her a very suspicious once-over.

There was movement behind the door. "They did not say anything about there being any housekeeping."

Rather than answer, she announced, "I have fresh towels." Cara saw the stranger looking at her empty arms. "You horn in on this and I'll cut your heart out," she hissed.

The next moment, she heard the sound of a window being opened from within the room. She knew what that meant. Her quarry was escaping.

There were tools in her small bag for moments like this, but with no time to extract them and use them on the lock, Cara took the easier, albeit noisier route. She pulled out her gun, flashing a long length of thigh as she secured her weapon. There was no hesitation on her part. Taking aim, she shot the lock.

Cara opened the door in time for her and the handsome stranger to see Weber leap from the back window.

Silhouette®

INTIMATE MOMENTS™
presents:

Romancing the Crown

With the help of their powerful allies,
the royal family of Montebello is
determined to find their missing heir.
But the search for the beloved prince
is not without danger—or passion!

Available in March 2002:
THE DISENCHANTED DUKE
by Marie Ferrarella (IM #1136)

Though he was a duke by title, Max Ryker Sebastiani had shrugged off
his regal life for one of risk and adventure. But when he paired up
with beautiful bounty hunter Cara Rivers on a royal mission,
he discovered his heart was in danger....

This exciting series continues throughout
the year with these fabulous titles:

Available only from Silhouette Intimate Moments
at your favorite retail outlet.

Silhouette®
Where love comes alive™

Visit Silhouette at www.eHarlequin.com

SIMRC3

This Mother's Day Give Your Mom A Royal Treat

Win a fabulous one-week vacation in Puerto Rico for you and your mother at the luxurious Inter-Continental San Juan Resort & Casino. The prize includes round trip airfare for two, breakfast daily and a mother and daughter day of beauty at the beachfront hotel's spa.

INTER·CONTINENTAL
San Juan
RESORT & CASINO

Here's all you have to do:

Tell us in 100 words or less how your mother helped with the romance in your life. It may be a story about your engagement, wedding or those boyfriends when you were a teenager or any other romantic advice from your mother. The entry will be judged based on its originality, emotionally compelling nature and sincerity. See official rules on following page.

Send your entry to:
Mother's Day Contest

In Canada
P.O. Box 637
Fort Erie, Ontario
L2A 5X3

In U.S.A.
P.O. Box 9076
3010 Walden Ave.
Buffalo, NY
14269-9076

Or enter online at www.eHarlequin.com

All entries must be postmarked by April 1, 2002.
Winner will be announced May 1, 2002. Contest open to
Canadian and U.S. residents who are 18 years of age and older.
No purchase necessary to enter. Void where prohibited.

PRROY

Two ways to enter:

• **Via The Internet:** Log on to the Harlequin romance website (www.eHarlequin.com) anytime beginning 12:01 a.m. E.S.T., January 1, 2002 through 11:59 p.m. E.S.T., April 1, 2002 and follow the directions displayed on-line to enter your name, address (including zip code), e-mail address and in 100 words or fewer, describe how your mother helped with the romance in your life.

• **Via Mail:** Handprint (or type) on an 8 1/2" x 11" plain piece of paper, your name, address (including zip code) and e-mail address (if you have one), and in 100 words or fewer, describe how your mother helped with the romance in your life. Mail your entry via first-class mail to: Harlequin Mother's Day Contest 2216, (in the U.S.) P.O. Box 9076, Buffalo, NY 14269-9076; (in Canada) P.O. Box 637, Fort Erie, Ontario, Canada L2A 5X3.

For eligibility, entries must be submitted either through a completed Internet transmission or postmarked no later than 11:59 p.m. E.S.T., April 1, 2002 (mail-in entries must be received by April 9, 2002). Limit one entry per person, household address and e-mail address. On-line and/or mailed entries received from persons residing in geographic areas in which entry is not permissible will be disqualified.

Entries will be judged by a panel of judges, consisting of members of the Harlequin editorial, marketing and public relations staff using the following criteria:
• Originality - 50%
• Emotional Appeal - 25%
• Sincerity - 25%

In the event of a tie, duplicate prizes will be awarded. Decisions of the judges are final.

Prize: A 6-night/7-day stay for two at the Inter-Continental San Juan Resort & Casino, including round-trip coach air transportation from gateway airport nearest winner's home (approximate retail value: $4,000). Prize includes breakfast daily and a mother and daughter day of beauty at the beachfront hotel's spa. Prize consists of only those items listed as part of the prize. Prize is valued in U.S. currency.

All entries become the property of Torstar Corp. and will not be returned. No responsibility is assumed for lost, late, illegible, incomplete, inaccurate, non-delivered or misdirected mail or misdirected e-mail, for technical, hardware or software failures of any kind, lost or unavailable network connections, or failed, incomplete, garbled or delayed computer transmission or any human error which may occur in the receipt or processing of the entries in this Contest.

Contest open only to residents of the U.S. (except Colorado) and Canada, who are 18 years of age or older and is void wherever prohibited by law; all applicable laws and regulations apply. Any litigation within the Province of Quebec respecting the conduct or organization of a publicity contest may be submitted to the Régie des alcools, des courses et des jeux for a ruling. Any litigation respecting the awarding of a prize may be submitted to the Régie des alcools, des courses et des jeux only for the purpose of helping the parties reach a settlement. Employees and immediate family members of Torstar Corp. and D.L. Blair, Inc., their affiliates, subsidiaries and all other agencies, entities and persons connected with the use, marketing or conduct of this Contest are not eligible to enter. Taxes on prize are the sole responsibility of winner. Acceptance of any prize offered constitutes permission to use winner's name, photograph or other likeness for the purposes of advertising, trade and promotion on behalf of Torstar Corp., its affiliates and subsidiaries without further compensation to the winner, unless prohibited by law.

Winner will be determined no later than April 15, 2002 and be notified by mail. Winner will be required to sign and return an Affidavit of Eligibility form within 15 days after winner notification. Non-compliance within that time period may result in disqualification and an alternate winner may be selected. Winner of trip must execute a Release of Liability prior to ticketing and must possess required travel documents (e.g. Passport, photo ID) where applicable. Travel must be completed within 12 months of selection and is subject to traveling companion completing and returning a Release of Liability prior to travel; and hotel and flight accommodations availability. Certain restrictions and blackout dates may apply. No substitution of prize permitted by winner. Torstar Corp. and D.L. Blair, Inc., their parents, affiliates, subsidiaries are not responsible for errors in printing or electronic presentation of Contest, or entries. In the event of printing or other errors which may result in unintended prize values or duplication of prizes, all affected entries shall be null and void. If for any reason the Internet portion of the Contest is not capable of running as planned, including infection by computer virus, bugs, tampering, unauthorized intervention, fraud, technical failures, or any other causes beyond the control of Torstar Corp. which corrupt or affect the administration, secrecy, fairness, integrity or proper conduct of the Contest, Torstar Corp. reserves the right, at its sole discretion, to disqualify any individual who tampers with the entry process and to cancel, terminate, modify or suspend the Contest or the Internet portion thereof. In the event the Internet portion must be terminated a notice will be posted on the website and all entries received prior to termination will be judged in accordance with these rules. In the event of a dispute regarding an on-line entry, the entry will be deemed submitted by the authorized holder of the e-mail account submitted at the time of entry. Authorized account holder is defined as the natural person who is assigned to an e-mail address by an Internet access provider, on-line service provider or other organization that is responsible for arranging e-mail address for the domain associated with the submitted e-mail address. Torstar Corp. and/or D.L. Blair Inc. assumes no responsibility for any computer injury or damage related to or resulting from accessing and/or downloading any sweepstakes material. Rules are subject to any requirements/limitations imposed by the FCC. Purchase or acceptance of a product offer does not improve your chances of winning.

For winner's name (available after May 1, 2002), send a self-addressed, stamped envelope to: Harlequin Mother's Day Contest Winners 2216, P.O. Box 4200 Blair, NE 68009-4200 or you may access the www.eHarlequin.com Web site through June 3, 2002.

Contest sponsored by Torstar Corp., P.O. Box 9042, Buffalo, NY 14269-9042.

Uncover the truth behind

CODE NAME: DANGER

in **Merline Lovelace's** thrilling duo

DANGEROUS TO HOLD

When tricky situations need a cool head, quick wits and a touch of ruthlessness, Adam Ridgeway, director of the top secret OMEGA agency, sends in his team. Lately, though, his agents have had romantic troubles of their own....

NIGHT OF THE JAGUAR
&
THE COWBOY AND THE COSSACK

And don't miss
HOT AS ICE (IM #1129, 2/02)
which features the newest OMEGA adventure!

DANGEROUS TO HOLD is available this February
at your local retail outlet!

Look for ***DANGEROUS TO KNOW,*** the second set of
stories in this collection, in July 2002.

Where love comes alive ™

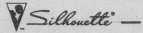

where love comes alive—online...

eHARLEQUIN.com

your romantic
books

- ♥ Shop online! Visit Shop eHarlequin and discover a wide selection of new releases and classic favorites at great discounted prices.

- ♥ Read our daily and weekly Internet exclusive serials, and participate in our interactive novel in the reading room.

- ♥ Ever dreamed of being a writer? Enter your chapter for a chance to become a featured author in our Writing Round Robin novel.

your romantic
magazine

- ♥ Check out our feature articles on dating, flirting and other important romance topics and get your daily love dose with tips on how to keep the romance alive every day.

- ♥ Learn what the stars have in store for you with our daily Passionscopes and weekly Erotiscopes.

- ♥ Get the latest scoop on your favorite royals in Royal Romance.

your
community

- ♥ Have a Heart-to-Heart with other members about the latest books and meet your favorite authors.

- ♥ Discuss your romantic dilemma in the Tales from the Heart message board.

All this and more available at
www.eHarlequin.com

SINTA1R2